MYSTERIES OF THE SOUTHERN GOTHIC

JESSICA CARRASQUILLO

SONGBIRD
BOOKS LLC

Cover by Theresa Chiechi

ISBN: 979-8-9905358-7-9 (Paperback)

ISBN: 979-8-9905358-0-0 (eBook)

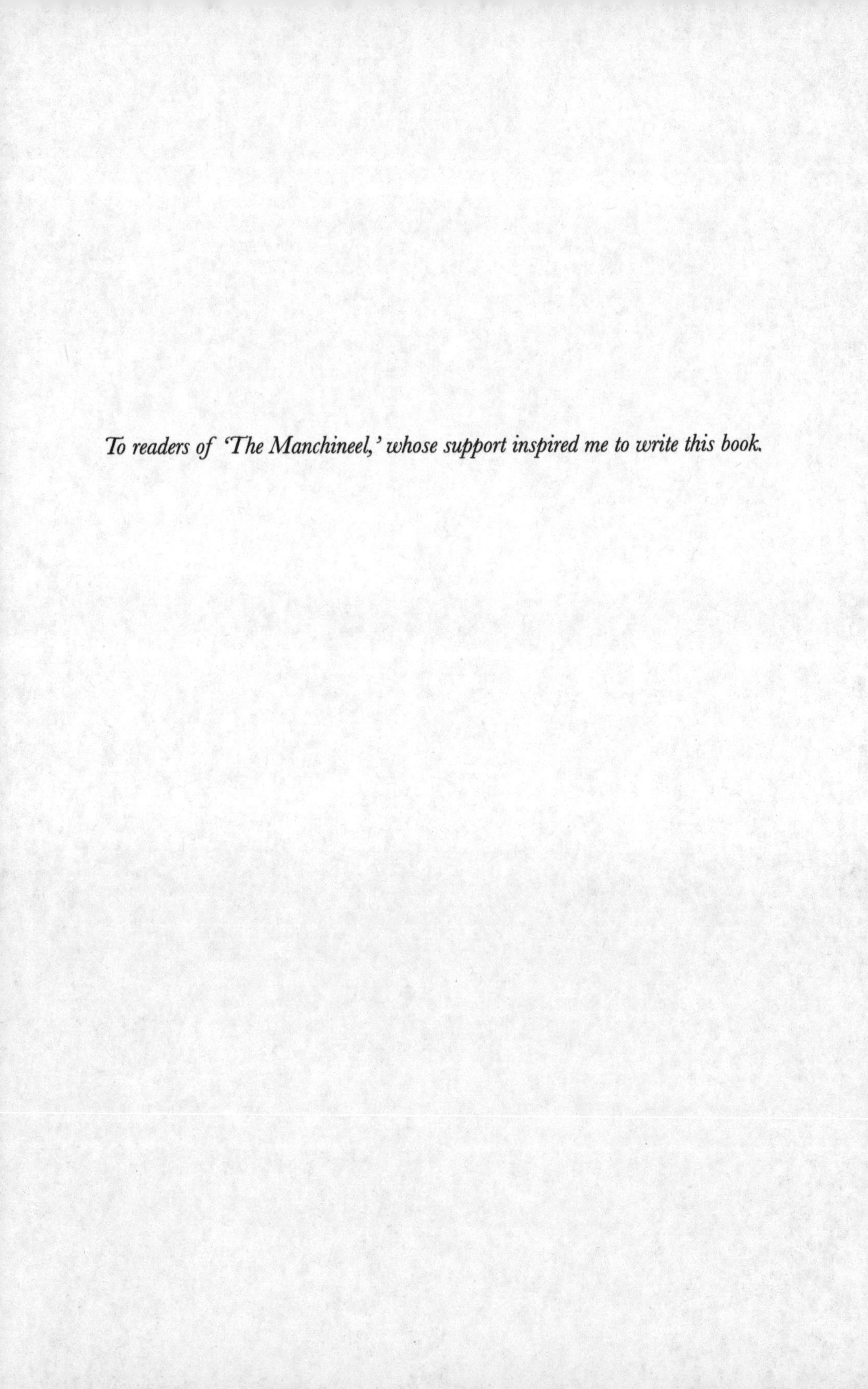

To readers of 'The Manchineel,' whose support inspired me to write this book.

Author's Note

Mysteries of the Southern Gothic is an interconnected standalone novel within *The Manchineel* series. While it's not necessary to read *The Manchineel* beforehand, doing so will enhance your experience and help you avoid potential spoilers. For maximum enjoyment, starting with *The Manchineel* is recommended.

Unlike *The Manchineel*, this story is a mystery-thriller with new characters, romantic elements, and deep emotional relationships, but it is **not** a traditional romance.

Please be advised the following work contains themes and scenes that readers may find distressing. A list of triggers is included in the back of this book and contains spoilers.

Chapter One

"WELCOME to Mysteries of the Southern Gothic, a podcast that examines real-life crimes and unsolved mysteries of the South. I'm Rosario Martinez. This episode is called 'Unaccompanied Minors.'"

A black manicured fingernail presses the touchpad on a MacBook and eerie music begins to play. The lights are off and the room glows with moonlight beyond a wall of windows. Twenty-three stories down, silver bands reflect against bay waters, and the downtown Tampa skyline glitters in the distance. Music fades, replaced with a man's voice, muffled and distant from an old tape recorder. He recounts in a charming southern drawl how he encountered the suspect just a mile from the penitentiary where the killer now serves a life sentence. "I could tell from the cold look in his eyes this man was pure evil."

Her voice returns, clear yet mysterious. "That's Deputy Beau Harris referring to Eric Mitchell Vernon, a registered sex offender and career criminal identified in connection with Carla's disappearance. I met Deputy Harris at Mickey's Diner in Thonotosassa near Vernon's former home. The small restaurant took residence in a converted motel painted coral and surrounded by overgrown palm trees overlooking a bleak parking lot. It's the kind of sleepy place where locals meet for coffee and the off-brand ketchup bottles are proudly American. This isn't a tourist destination. There's no frills and no cell phone service." The sounds of the diner's conversations, clattering silverware and plates interrupt her peaceful voiceover.

"All the hair on the back of my neck stood up as soon as we locked eyes," Deputy Harris continues. "I felt a chill. I knew then that Eric Mitchell Vernon was our man."

The audio cuts off, and a series of news anchor voices from various broadcasts follows.

Breakthrough in the case of a missing Thonotosassa girl.

A suspect has been identified in the case of missing eleven-year-old Carla Whitman.

Law enforcement tells us the suspect, Eric Mitchell Vernon, is in custody and has been charged with the murder of eleven-year-old Carla Whitman.

Rosario's phone vibrates on her desk. An unsmiling photo of Shawnee, her co-producer, appears on her phone. Glancing down at it, she curses under her breath, then reluctantly answers. "Hey."

Chapter Two

BEFORE IT BECAME dangerous for her to live alone, Eleni Katsaros's home was a church. Candles flickered constantly on a side table in her living room. Photos of her daughter Calliope formed a shrine around a Holy Cross. Eleni and her son Ulysses never passed Calliope's altar without genuflection—a brief bending of the knee and a sign of the cross. It was a sign of respect. An acknowledgment of God's presence.

The communion bread Eleni kept was consecrated by The Church of the Ninth Order, to which the Katsaros family once pledged allegiance. While The Order added its own colorful spin on Catholic formalities, they, too, believed a wafer could signify the Body of Christ. Though Calliope's body was never found, her memory was ever-present in that place.

The walls of Eleni's new room are white, a blank space as stark as her memory, with not a single photo of Calliope. Despite his many requests, the memory care facility staff discouraged Ulysses from bringing in personal effects. Holding a framed picture in his hands, he argued with the nurse in his mother's room. The nurse's heavy brow creased, her words firm. "The edges are sharp," she warned, then tapped a fingernail against the surface. "This is glass. It's a safety risk."

"What if I take the photo out? She can just keep it in her drawer."

Peeking her head out into the hall for a moment, the nurse softened and lowered her voice. "They misplace things a lot here. If it's an important photo, you'll want to leave a copy."

"Yeah, fine. Thank you."

A week later, he's greeted by the smell of ammonia. He hates it here. He'd give anything to provide her better than this, but even this place, with a shared room and scant staff, claimed her entire social security check plus eight-hundred dollars a month from Ulysses.

"Mom?" He found her sitting in a chair, her gaze lost out of a window with a view of the parking lot. Her hair, once neatly swept into an elegant style, was in disarray, though not a single strand has yet turned silver. Turning to him, her eyes lack any glint of recognition. "Hey," he presses on. "Mom, it's me. Ulysses. Your son. Do you remember me?"

"My son?"

"Yeah." He approaches to sit at the edge of her bed, beside her. "Can I sit with you?"

"Go ahead," she says with a flippant wave of her hand, as if she were inviting a stranger to take the seat beside her on the bus. She takes him in, and he can see her calculations and judgements. His long hair worn up in a bun atop his head, his beard, his arms covered in tattoos are absorbed with a look of curiosity and disapproval. "You don't remember me?"

"No," she says, motioning toward her head. "I have trouble remembering things."

"I know, Momma," he says, taking her hand. When they touch, her eyes warm at him. His eyes well with tears and his vision blurs. The grief overwhelms him, but he tries to swallow it down. He doesn't want to confuse her. But her maternal instincts seem to return as she squeezes his hand, leaning forward to press a palm to his cheek.

"It's alright," she says, comforting him. "Don't cry."

He wipes his face with his sleeve. "What about Calliope? Do you remember her?"

"Calliope?"

"Yes, your little girl."

She frowns apologetically and shakes her head, a lack of emotion adding weight to the blow. Motioning toward a small dresser, he says, "I think there's a picture in there. Is it alright if I find it for you?"

"Sure," she says.

Going over to the dresser, he pulls open the top drawer. He remembers leaving the photo, Calliope standing in front of her bicycle with streamers on the handlebars, an inch wide gummy gap where her two front teeth should be, tucked under a stack of folded cotton shirts. But after lifting each pinch of pastel fabric in the stack, he meets the white particleboard of the drawer. He pulls open another, and another. Realizing it's gone, he regrets not taking the nurse's advice. But there are many more photos of Calliope, even if that one is lost.

"I guess it wandered off," he says, sitting back beside her. Reaching for his cell phone, he considers searching through the depths of his photo albums, but as he looks at her, peaceful and unaware, he wonders if it's better she doesn't remember. He, too, struggles to remember the happy times. Time before a stretch of years so dark, he's willed his own mind to forget, having replaced the evils with palatable lies.

The thought stirs up many questions. They spin in his mind on the quiet drive to work. No music plays in the background. Just the muffled sounds of the cars whipping by on the causeway. It's beautiful driving east with the sunrise ahead of him, even shrouded by clouds. The placid bay waters are flat and white like milk under a silver sky. Palm trees sway in the breeze. His chest aches as he wonders if this burden will ever go.

Over his designated parking spot, a sign reads *Ulysses Katsaros, Palms Waterside Recovery*. Setting his coffee on top of his Jeep, he straightens his fitted, black button-up shirt, tucking it into his black chinos. The sleeves are rolled up to his elbows to subtly display his tattoos—shattered Greek busts, with roses growing from the cracks. Glancing at himself in the reflection of his side mirror, he pulls himself together and puts on a hopeful face for his clients to find solace in. What he offers is hope. The reassurance that if they hang on, if they try and put in the work to clear a path for themselves, they too can live better, healthier lives. But preparing to head inside, he doesn't know how to pour from an empty cup.

Laura, a fit middle-aged woman who works as Palms Waterside's admissions coordinator, is on tour with a young man. Eyes sunken, skin sallow and cheeks hollow, his thin frame is swallowed by a faded Balenciaga hoodie that could probably cover a month of Ulysses's rent. The young man's eyes glaze with boredom as he trails behind a middle-aged couple in neutral toned sweaters. Ulysses overhears Laura selling them on the faith-based recovery center's fully equipped gym and spa treatments as he politely squeezes past them in the hall toward staff offices.

Once at his desk, he checks his calendar and sips his coffee. Through the slivers in the blinds, he can see the morning sunlight is shrouded by a blanket of clouds. Art therapy at ten. One-on-one with Lily at eleven-thirty. Lunch, also known as paperwork at his desk with a sandwich. Prayer group at one. A quick knock pulls his attention toward the open door. It's Dr. Okafor, his supervisor and Palms' Medical Director.

"Good morning, Uly," Dr. Okafor, a burly Nigerian man with a sporadic gray patch of hair and thick clear round frame glasses, greets in his signature baritone. "How you holding up?"

Ulysses smiles at him. "I'm good. Thank you."

Dr. Okafor leans against the metal door frame and tugs at his dark wooly beard as he studies Ulysses's bookshelf. "Your fern's looking a little thirsty."

The potted fern near the picture window is wilted and brown. "Ah. Thanks for the reminder."

"How's your mom?" Dr. Okafor asks.

Ulysses offers a weak smile and a shrug. "Not great."

"You know I'm around if you ever need anything."

"I do. Thank you."

"Hang in there," the doctor says with a nod and pats the door before sauntering away.

Ulysses takes a half drunk Aquafina and starts to unscrew the top, planning to dump it into the parched soil. Sofie, his ex-girlfriend, got him this plant. It was a congrats-on-completing-your-internship fern he'd kept alive for three years. He hesitates, wondering if it's worth the effort, then empties the bottle, watching the dry soil soak up the liquid.

Heading to the art therapy studio, he tries to be in the moment, to get out of his own head, and notes the weather, his surroundings. It's a dreary day. Already he can hear the shouts of agitated clients suffering through detox. Setting up the studio, he places square canvases in each easel, lays out metal tubes of acrylic paint. Cadmium red, yellow. Burnt sienna. *The color of Sofie's eyes*, he thinks, but quickly dismisses the thought. Mars black. Burnt umber. Cadmium orange.

He counts out brushes and sets them on utility carts. Clients filter in looking weary. His first session is always the least enthusiastic. Taking a breath, he slips on a mask of a smile and addresses the group. "There's no deep introspective assignment today. Sometimes just creating something is enough. It's a distraction, an outlet. So don't overthink it. This is less about creating a masterpiece and more about allowing a conversation between your heart and your hands."

Ulysses watches as the session progresses, noticing the lack of interest. Some clients doodle aimlessly, a few paint nonsensical images, and others just smear paint across their canvases. The energy in the room is palpably indifferent. As the time comes to an end, clients exit one by one, leaving behind a mess of paints and unwashed brushes. Ulysses takes a deep breath, trying not to let the apathy get to him. As they go, he catches glimpses of their works: a canvas with only a big blob of black paint in the center; one has words scribbled with evident frustration; another is just a series of crudely drawn veiny dicks and balls. Sighing, Ulysses begins the task of cleaning up alone.

That night, lit by the glow of his phone, Ulysses swipes. It's dark in his apartment, and the only sound is the ting from the metal buttons of his jeans clanging against the drum of his dryer. Domino, his fluffy border collie poodle mix, is curled in his lap. Eyes fixed on the phone screen, Ulysses sees Sofie's text the moment it arrives. It's a day and a half later, but she's finally responded. Seeing her name on the screen sends his heart into his throat. For a moment, he's flooded with the hope this message will be the lifeline that will lead them back together.

It had been forty-two days without contact before Ulysses finally gave in to temptation. It seemed like a plausible enough excuse to find out if she had any second thoughts. He'd asked about her old bookshelf that sat empty in his apartment after she'd left with all the books.

Now, drawing in a deep breath, he taps on her response.

Donate it. Sell it. I don't want it.

The weight of her rejection sinks into his belly. With a flick of his thumb, he disappears the offensive message and sets down his phone. Once its light is gone, he realizes the sun has set. It's only six o'clock. Another reason to despise this time of year. It's mid-December in what passes for winter in Florida, and there's only the slightest chill in the air. With a slight nudge, Domino jumps from his lap and watches intently for Ulysses's next move, his astute brown eyes peeking through a black mask of fur. This dog is the last creature on the planet to give a damn what Ulysses does. He only just has time to eat a sandwich and take Domino for a quick walk before leaving to his second job.

The sun has barely set, but it's so dark, it might as well be midnight. Funk music and the murmur of conversations and laughter from nearby bars seep into the streets. The air is dense, and the scent of cigars lingers on the air. He crosses the narrow brick road toward an old storefront in the historic district, the sidewalk punctuated with tall, skinny palm trees. The glass doors he unlocks are etched with the words *Ybor City Fine Arts Center*.

Inside, he flips on the lights where oil and turpentine waft in the air. Ulysses retrieves a stack of small canvases from a storage closet and carries them into the studio, where five easels are set up in a semi-circle. Running on auto-pilot before class begins, the sound of someone clearing their throat seizes his heart in his chest and he jumps slightly. It's a young woman.

"Oh," she says, seeming to realize she's startled him. "I'm sorry. Is this Classical Training for Artists?"

He relaxes and chuckles to himself thinking how someone with such a soft voice could have frightened him the way she just did. "Yes, it is."

Big brown eyes gleam at him with a reverent intensity that's both intriguing and slightly unsettling. Her hands clasp in front of her to steady a slight tremor, her fingers nervously intertwined. The longer she looks, the more familiar she seems to him. It's odd he can't place it.

"Have we met?"

"Uh, I don't think so." Her gaze momentarily drifts away, then back to him, as if caught in an internal debate. The woman steps further into the studio, her movements carrying a tentative grace. Scanning the room, her attention lingers on his painting, a simple still life of a bowl of moldy oranges. The corners of her red painted lips curve into a shy smile. She tucks a stray piece of her thick, shoulder-length platinum hair behind her ear. Her dark brows, eyes, and olive skin suggest it's bleached. "Maybe I just have one of those faces."

It's a pretty face. One he'd be sure to remember, he thinks, while looking at her oddly reminiscent and delicate features. Though, he knows now more than ever the mind makes no guarantees about the things it holds on to, the things it lets go.

"Maybe. I'm Ulysses, by the way." He extends his hand.

"Rosario," she says, accepting the handshake. There's an excitement to her energy that's contagious, the doldrums of the evening momentarily charged. As Rosario releases his hand and moves to set up her workspace, Ulysses finds himself watching her. Against her torn and tight black jeans and Doc Marten combat boots, there's a poised elegance in her posture, a refinement. Every so often, she steals glances his way, quick flickers of her eyes that speak of curiosity and something deeper, something unarticulated.

The room begins to fill with more students, the buzz of conversation growing, but Ulysses's attention remains partially anchored to Rosario. The night's focus is on Classical techniques—Rembrandt's soft edges and forms, DaVinci's proportions—but part of his mind struggles with the itch of this puzzle.

Once they've started, he wanders the room to take in the work happening at each easel. It's a beginner's class, and the images forming on the canvases are mostly rough. Pausing beside Rosario's easel, Ulysses looks at her and she stops, brush mid-air, with a small curious smile. Her eyes widen, as if to ask him why he's looking at her that way.

"Did you grow up around here?" he asks.

Her mouth falls open slightly and she seems to struggle to process the random question. "Yeah," she says after a beat, and a nervous laugh escapes her lips. "Did you?"

"Yeah. Where'd you go to high school?"

"Tampa Prep," she says, a slight blush tinging her cheeks.

He didn't know anyone who went there, a school for rich kids in an upper-class neighborhood. Working through the possibilities, he agonizes over the mystery. "Hmm." He laughs and shakes his head. "I know you from somewhere." Her eyes flutter and she looks away. He's made her uncomfortable, and he decides not to prod further.

On her way out, Rosario approaches him. "Thank you. I've been looking for a group like this. A chance to meet new people." Her wide, expectant eyes hold him as she lingers.

"I'm glad you found us. See you next week?"

"Yeah, see you next week."

He tidies up and locks the studio behind him before heading home. Domino jumps erratically, letting out a shrill whine. "I know, bud." He unhooks his leash from the wall and clips it to the dog's harness. They go for a walk, passing the twinkling lights in festive colors, inflatable Santas and cutouts of reindeer stuck into the lawn of his apartment complex. He sits on a bench and lets Domino tire himself around the small dog park enclosed with a chain-link fence, repeating the motion of throwing a ball and letting Domino retrieve it. His phone vibrates in his pocket. A message from Brody, his childhood best friend and Sofie's older brother.

Warren's coming home. Mom's throwing a big party after Christmas. It's been a while since I've seen you and it'd be nice if you could make it.

The prospect makes his chest seize up. Staring down at his phone, he jumps to his photos and swipes through his album of Sofie. Concerts, friends' weddings, vacations in the Georgia mountains. Her period was late after that trip, and for a couple of weeks, he'd thought he might be thrust into the next phase of his life. Thought about engagement rings. But then her cycle started, and when they both felt relief, he figured it wasn't the right time. He should have asked her then. *God, what if she's already seeing someone else?* The thought crushes him.

Will Sofie be there?

It's just cold enough that his breath expels faint, milky clouds that dissipate in the air. He takes in the scent of burning wood. The smell, the cool air against his skin, and the thought of facing her makes an ache radiate inside him. All his senses remember even as his mind tries to forget.

Returning inside, he makes dinner—microwaved meatballs and a prepackaged salad. While eating in the quiet solitude of his kitchen, Brody texts back.

It wasn't Ulysses who'd left without a word. No explanation. No note. One day he had someone to come home to, and the next, he didn't. He still doesn't know why.

Chapter Three

"HOW WAS ART CLASS?" Shawnee's voice is as deep as a woman's voice can be while still being recognizably feminine. From the gentle whir of traffic in the background, Rosario can tell Shawnee's on the road. She glances at the time. "It's after midnight, where are you?"

"I'm almost home. Met up with Veronica from Channel Ten."

"What about?"

"Another data breach story. Gave her some infosec commentary," she says. "No luck with Persephone?"

"Calliope and no, didn't get very far." She's been avoiding this conversation. It went so much worse than she ever thought possible. Never did she think he'd recognize her, and she didn't anticipate he'd be…the way he was.

"Why? What happened?"

He wasn't anything like she imagined, that's what happened. Though she's not sure what she expected. Normally, she'd have fully researched the source before ever approaching them, but Ulysses was completely off the grid. No social media accounts. No staff photos on the Palms Waterside or art school websites.

"I don't know, showing up to his job like that. The vibes were off," Rosario admits. There's a long silence, one Rosario knows is filled with Shawnee's curious judgment. The truth is, they do it all the time. When a spree of package thefts hit the community, Rosario knocked on victims' doors, gathered doorbell camera footage, and was led to a suspect. She trailed the young woman one morning to confront her at work, only to arrive at a high school. It wasn't until they were face-to-face, the suspect's youthful eyes widening in surprise, that Rosario noticed the backpack slung over her shoulder and realized she was a student. Rosario probably would have been arrested for trespassing were it not for the girl porch pirate wearing a stolen necklace.

When they'd decided to cover the Carla Whitman case, Rosario strolled right into the police station and found Deputy Harris herself. She wasn't one to wait for permission.

"Mm," Shawnee hums skeptically.

"He thought he recognized me from somewhere, and I freaked out," Rosario explains. "I hadn't considered he might remember me from that *Deadline Discovery* special."

"He recognized you? Well, we had no control over what that show did."

"I know. He just said I looked familiar. I panicked. Plus, he has Calliope's name tattooed on his neck and it threw me off." In the moment, it just felt too personal. Which, thinking of it now seems ridiculous. Her whole deal is getting too personal. That's kind of the point.

"Oh?" Shawnee says, with interested surprise. "Tattoos, huh?"

"Yup. Tattooed arms, hands. Long hair. He's got this kind of artsy-grunge vibe going on." *Smoking hot*, she thinks, deciding to leave the color commentary out of her debrief. "I choked. I was scared he'd be angry."

"Mm," Shawnee hums again. "So now he thinks you're an art student?"

Rosario cringes and groans. "I guess. Don't worry about it. I'll smooth things over."

"You're getting sloppy, Martinez."

"Shut up. Any news on Belladonna?"

"Still waiting to hear back. If this missing kid case doesn't work out, I think we're going to nail this chick to the wall."

"It's going to work out. I gotta go, I'm editing."

They hang up. Now that the case is front of mind, Rosario reaches into her desk drawer to find the Calliope binder. Retrieving it, she sets it on her desk and flips it open. Her fingers gently trace the lines of a faded newspaper clipping protected in a plastic sleeve, eyes scanning the text with apprehension.

Investigators continue to search for Calliope Katsaros, a missing eight-year-old girl from Hillsborough County, and on Monday announced a tip line for anyone able to offer information in the case.

But she was more than a headline. Over the years, Rosario had watched countless news stories and interviews on Calliope's case. The little girl was beloved. Her friends and family wept on television, teachers sang her praises and grieved her potential. Rosario hoped to finally uncover answers, but she's screwed this up already. Showing up and asking questions felt intrusive. Even though he greeted her with a scowl, his pretty eyes, green as sea glass, carried such serenity. Bringing up this sore subject felt like she'd be sticking her finger in a wound.

The rainbow wheel on her screen spins as it saves the audio file. Her first attempt to talk to Ulysses was a disaster, and she fears she's blown her chance to gain his trust. Now, no matter what she does, it will seem like she intended to deceive him. She pauses, leaning back in her chair, lost in thought, envisioning the bright young girl at the heart of this mystery, and the scared little boy Ulysses once was. She takes a deep breath. She can fix this.

Chapter Four

AT WORK, Ulysses finds himself seated across Dawson, the lanky teen in an oversized designer hoodie he'd observed on tour. "Who's Calliope?" Dawson asks with a smirk, regarding the inked letters embedded in the skin beneath Ulysses's ear. Sprawled across the side of his neck in large cursive letters and classic flourishes is her name, a form of punishment and reverence all at once. Hurt like a bitch, but the worst came later. Each day after, looking in the mirror. He was used to the constant reminders living in that house, but one drunken afternoon, he'd decided that if her memory was on his body he could never truly be free of it. Now it's been there so long, it blends into his sense of self, innocuous as a freckle.

They'd only just sat down and settled into their seats for their first one-on-one session when Dawson lobbed the question at him and dredged her up. The smirk on his face suggested he hoped it was intrusive. He wasn't the first person who turned their inner pain outward and directed it at Ulysses. In detox, it's a daily occurrence. And he's heard much worse.

A short silence hangs between them. Clearing his throat, Ulysses meets the young man's gaze, choosing his words carefully. "That's…

personal." His tone is firm yet polite, revealing nothing. He offers a warm smile. "Let's focus on you."

"Strange to get a name tattooed on your neck if you don't want anyone to ask you about it, don't you think?" Dawson spits back, ignoring Ulysses's attempt to redirect their conversation. He curls up, dragging his expensive sneakers against the seat's upholstery to sit cross-legged. His dark eyes gleam with a mix of defiance and curiosity.

The bratty front is just a coping mechanism, Ulysses reminds himself, a way to keep people at arm's length. After all, if he pushed them away first, they couldn't abandon or hurt him. He was Dawson once. Sort of. A poorer version. But the anger, the testing of boundaries, the drinking until blacking out—that was all the same. Alcohol was a way to destroy the shame, the feelings of powerlessness and loss of control. All the emotions associated with trauma. As fortified as Dawson's defenses are, Ulysses sees right through them.

"Why do you think you're here?" Ulysses asks.

Returning home through the colonnade of his apartment building, Ulysses notices a paper posted to his front door. It barely registers, and he brushes it off as some maintenance notice. The manager probably needs to shut the water off for a repair or something. He yanks the paper from the door.

Notice to Pay or Quit for Non-Payment.

You are notified that you owe rent in the amount of $4,200. This amount does not include any late fees you may also owe. If you do not pay $4,200 by the date stated below, your tenancy will be terminated, and you will be required to move.

Due the fourteenth of December. Three days from now. It's right there in black and white, and yet, he can't believe it. His stomach sinks. This must be a mistake because his landlord, Mohammed, hasn't even called him. Domino jumps at him excitedly as Ulysses paces, his nerves tangled in a knot. He doesn't have $4,200. He finds Mohammed's number and taps in the digits. The phone rings and rings, each warble hastening his heartbeat. *Come on,* he pleads with the universe.

"Hello?"

"Hey, Mohammed. It's Ulysses at twenty-two hundred Bayview. I just got your notice."

"Uh-huh."

"Well, I'm trying to figure out what's going on here because the rent's been paid."

"I received your December rent, but you did not pay in October or November."

Ulysses gave the money to Sofie. He gave the money to Sofie, he's sure of it. "Mohammed, this is the first I'm hearing about this."

"I have been calling."

"Who?" Ulysses yells, frustration getting the best of him. "I have no calls from you."

There's some rustling in the background and the sound of Mohammed's labored breath before he recites a phone number. Sofie's phone number. Ulysses fights the urge to throw his phone against the wall across the room. "That's Sofie's number. She doesn't live here anymore. Look, I gave her the money to pay the bills. She was supposed to pay you."

"I'm sorry but she didn't."

A cold sweat breaks over his skin and his chest tightens. He's going to be sick. "I need more time."

"I'm sorry. I can't make exceptions."

"Please. I've lived here for years. It's Christmas. I don't…I don't have anywhere to go. I pay for my mother's assisted-living facility. I'm working two jobs. I swear I will pay you. I'll borrow the money if I have to, just *please* give me some more time to get this together. Three days is not enough."

There's a long pause, and Ulysses holds his breath. Mohammed sighs. "One week."

It's not much better than three days, but he's not in a strong negotiating position. They hang up and Ulysses calls Sofie. It rings once before he gets a recorded message. *"We're sorry but the number you have dialed has been disconnected or is no longer in service."*

At that moment, the closest breakable object is a ceramic mug on the kitchen counter. He slams it against the wall, and it shatters into pieces with a high-pitched crash. He lets out a guttural scream. Domino whines and skitters away. She knew. She knew he wouldn't have the money, that he was supporting his mother. She knew this would ruin him, yet she stole from him.

He loved her. Why would she do this? What did he do to deserve this? He can't breathe. Falling to his knees, he doubles over and weeps. Domino's paws patter across the floor as he approaches him and sniffs at his neck. Ulysses reaches for him and wraps his arms around him. Hugging his dog, he cries until he can't anymore, until he's depleted. What is he going to do?

A payday loan would solve his immediate financial crisis but put him in deeper trouble in just a few weeks. He'd have to take another loan to cover the memory care facility fee. Scrolling through his bills online, he looks for places to cut. Student loans—he can request a forbearance. That'll free up a couple hundred bucks, but he's already paid for December, so it won't help today. He rarely dines out. His biggest splurge is a gym membership, but it's only thirty dollars a month. Water. Electricity. Gas. Groceries. He can skip a few meals, eat a lot of rice and beans. Cell phone. Car payment. Car insurance. Memory care. Tithes to the Church.

Sitting on his bedroom floor, back to the wall, he stares at his phone for a lifeline. His first call is to Brody. "I gave the rent to Sofie. I guess she wasn't paying it. Now that she's gone, dude, I don't know what I'm gonna do."

"Goddammit." Brody breathes hard into the phone, his frustration with his sister palpable. The word makes Ulysses wince. "She hasn't come here." He sighs. "Look. I'll try to get in touch with her. See if any of this can be fixed."

"I appreciate it. I'd never ask but…" He trails off, regroups. "Do you think you could help me out on a short-term basis? I've only got a week to pay this. If you can float me for a month or two, I'll do whatever I have to do. I'll get another job. Sell my stuff." He already has few possessions, mostly worn-down furniture he'd have trouble giving away for free if he tried.

Brody lets out a tense sigh, and Ulysses already knows the answer. "It's Christmas, money's tight. I could barely get the kids presents this year."

"I understand. Don't worry about it. I know you would if you could."

"Sorry, man. I'll try to get ahold of Sofie. If you need a place to stay, I'll shuffle the kids around. We'll figure something out."

"Thanks." He ends the call and stares blankly ahead. He's barely scraping by as it is, nothing leftover to save every month. Maybe six months living in his Jeep would buy him time to save for a new place. It's winter, at least. He won't sweat to death sleeping in the back seat without air conditioning like he would in the Florida summer. If he keeps his gym membership, he can shower there, get ready for work. He buries his face in his hands, never expecting it would come to this.

There's the matter of his mother, too, and the awful places she might end up if he can't find a solution. He feels sorry for himself for a while, before finding what's left of his Jack Daniel's in the kitchen and drinking straight from the bottle.

He wants his mother. To be hugged by her, reassured. To see the deep love in her eyes that can only come with the recognition that he's her son. But he never will again. Once that levee has burst, the rest floods in. Every embarrassment. Every relapse, every failed relationship. His loneliness. The terrible truth—*Sofie stole from me and she's never coming back.*

He falls asleep wrapped in grief, but by daylight, he's resolved to pull himself out of this mess. Getting ready for work, he focuses on the tasks ahead and puts the ugliness out of his mind. It's a new day. At his desk, Ulysses signs off on his notes and closes a file before moving on to the next in his tall stack. Laura knocks. "Come in," Ulysses mutters.

"That plant of yours has seen better days."

Glancing over at the fern Sofie gifted him, Ulysses observes the drooping yellowed leaves, lifeless and sad against the plastic pot. Getting up, he crosses the room and picks it up at its base. He walks it to the trashcan, then unceremoniously dumps it inside. Wiping his hands, he pats off the flecks of dirt.

Laura gives him a worried look, resting in the chair in front of his desk. "You alright?"

"I'm fine," Ulysses says dismissively. "What can I do for you?"

"New client. Came in today, but he's in detox right now. Thought you might want to take a look before he comes to this side."

"Thanks."

As Laura leaves, placing a manila folder on his desk, Ulysses rubs his temples, feeling the weight of his existing caseload. Opening the folder, he skims through the details. Another young man. Opioids.

At the end of the day, he sits with Domino in his lap, his hand mindlessly passing strokes across his plush black and white fur. Looking at his phone, he scrolls through odd jobs online. Finding nothing worthwhile, he checks his messages. Nothing new. Spam emails flood his inbox with holiday gift offers. His eyes catch the empty bookcase.

Getting up, he flips on every light switch and lamp in his living room, then takes pictures of the few possessions he owns worth anything—an electric guitar, an acoustic guitar, and the empty bookcase. He posts them all to the marketplace and shares with a message to his art group. It's a start.

Setting his phone on the kitchen counter, he reaches for a glass from the cabinet. His phone buzzes as his hand makes contact with the glass. It's Rosario.

I've been looking for a bookcase just like that. Is it still available?

Of course it is. He posted it half a second ago, he thinks, smiling to himself.

He pours a drink and his smile curves around the glass. She's eager. Pretty. Too bad his life is fucked. With a defeated sigh, he returns to the couch.

Chapter Five

HE WAKES on the bedroom floor. A pain from deep inside his brain aches. His phone vibrates under his thigh. Retrieving it, he squints at the screen with dry, blurry eyes. Messages from Rosario.

> Hi, I'm outside. Did you still want to sell the bookcase?

> Saturday at 10, right? Did you mean next Saturday?

Oh fuck. He climbs to his feet, tense muscles resisting his stretch as his joints pop. Closing Domino in the bedroom, Ulysses darts toward the front door. He'd planned on scrubbing the house like a surgeon before she arrived, insecure about his sad little apartment. Catching a glimpse of himself in the mirror, he looks like a man who drank himself to sleep on the floor last night. This wasn't the impression he'd hoped to make.

When he opens the door, she's standing there, dressed comfortably in leggings that hug her body and a plain white shirt, sneakers and a denim jacket. Her dressed down appearance puts him at ease, although he's not sure what he expected. They're moving furniture.

"I'm so sorry, did I wake you up? Did I come on the wrong day?"

"No. Don't apologize. I'm an idiot, I overslept."

Welcoming her inside, it's a short tour. With a clipped, "Welp," he gestures toward the bookcase where it sits against one wall of the living room, his mind still in a fog. Hearing a new voice in his space, Domino whines and scratches from behind the bedroom door.

"Oh, you have a dog?"

"Yeah. I don't normally keep him locked up, I just didn't want him running around bugging you. He doesn't bite or anything like that."

"I don't mind."

Ulysses opens the bedroom door and Domino launches himself at Rosario. "Domino," he scolds. "Down."

Rosario's smile and laughter are bright. She crouches on the ground and makes her voice sweet as she digs into black and white fur and accepts his licks on her face as his fluffy tail shakes. "Hi, Domino, thank you for the kisses."

"Domino," Ulysses calls again, and the dog rushes back to him. "Calm down, bud."

"He's sniffed me well and good by now," she says, looking around. "The bookcase is perfect. Thanks for letting me pick it up."

"Of course. Thanks for taking it off my hands. It was—" he starts but stops himself. *Do not mention the breakup*. "Not getting used obviously. Everything's on the Kindle," he says, giving her more information than she needs. "I'll give you a hand taking it down."

"Are you sure? I've got it."

The bookcase is bigger than she is. He kind of wants to let her do it just to see if she can, but he resists the temptation. "Of course, it's no problem."

As soon as he lifts, the spike in adrenaline makes him nauseated, and he fights against the spinning sensation. He realizes he would look a lot cooler doing this if he wasn't horribly hungover. Taking one end, Ulysses descends first to bear the greater weight. When they pause on the first floor sidewalk, the contents of his stomach threaten to erupt, and he forces down the urge to vomit. She rushes over to a U-Haul and lifts the metal door, revealing an expanse of nothing. Seeming to notice his amused curiosity, she says, "It was the smallest one they had this morning," with a slight flush and tucks a stray section of hair behind her ear.

"Wish I'd known you were going to rent a U-Haul. I'd have brought it to you myself and saved you the trouble."

"Oh, no. Don't be silly. It's no trouble at all."

"You going to be able to get it into your place? You need help?"

"It's okay."

"You sure?"

She lets out a nervous laugh. "Help would be nice. Yes, thank you."

Rosario texts him her address, then drives the U-Haul as he follows her in his Jeep. Plugging the address into his GPS, it points him toward a dot near the water. *Hmm*, he thinks, *nice neighborhood*.

Following her into a concrete parking structure attached to an elegant high-rise, he discovers it's even nicer than he assumed. They park and he meets her at the lift gate once again. Carrying the beat-up bookcase through the lobby, where marble floors gleam under a modern helix chandelier, he's hit with an unexpected zap to his confidence. Suddenly, he becomes hyper aware of how grungy he must look compared to the elegant surroundings.

The doorman rushes over. "Miss, do you need a hand?"

"We've got it, thank you."

Entering the elevator, they maneuver the case inside. His gaze drifts to the stainless steel panel of buttons and where her finger lands. The twenty-third floor. When they arrive, they carry the shelf out into a corridor. Walnut double doors are adorned with large foliage wreaths with red and gold ornaments, flanked by two flocked evergreen trees in pots with white twinkle lights. A hotel-style key reader unlocks her doors. When they swing open, he's immediately struck by the breathtaking views of the water through a wall of floor-to-ceiling windows. Looking around, there are so many beautiful details to take in. The glossy marble floors are designed with muted pinks and greens in elegant patterns. Overhead, the amber glow of spherical pendant lights in mercury glass cast a warm, inviting light. It's like a trendy luxury hotel. This is her apartment.

The bookcase, likely made of particle board, stands out in the space like a hangnail against the backdrop replete with custom shelving and accoutrements. "Where did you want this?"

"Um, I think probably in the office," she says and scurries off. He follows her, leaving the bookcase in the entry. As he tries to keep up, he realizes the apartment is huge. She leads him to an office. One that looks like it's been carefully curated by an interior decorator, complete with custom built-in bookshelves and a desk with a row of sleek monitors mounted to a reticulating arm. A webcam is mounted on the center monitor. A professional-looking microphone rig rests nearby, along with mounted ring lights. Behind the desk, a wall features framed posters of vintage pulp fiction novel covers, and a pink neon sign that reads *Mysteries of the Southern Gothic*.

He's heard that name before. Where has he heard that name? As the realization settles in like a lead weight on his chest, he lets out a weary sigh. Pointing to the sign, he asks, "This is you?"

She nods tentatively and takes slow steps toward the desk. Leaning against it, she offers a sheepish smile. "That's me."

"Now I remember where I know you from. You did an interview with those *Deadline Discovery* people. That special they did on Calliope. I guess it's just a coincidence you'd walk into my class. Drag this ugly bookcase across town to your palace." His voice drips with distain.

Her shoulders slump as she covers her face with her hands. After a beat, she takes a deep breath and faces him, cheeks flushed. "I screwed up. But I just want to help you get answers."

A mix of anger and embarrassment stew in his gut. He should have known. With a sneer, he starts to back out of the room. "You thought you'd help by lying to me? Tricking me into coming here?"

"I didn't know how to approach you. I thought if we could talk in private we could—"

"We could what?" he interrupts, pulse quickening. "Talk about my sister's case? You're unbelievable." Turning his back, he bolts toward the front doors. Her footsteps linger behind him, keeping pace. Finding himself cornered at the elevator, he slams the button.

"Please let me explain," she pleads.

Ignoring her, he glances up at the lights telling him the elevator is ten floors away. He remembers the things those people said. The way it crushed his mother. "My mother worked day and night to keep me and my sister fed. Those *Deadline Discovery* people painted us to be trailer trash. Like she was some kind of a neglectful parent for not being there that day."

"I'm sorry they did that but —"

"*You* helped them do that," he says, an accusatory finger pointed at her. "You harped over and over again about those *unsupervised children*."

"I never meant to hurt you or your family."

The elevator doors open and Ulysses rushes inside. She follows him in, and he groans in frustration. "Please. I just want to be left alone."

"No, Ulysses. You want answers. I know you do. You want to find her."

All he can see are those photographs on the shrine lit up with candles. Calliope eternalized with blonde pigtails, missing her two front teeth. "It was twenty years ago. I was a kid. I was traumatized. I don't remember anything from that time. Even if I wanted to help you, which I don't, I couldn't."

The doors open in the lobby, and she follows him on the walk to his Jeep. Continuing her attempts to convince him, she trails behind. "You specialize in this, so you know the memory is an unreliable thing anyway. Crime scene witnesses, they fill in the details because the mind tries to add things in, bridge gaps on its own, even if it's inaccurate. But how you felt, the way you were made to feel—you'll always remember that."

Specialize? *Fucking hell.* Of course she's investigated him. Knows where he works, that he's a mental health counselor. He won't admit it, but she's right. He'll never forget how he felt. Terrified. Sick to his stomach. "Sorry, you'll have to promote your little podcast some other way. Can't help you."

"You think this is about the show? The show is a means to an end, to raise awareness. Listeners have emailed me with tips. We've aided real investigations, Ulysses. This isn't about the show, it's about finding Calliope."

Hearing her say his sister's name makes him want to scream. She's a liar. Concealing the truth from him like this. Letting him feel like a fool. He doesn't have time for this. His life is falling apart, one disaster after the next. He clenches his jaw and stops mid stride so abruptly she crashes into him. Facing her, he makes his message clear. "Leave. Me. Alone."

Her eyes widen with a frightened expression and he backs off. Climbing into his Jeep, he slams the door and she steps away, a hurt look etched on her face. Tires squeal as he peels out and drives away.

Chapter Six

THE BAY WATERS sparkle in the distance, light shining off them like scattered diamonds. Shawnee stares through the window of Rosario's office, a deep stitch in her brow nearly hidden behind her retro black framed glasses. Towering over Rosario where she's sitting at her desk, Shawnee is an intimidating figure—Amazon-like, with toned muscular arms crossing her chest in clear agitation.

"We can't move forward with this investigation if he's not on board," she says, her husky voice carrying a tense edge. "He's our way in. You should have let me talk to him."

"Give him some time to cool down. We have other stories."

"The Candy Bandit?" Shawnee snaps, her voice filled with condescension.

"It's a good story." A burglar whose calling card was leaving empty candy wrappers behind wasn't exactly bone chilling, but the goal of the show wasn't to titillate or horrify, it was to get answers. "What about Belladonna?"

"They're big shit out there. It's impossible to get anyone on the phone. Ulysses is low-hanging fruit. He's right there, we just need to snatch him up. We need new content. Unlike you, Plantain Princess,

I don't have a trust fund paying my bills. I survive on those sponsor payments."

It stings like a slap. Maybe Rosario didn't have the same problems, but she hated it when her privilege was thrown in her face. Especially when it came to making decisions about the show. Rosario rolls back in her office chair. "Forcing him isn't going to make this any better. He'll never talk to us if we do that. Just…let me fix this."

Shawnee softens, the way she normally does once she's snapped at Rosario and feels remorseful. She flips open the thick, green Calliope binder sitting on the desk. Inside is a map they'd drawn of the mobile home park, identifying the residents at the time of Calliope's disappearance. It was a small, private park off a busy road in Tampa, with five doublewide trailers shrouded by tall oaks dripping with Spanish moss. A ten-foot stockade fence concealed the structures from view, with a single-lane gravel road to enter and exit by. Near it, a metal sign read *Water Oak Mobile Home Community LLC.*

Of the five residences, two were vacant. One was rented by the Randall family. Nadine Randall, the mother, was a food service worker at an assisted-living facility. The father and Nadine's then husband, Lang Randall, was a long-distance truck driver who was on the road at the time of Calliope's disappearance. Left at home alone that day were their two sons, Warren, aged sixteen, Brody, aged thirteen, and their daughter, Sofie, aged eight.

In a neighboring unit was the McNichol family. A teenage girl, Chelsea, and her mother, Debra, were away from the residence with confirmed alibis.

"Eleni was at work. The father has never been in the picture. So that leaves, Ulysses, Calliope, Brody, Sofie and Warren. That we know of." Shawnee shakes her head in confoundment. "Boys that age can't even keep their tighty-whities streak free, how were they able to hide a body and eliminate any evidence?"

"Why do you assume she's dead? How do you know she's not alive somewhere?"

"After twenty years? No way. She's gone, and one of them did it."

Rosario spins slightly in her chair, then stops herself with her toes on the wood floor. "The oldest one. Warren. I always wondered about him. He's doing time right now for armed robbery."

"He was sixteen. Kids that age would have made mistakes. There would be evidence. Crimes like this are crimes of opportunity. Someone visiting the neighborhood. A predator. This is my point, Rosario. The podcast will get people thinking. You never know who might send in a tip about something they remember about that day. Someone who might know where she is now."

"I know. I'll try. I'm just giving him some time to cool down, that's all."

That weekend, Rosario makes a trip to Ulysses's apartment unannounced. She parks her sleek, cherry-red convertible in the spot where she'd parked that ridiculous U-Haul. Just thinking about it sends a heat of embarrassment up her neck. What was she thinking? Her mind nearly melts from the mere prospect of seeing him again, looking into those eyes. The image of him that flashes in her mind makes her stomach flutter, but she shakes it off. Losing her nerve now cannot happen. Failure is not an option.

Rushing up the stairs to the second floor units, she finds his door and knocks, expecting it to rouse Domino into a fit of barks. A wind picks up and rustles through the nearby palms, then complete silence. Maybe they've gone for a walk? She turns around, surveying the apartment complex grounds, hoping to catch a glimpse of him. She hears a door open, but it's not Ulysses. It's someone else on his floor. A man with too much gel slicking his dark hair back like it was soaking wet. He makes eye contact with her, seeming to size her up.

"*¿Vienes a ver el apartamento?*"

"No," she responds, confusion setting in. "*Vine a visitar a un amigo.*"

"*Ah, nadie vive aquí.*"

She looks at the door again and confirms the number. "*¿Esto es Bayview?*"

"Sí, pero el hombre que vivía aquí se mudó. Han estado mostrando el lugar. Pensé que buscaba a Mohammed."

He moved? "Oh, I didn't realize."

Once the man confirms she's not there to meet Mohammed about the empty apartment, he nods and continues his stride through the walkway and down the stairs, leaving her stunned. Ulysses wouldn't have moved to get away from her, would he? That seems a little extreme.

Getting back into her car in a daze, she sits in the driver's seat in silence. Now what?

Chapter Seven

ULYSSES CRAMS his clothes and toiletries into a large suitcase. Whatever doesn't fit is folded, then neatly placed into two large trash bags. Bins of sentimental items and a laptop bag are all carried to his Jeep. Stacks of canvas—some completed paintings, some incomplete—are stacked in his trunk along with banker boxes filled to their lids with art supplies.

Ulysses checks into a pet-friendly extended stay motel near work and pays for the week. It's nice. Clean. Cramped, but in some ways nicer than his apartment. His *former* apartment. It's so strange that a place he'd called home for years is no longer accessible to him. He never thought it was possible to feel rejected by a place, but somehow everything about his thoughts of home feel tainted.

It's not fair, but it's not the end of the world. The lobby has vending machines. Free coffee. Maybe it's not home, but it's not the street. He'll get through this. Though, paying ninety bucks a night is not ideal. For a month, it'll be more than his rent was. And he isn't sure how long it'll take him to scrape together enough money to find a permanent place. But for now, at least, he's surviving.

For the first week, life proceeds otherwise as normal. He goes to the gym, to work, Dr. Okafor and Laura none the wiser. He takes

Domino on long walks at night until his evening job. Their last art class of the year comes and goes without incident. To his surprise, Rosario is smart enough to keep her distance.

Dinner is a packet of beef ramen. Just as he fills an old saucepan with tap water and sets it on the burner of his efficiency stove, there's a knock at the door. Domino barks, and Ulysses brims with unease. No one knows he's staying here. This transient place isn't in the best neighborhood, and his mind imagines the kinds of trouble that might be on the other side. He looks for a heavy object, settling on an iron he'd left out when pressing his dress pants that morning. The peep hole, fogged and darkened, allows him only to see distorted shapes and shadows. The door's latch is closed, letting him safely open it an inch to peek out as Domino tries to shove through his legs.

Standing there in a hoodie, torn jeans and combat boots is Rosario, a six-pack of beer dangling from one hand and a Chinese takeout bag in the other. Just as the shock of her audacity swells, the exhaustion of the week's events draws him back and he lets out a long, weary breath. He closes the door to remove the latch, then opens it again to face her. Domino whines to greet her, but all Ulysses can offer is a defeated look and a shake of his head. "Seriously?"

"I brought gifts."

"Are you following me now? You think this is okay?"

"Look, I fucked up. I should have told you who I was when I met you. But those shows, they take pieces of what you say to build a narrative. I would never do anything to paint your mother in a negative light. By all accounts, she is a wonderful and caring person. And with our show, you will have a chance to help people see that."

"You showing up here unannounced is crossing a line." His voice is firm.

She shifts uncomfortably. "I know, but I needed to explain in person. Those shows, they twist things. I respect your family's struggle, Ulysses, truly. And I want to do this story justice. I want to get your case the attention it deserves."

"Why me? Why Calliope? Don't you have another mystery you could focus on?"

The air is cold and her breath appears as she speaks. "I grew up here. I grew up seeing your sister's face everywhere. She stayed with me. Her story stayed with me, and the person responsible for her disappearance might still be out there. Calliope might be out there. What if we could solve this once and for all? What if we could find her?"

He scoffs lightly. This is pointless. "I've told you. I don't remember any—"

"Try," she interrupts gently. "Let's just have a conversation. We can start there. Please? It's cold out here."

Though her mere presence here is infuriating, what's worse is that her appeals are starting to wear on him. There's a pause, a silent battle within. Maybe it's because she's pretty, or because this might be a chance to fix his mother's reputation, but he can feel his defenses begin to recede. Finally, Ulysses steps back and holds Domino by his leash to keep him from running out as he opens the door wider. "Alright. Come in."

Chapter Eight

AS ROSARIO STEPS INSIDE, Domino sniffs curiously at her and the takeout bag. Ulysses's bed is made, pushed up against a wall painted apple green. He leads her to the small kitchenette, clearing a space on the cluttered table. He turns on a standing lamp to brighten the space. As she sets down the beer and food, his gaze follows her with a look that's almost cautious.

"You didn't have to bring all this," he mutters in a low, gravelly voice.

She eyes the packet of ramen resting on the edge of the sink beside the stove. "I wanted to," she replies, unpacking the containers. "Consider it a peace offering."

They sit in an awkward silence, the tension slowly dissipating as the aroma of the food fills the cramped room. With a nod and a low grunt of acknowledgement, he settles into his chair. Rosario hands him a fork, which he accepts gingerly. His fingers brush hers briefly, and a small shiver travels up Rosario's back.

They sit across from each other at the table, eating from plastic takeout containers of cashew chicken and fried rice, lo mein and other dishes she ordered in the gamble of finding something he might actually like. He cracks open a beer and brings it to his lips.

Domino sits nearby with sharp eyes, patiently waiting for a scrap to fall. Scanning the room for details, Rosario tries to fill in her narrative. Boxes and garbage bags are filled with his things.

Her eyes catch a series of canvases resting against the wall facing outward. Dark Sailor Jerry-style takes on classical works in various sizes. In the largest one, a woman kneels by the body of a fallen man, her posture suggesting she's performing some sort of ritual or act of mourning. The color palette is limited to shades of blue and orange. Stormy skies and a sparse landscape littered with skulls give the scene a sense of foreboding. It reminds her of a vintage illustration in an old textbook, just classic enough to seem familiar but with a twist, an unsettling detail she can't place but that gives her the sense something is about to go terribly wrong. "Did you paint that?"

He glances over his shoulder at it, then nods through a chew.

She studies it more, hoping to make a connection. "What's it mean?"

A lump of food in his cheek, he speaks from the corner of his mouth. "It's Antigone." The name sounds familiar, but she can't remember why. He swallows hard and quickly changes the subject. "I assume you didn't come here to talk about my art." His voice is low and rough, letting her know he hasn't warmed to her enough for small talk.

Rosario pulls a small mic from her bag and sets it between them, the distance short enough for the powerful device to clearly capture both of their voices and record it to an app on her cell phone. "Is it alright?" she asks, gesturing toward the mic.

"That's why you're here, right?"

She nods and presses the red circle on her screen. "We're recording now. I was hoping you could tell me what you do remember about the day Calliope went missing."

He sets down his beer and leans back in his chair, crossing his arms. His eyes briefly scan upward, as if retrieving the details from a deep forgotten place in his mind. "Brody, my best friend, lived next door. He'd just gotten a new PlayStation. We were playing Smack-Down vs. Raw. Edge versus Bubba Ray Dudley in the WWE Championship." He snickers to himself but it's humorless. "There's so much I've forgotten, but it's the silly shit like that I remember." He rubs a thumb over where his fingers meet his palm. Staring into his hand, his eyes grow distant and he seems to get lost for a moment. "She was out there hopping around on her little skip-it thing. She never screamed. Cried. Whoever took her probably led her away somewhere."

"What about the other little girl?" Rosario asks. "Sofie. Didn't she play with Calliope?"

"Yeah," he says gruffly. "Sometimes. But she's always been a little...manic. Running around from thing to thing. We couldn't keep track of her. Brody didn't even try."

It strikes Rosario as odd. Two unsupervised little girls. One goes missing, and the other remains safe and sound without any knowledge of what happened to the other. "So, then what happened?"

"We played for a while, then we got hungry. I figured if I was hungry, Calliope was probably hungry, so I shouted for her. But she wasn't out there." He stops, shaking his head. His eyes lost on something on the table, he lets out a soft sigh of regret. "I didn't think anything of it at the time. I figured she'd gone back inside. If she really needed something, she'd come knocking like she had before. But then it got late. Then really late." He stops. From his tone, she suspects the bitterness isn't from the memory itself but from being asked to recount it. "Called the cops. They searched everywhere. Interrogated me like I was a suspect. 'You get into a fight with your sister? Did you hurt her? She fell down and hit her head, didn't she?'"

Rosario hadn't realized the police had considered him a suspect at thirteen years old, but thinking about it now feels absurd. The lack of evidence. No signs of a struggle. No body. No blood or hair. Nothing.

"They searched every inch of that park and everywhere in the neighborhoods around it. Every patch of woods, the surrounding ponds, anywhere a distance she could have possibly traveled nearby on foot." He shrugs, and his eyes study her with a hint of expectancy, a signal that he's done. "You know the rest."

"I'm so sorry," she says, unable to imagine the weight of the guilt he must carry. Her heart aches for him, and she wants to end things on a happier note. "What was she like?" It was something Rosario always wondered herself. Even after all the news stories and interviews, there is something special about being here with Ulysses now, Calliope's own flesh and blood.

Then a gloom casts over his eyes, and he drifts away somewhere distant. "I don't remember her much. I know that must sound terrible. The years, what I've been through in between. Took me pretty far away, you know? Not just the time going by either, but who I was then doesn't even exist anymore."

"Not anything? Not even like…" She pauses to think up an example. She doesn't have any siblings but she tries to imagine. "Like, who was mom's favorite?"

The question presses firmly on a nerve and he flinches. A moment passes before a small smile creeps across his face, not quite reaching his eyes. "Definitely Calliope."

The words are loaded with something that sounds like grief or resentment, but he's so serene. Calm and unreadable. Her instinct is to press on. She's found the crack in the ice, now's the time to hammer it until she breaks through. But instead, she says, "Thanks for sharing all this with me. I'm sure it's not easy."

He doesn't look at her but nods in acknowledgement with a gruff sound, which she assumes means, *you're welcome*. Bringing the beer to his lips, he takes a long thirsty sip. She waits for him to set the beer down before she presses further, and when he does, it lets out a hollow *clink* that says its empty. He reaches for another.

"Do you still keep in touch with Brody?" she asks.

"Yeah. When I can. It's been a little while, you know. He's got a family now."

"Do you think he'd be willing to talk to us?"

Eyes widening, he stretches back with a reluctant groan. "I don't know."

"Can you ask him?"

"It's complicated."

"Why?"

With a cold glare and a hiss, he snaps, "It's personal."

"You two had a falling out?"

"Not exactly. Are you still recording this?"

She leans forward, quickly tapping the button to stop. "Not anymore."

His demeanor shifts, slouching a little in his chair. Domino has nuzzled his head against Ulysses's lap, and Ulysses absentmindedly rubs Domino's ears. "Sofie and I…we were together for a while. But like I said, she's always been a little manic. We broke things off, she moved out." He waves his hand around at the surroundings. "Properly fucked me over by pocketing the rent and now I have her to thank for my current living situation."

Rosario has a selfish moment of relief realizing he hadn't moved out because of her, but it quickly wanes when she imagines how unbelievably fucked up it is to screw someone over that way. Then again, she doesn't have the whole story.

"Things are a little awkward with me and the Randall family at the moment."

"I see." She decides to take things slow, not wanting to push her luck so soon. "And your mom? How's she?"

The mention of her summons a dark cloud over him, and he winces slightly. She can see how the years of living with tragedy have weighed on him. He pulls at the hem of his T-shirt. On it, *Deftones* is written in cursive, beneath it a skull surrounded by roses. "Physically she's fine. But mentally, she doesn't remember much. Not me, not…" He trails off, letting the end of his sentence die on his lips.

"Do you have any other family?" It's a question she asks not for the show but because it's just days before Christmas. Sitting here in this dingy motel room filled with hastily packed possessions makes her heart break for him. His tight, restrained expression returns with his response. "No."

She folds up the mic and places it back in her bag. "I'm having people over for Christmas Eve. You and Domino are welcome to come."

He chuckles dryly, a sound devoid of any real humor. He glances at Domino, who has settled down at his feet, then back at

Rosario. "I appreciate it, but…" He averts his gaze, focusing on the beer can in his hand.

Rosario waits, giving him the space to mull over the invitation. She knows it's a long shot, inviting someone who's clearly wrapped in his own world of solitude and isn't her biggest fan.

Ulysses takes a deep breath, and for a second, it seems like he's about to decline outright. But then his eyes meet hers, a flicker of something like gratitude flashing within them. "Maybe," he says finally, the word not a commitment, but not a dismissal either. "I'll think about it."

Rosario nods, understanding the weight of even that non-promise. "Okay. Door's open. Just let me know." She continues packing up her things. "Shawnee, my co-producer, might have some questions after we go over this audio. Is it okay if I reach out over the next day or two?"

He nods, a slow tilt of his head that conveys a silent 'yes.' "Just warn me before popping up here again, please." His voice is softer now, the guarded walls showing cracks of warmth.

Rosario pauses, her hand on her bag, and offers him a smile. "I promise not to show up unannounced again." She zips up the bag and slings it over her shoulder, ready to leave but lingering on the threshold of departure.

"Thanks for the food," Ulysses adds, gesturing toward the containers. There's a hint of sincerity in his tone that wasn't there before, a subtle shift that offers her a bit of hope she's making progress toward earning his trust.

"It's the least I could do," Rosario replies, moving toward the door. She waves toward the painting. "That's a really cool painting, by the way."

He turns to it again and chuckles. "Thanks." A tattooed hand grips the back of his neck, and she can't help but notice the flex of his bicep, around which the sleeve of his shirt becomes taut. "It's been in my closet for years. Sofie didn't like it. Said it freaked her out."

"There's definitely something creepy about it."

"Good. That means it's working."

To her surprise, he cracks a smile that rises to his eyes. She can't help but smile back, and a rush of warmth washes over her. "Take care, Ulysses. And remember, Christmas Eve, if you want. Especially if you like Spanish food. We'll have a lot."

"I'll let you know."

With a final nod, she steps out into the chill of the evening, the click of the closing door a gentle conclusion to the night. Shutting the driver's door, she waits until she's in the quiet privacy of her car before she asks, "Hey, Siri, who's Antigone?"

"Antigone is the mythical daughter of Oedipus," it says, and an image pops up with a Wikipedia entry. She skims it. In the Greek tragedy, Antigone breaks the law to give her brother Polynices a proper burial. As punishment for her crime, Antigone is sealed in a tomb alive. *Dark*, she thinks. Most of his art is. There's something about him that's so fascinating. And, finally, she's begun to earn his trust. Thinking of him, his smile and the flex of his tattooed arm, floods her body with heat. But if he's helping the show, then she can't like him. Not romantically. It'll only complicate things. Pushing the dreamy thoughts of him from her mind, she focuses instead on the road ahead as she starts her car.

Chapter Nine

NOW THAT HE'S DESTITUTE, Ulysses is painfully aware that going outside costs at least a hundred dollars. Despite his efforts to be frugal, he can't bear another moment in his motel room, so he takes Domino on a short scenic drive to get some fresh air. They're on the road with the Jeep's top down when Rosario sends him a text.

> Are you free today? Shawnee and I are at my place going over your interview and we were hoping you'd come by to answer a few follow up questions.

> We'll pay for gas.

An unexpected smile quirks up the corner of his mouth. What does she want now? He's already told her everything he knows. But, he's in it now. He'd rather they get it right than repeat the *Investigation Discovery* debacle. Besides, it's not like he has anything else to do.

He agrees, and navigates to Rosario's place by memory. Catching a glimpse of his reflection in the double entrance doors, he's reminded how out of place he looks in his *Nirvana* T-shirt, slouchy shorts and flip-flops. He probably should have stopped at home to make himself a little more presentable. The doors *whush* open and a blast of cool air hits him, carrying a herbal citrusy scent. Sliding a hair tie off his wrist, he quickly pulls up his thick, wavy hair into a tidy bundle on his head. He nods to the doorman with a confident grin, hoping that in doing so he won't be questioned. It doesn't work.

"Can I help you, sir?"

"I'm here to see Rosario Martinez," he says, holding Domino tight on his leash as the dog looks curiously at passing residents, ready to lunge excitedly at any moment. "She lives up on twenty-three. She's expecting me."

"Ah, yes. Go ahead."

With a tight smile, Ulysses proceeds to the elevators and is grateful to ride up alone. He gets to the door, rings the bell, and after a moment, he's greeted by a large woman. Taller than him, and solid like a professional wrestler.

"Hey, I'm Shawnee. You must be Ulysses." Her voice is feminine but deep, husky with a slight rasp.

"Hey," he says. "Where's—"

Before he can finish his sentence, Rosario appears from around the hall corner. The room is open and bright, lit by the natural light flooding through the wall of windows. The view is impressive and seeing it for a second time doesn't make it any less breathtaking.

"You brought Domino," she shouts excitedly.

"I did. I hope that's okay."

"Of course. Let that floofy boy off his leash."

Ulysses reaches down to unclip him, the leash taut from Domino's eagerness to sprint at her. As soon as he does, Domino fires toward her like a slingshot. His nails click against the polished marble as she crouches to greet him.

"Anyone ever tell you that you look like Jesus Christ?" Shawnee asks. It distracts him from Rosario and Domino's adorable moment of reunion.

"Yes, actually."

As he answers, Shawnee's already reaching toward his head with an apparent lack of respect for personal space. "I bet it's even better with your hair down." Taking a step back, he narrowly avoids her touch.

"Will you leave him alone," Rosario says, arriving in time to smack Shawnee's hand away from his hair, allowing him to breathe a little easier.

They gather in Rosario's office, where he's surprised to see the bookcase in use, filled with books. "Wow, you actually used that piece of junk?"

"What do you mean? It's my favorite piece of furniture in the whole apartment."

He shoots her a playful and skeptical look. "Continuing the ruse, I see."

Shawnee pulls back a comfortable, modern-looking armchair and waves for him to sit. He quickly obliges. Once seated, Domino sits on the floor beside him. Reticulating mics flank their chairs, giving the interview a professional quality.

"You're an artist, right?" Shawnee asks, interrupting his examination of the room.

"Yeah."

"What do you think of this poster?"

She presents a framed poster behind clear acrylic to him. It's filled with magnolia flowers. At the center it reads *Mysteries of the Southern Gothic* written in flourished cursive. He's reluctant to judge it, not knowing the story behind it. "It's...pretty."

"See," Rosario says.

Shawnee snatches it back and gives him a cold look. Seemingly flustered, she flips her long, raven-black hair over her shoulder. "Pretty is good though."

"If that's what you were going for."

"It's not," Rosario adds. "Where's the gothic? It's southern *gothic*. Not southern belles talk about crimes and such."

Ulysses bites his lip to conceal a smile, worried Shawnee might crush him for taking Rosario's side. Shawnee rests it against her thigh and studies it. Pushing her thick cat-eye glasses up her nose, she sighs. "I commissioned this. I don't think the designer understood what we were going for."

"You should see Ulysses's work," Rosario says. "It's amazing." All the flattery is a little much, and he wonders if she's sweetening him up for something bitter later. "You should have hired him to do it."

"Would you be willing to take a stab at it?"

"That's an interesting choice of words for a crime podcast. But yeah. Sure."

Shawnee rubs his shoulders and squeezes firmly. She's strong. Pulling a chair up beside him, she gets right to business. "Are we rolling?"

"Not yet. Are you ready?"

Ulysses nods and Rosario joins them. She hunches over toward her laptop sitting on a low coffee table between them, then gives them a thumbs-up when they're recording.

"Alright. I wanted to get in the weeds here. I listened to your talk with Rosario, and I was hoping we could walk it back a little bit. I'll ask some questions, and you let me know what you remember. Sound good?"

"Yeah." He shrugs. None of this is good, but he's already agreed to participate in this having been won over by Chinese food and Rosario's feminine wiles.

"You said you went over to play video games that day. But go back to that morning. Did you wake up at home? Did you sleep over at Brody's?"

"I was home that morning. My mom was pretty firmly against sleepovers."

"My mom too," Rosario says, then adds mockingly, "*Que crees, para que tienes casa?*" applying a pronounced Spanish accent.

Ulysses laughs, although he doesn't understand what she's said other than *casa*. He assumes from the tone it's something along the lines of what his own mother would say: *you have a home*.

"Rosario," Shawnee scolds. "This is serious."

"Sorry," she says, then turns to Ulysses and shyly tucks her thick blonde hair behind her ears. She wears little skull stud earrings with diamonds for eyes. "I'm sorry."

"I thought it was funny." He and Rosario exchange a fleeting glance and smile at each other. "But yeah. I never slept over anyone's house as a kid."

Shawnee raises an eyebrow and exhales with frustration, eyes fixed on Rosario. Rosario shrinks back a little and any trace of humor is sucked from the room.

"Do you remember what time you got to Brody's?"

He shakes his head, but then realizing his physical gesture is useless on a podcast, he leans toward the mic and says, "No. I just know my mom had already left for work."

"Had Nadine?"

Hearing her say that name takes him by surprise. Of course she'd know Brody's mother's name is Nadine. They've done their research. His memory of that day is a blur. He remembers the events directly around the time Calliope disappeared only because he had it dragged out of him repeatedly by his mother, by the police. He'd never forget those few hours that afternoon, but the details of the morning and everything after are gone. "I don't remember."

Shawnee looks at Rosario, like a silent signal, and Rosario turns to him. "Brody had a mom and dad, didn't he?"

Something about the way she says it takes on a maternal quality. As if she's asking the little boy he was back then in a gentle way to spare his feelings. To his surprise, it aches. It makes him remember that sense of loss, of something missing in his own life while watching Brody with his family. A mom, a dad, and their kids. Of course, it wasn't perfect. They fought plenty, but other times, he'd felt so jealous watching them. Especially at holidays. Or on Brody's birthday when his father got him a giant Super Soaker, and Brody was so excited, he ran up and hugged him. Ulysses went home and cried that night. He was so hurt to be without a father, but he never let anyone know.

"Yeah, he did."

"But his father was gone most of the time?"

"Yeah, he was a long-distance truck driver." During those periods, Ulysses felt a little normal. There wasn't the constant reminder Brody had something he didn't.

"And he was gone the day Calliope went missing?"

"Yeah." Ulysses was acutely aware of the times Lang, Brody's father, was around back then. But now, while trying to remember, there are only flashes. Images. The way the lattice under Brody's house crisscrossed; the air conditioner unit that was duct taped in a window and dripped; the screen door and the bright hibiscus bushes planted beyond it. He's never sure if these are his own memories or memories reinforced through old photographs he'd revisited over the years. Having the facts of that day drilled over and over, it's all he can remember. "I'm sorry I wish I had more details."

"You're doing fine," Rosario reassures him.

"Nadine, did she come home before or after your mom did?"

He stares at his hands, hoping the images will appear. "I think it must have been after because I remember my mother being really upset that—" He stops, remembering that this is being recorded. But it's the truth. "She disliked the fact Nadine never checked in on her. Never offered any condolences."

"That's a bit odd, don't you think?"

They didn't know Nadine. She was a cold woman. Still is. It never surprised Ulysses that she'd be incapable of showing warmth in a crisis. Thinking about her one day being his mother-in-law, or the grandmother to his children, had been an unpleasant thought. One he doesn't have to worry about anymore. "She's got a way about her."

"What about Lang? Did he ever offer condolences?"

"Uh…" He struggles to remember. "Actually, they moved away not long after. Ended up splitting up. Divorced."

Rosario and Shawnee exchange glances. It never crossed his mind the breakup could be remotely related because he'd seen first-hand how dysfunctional they were. How they'd scream at each other. It made his stomach hurt, and he remembered feeling sorry for Brody and Sofie having to listen to it.

"I'd love it if we could talk to Brody," Shawnee says. "Could you call him?"

She doesn't even finish asking her question before Ulysses is shaking his head with emphatic refusal. "Things are awkward right now."

"Right. Sofie broke your heart. Displaced you. I get it."

It's a cold summation of his pain and gives him a jolt of resentment. Maybe because he'd never told her these things. They were facts for their story. Despite the contempt that should be visible to her and the tension of his tightened jaw, she continues.

"We're talking about getting justice for Calliope. I'm sure you'd agree that trumps a little discomfort."

Looking to Rosario for support, he finds her staring intensely at her laptop where it rests on the coffee table, either blissfully unaware of or willfully ignoring his uneasiness. "Of course there's nothing more important to me than Calliope. But I don't see how talking to Brody is going to—"

"Leave that to us. As kids, you weren't the most reliable witnesses. Now, I'm hopeful a little nudging of your memories will help us uncover new details your younger selves may not have found important."

Ulysses scoffs but can't find the words to push back. "What am I supposed to say?"

"Don't worry about it. Let us do the talking."

"You want me to call him right now?" he says, his voice tense with disbelief at her audacity.

Shawnee leans forward with a firm, unwavering stare. "Right now."

Chapter Ten

PRESSING his lips into a thin line, Ulysses's nostrils flare and he emits a long resigned sigh. His flip-flop oscillates on his foot from how his leg shakes, crossed over his thigh. Rosario had been pretending to be busy on her laptop to avoid the awkward business of strong-arming him, a skill Shawnee exhibits more readily. Once Shawnee has clearly won, Rosario leans back into her seat and offers him a compassionate look.

"Fine." He pulls out his phone and dials. It rings on speaker-phone twice before Brody answers. After explaining the purpose of his call, Brody eagerly accepts in a distinct country twang. "Yeah. I'll talk to 'em. You should bring 'em over."

Ulysses's expression grows serious. Locking eyes with Rosario, he shakes his head to let her know that isn't going to happen. "I already told you I'm not coming over there."

"We're gonna get you the money, man. I promise. She lost her damn mind, went and bought a van to live in like one of those people on the internet. Said she was going to travel the world."

Ulysses buries his face in his hands as Rosario and Shawnee lean in, thanking the heavens they're recording. Ulysses's words come out dark and flat. "I'm living in a motel so Sofie could start a fucking travel blog?"

"You know how she is, man. I warned you."

He leans back, the heels of his hands pressing into his eyes. "I'm hallucinating. This can't be real life."

"We're handling it. We're gonna pay you back. Just give us some time."

"Who is *we*?" he asks.

"Momma, Warren and me."

Shawnee catches Rosario's eye at the mention of Warren's name, and she raises an eyebrow. Having access to Brody and Warren together is a unicorn of a perfect opportunity. If nothing else, she can make observations. Connections.

"I'm not coming," Ulysses repeats. This time he's firm.

Shawnee leans in, shoving her glasses from where they'd slid down the bridge of her nose with her index finger. "Brody, this is Shawnee. We'd love to meet with you. Just tell us when and where."

"Well, if you show up now, my wife is gonna have me publicly executed. It's practically Christmas. We got a lot goin' on. But we're hosting a get-together after. It's kind of a welcome home party for Warren. Y'all are welcome to come by."

"Sounds perfect."

They hang up, and Ulysses seems overwrought, his shoulders tense, expression cold. "Are we done here?"

"Why *did* Sofie end things?" Shawnee asks.

Whoa, Rosario thinks, sitting up in her chair with a mixture of pity, shock and a pinch of morbid curiosity.

"That has nothing to do with Calliope."

"How do you know?"

He doesn't react to the intrusive question, instead he politely responds, rubbing Domino's ears. "That's personal. And private."

"I'm sorry," Rosario interjects, then glares at Shawnee. "You don't have to tell us about Sofie. How about we take a break?"

• • •

LOOKING OUT OVER THE BAY, Ulysses leans against the metal railing separating the balcony from a twenty-three-story drop. Beside him, Domino shoves his snout between the narrow railing's bars and curiously sniffs at the air as Ulysses scratches the fur around his collar. What is it about this guy that's making her this way? He projects a laid-back nonchalance that's attracted her since she met him. He's seemed so comfortable in his own skin, too authentic and confident to try to conform or impress. Watching him and his pensive expression through the window gives Rosario an unexpected flutter in her stomach. He'd fought this all the way, but he was here, suffering through this for Calliope. Damn Shawnee for making this more difficult for him.

"You shouldn't have pushed him like that."

"What if Sofie remembered something about that day that made it impossible to stay with him?"

"What do you mean?"

Shawnee shrugs. "We can't rule anything out."

"He was a kid."

"Yeah, and sometimes adults help kids cover up really bad things."

No. She can't explain it, but she knows in her gut Ulysses is innocent. "You're wrong," Rosario says, leaving Shawnee in the office. She approaches the sliding glass door and opens it quietly. Still, the sound causes Ulysses to look over his shoulder. "Hey," she says gently. The air outside is damp and briny. The smell of car exhaust mingles with a hint of fishiness in the bay breeze. He turns and looks back out at the water.

"I'm sorry," she says, standing next to him. "I told Shawnee to lay off. She can be a little…"

"Intrusive?"

"I was gonna say pushy."

"She's that too."

They're quiet for a lull, and the sun that had been warming the balcony gets hidden behind a cloud. A cold wind breezes through. "You handled it well though. Shawnee's questions can make people pretty angry sometimes, but you held it together."

"I work with teens and young adults, usually in the middle of a brutal detox. She'd have to say a lot worse to get a rise out of me."

"That's honorable work."

He shrugs. "I had no idea podcasting was so lucrative. I'd have gone into communications instead of counseling."

"It's not, really. My parents bought this place."

"Ah, I see."

Letting out a long breath, she leans against the railing with him. "Guess that tells you everything you need to know about me, huh?"

Turning to her, his eyes hold a warm sincerity. "In the short time I've known you, you've already surprised me more than once. I'm not going to make the mistake of assuming anything about you."

Most people stop trying to learn anything else about her once they know about her family's money. They assume her life must be easy. She can feel a smile tugging at the corners of her mouth as her heart swells with affection for him. "Thank you."

"What's your family do?"

She laughs to herself. "Plantain chips. My great-grandmother had a whole farm in Puerto Rico. They lived off of it, but when my grandfather inherited it, he turned it into a business. Now my family runs it."

"Seriously?"

"Yup. Shawnee likes to call me the plantain chip princess," she says jovially.

There's a comfortable silence as they both gaze out over the bay, lost in their thoughts. Finally, Ulysses breaks the quiet. "She never told me why. I came home one day and all her shit was gone."

A pang of sympathy squeezes in Rosario's chest. How awful to be abandoned like that without an explanation. "I'm so sorry. And you have no clue why?"

"I mean, things had cooled, but we didn't argue. It just got comfortable. Familiar. You know?"

"Not really. I haven't really...I've never had a live-in boyfriend or even a long-term relationship."

"No?"

She shakes her head. "It's not like no one's ever tried. But I go with my gut. If it doesn't feel like it could be forever, then I don't want to waste my time. And I haven't met anyone who's felt like forever. So I focus on what I love." She gestures toward the office window. "This podcast and the stories we've shared are the best things I've ever done."

Looking off toward the bay, he nods. "I think that might have been it. I just wasn't forever to her." A moment passes, stretching on from a sense of his melancholy. "We've been off and on for a decade. You know, there was a time I thought about asking her to marry me, but I didn't do it."

"Maybe she wasn't forever for you either, and deep down, you knew it."

"You might be right."

"Is that why you don't want to see Brody? You're afraid Sofie might be there?"

A smile moves his close-cut beard slightly. There's something boyish about him, vulnerable. "Of course that's why."

She knocks into him with a light swing of her hips. "We'll be there with you. Won't you feel better if you can face her? You're not the one who did anything wrong." His eyes soften and she thinks she might be getting somewhere, so she goes in for the kill. "Might even make her a little jealous," she adds as a cherry on top and winks at him. He chuckles. If the sun were shining clearly on him, she might even see a hint of a blush on his cheeks.

"Alright."

"You'll go?"

He holds her in his gaze. "Shawnee might be the muscle in this operation, but you are very persuasive."

She decides to double down while he's agreeable. "And Christmas Eve?"

Ulysses watches her, a charmed smile spreading across his face. Her insistence clearly strikes a chord with him. "You're not leaving anything on the table, are you?"

"Absolutely not."

"It's a very sweet invitation but—"

"But what?"

He seems to struggle. "It's your family Christmas Eve, I don't want to impose."

"It's not imposing. We're a *more the merrier* kind of family, and I'd really like it if you came."

There's a lengthy pause, a breath held in suspension, before he finally lets it go with a long sigh. "Christmas Eve it is."

Chapter Eleven

THE MOTEL ROOM fills with the scent of cinnamon, cloves and honey as Ulysses boils his syrup. It's a recipe he's helped his mother prepare dozens of times, but the first time he's tried it completely on his own. His hands hover over the tiny counter, looking for a bit of extra space. He resorts to clearing the small table that doubles as a desk. He whisks his dry ingredients, then his wet ingredients separately, before forming his dough.

He'd agonized for days over it, but ultimately decided to keep his word and go to Rosario's for Christmas Eve. He still wasn't certain he could trust her, but the thought of being alone with his thoughts in this crappy motel room was bad enough to tilt the scales in her favor. Even if he was apprehensive about it, he can't show up empty-handed.

After rolling, baking, and soaking batches of hot cookies in chilled syrup, he covers them in finely chopped walnuts and seals them in a Tupperware container. It gets tucked under one arm when he knocks on Rosario's door, the sounds of laughter and salsa music emanating from inside. Rosario greets him with a bright-red lipped smile that matches her vibrant dress.

"Wow, I am underdressed," Ulysses says, feeling like a schlub in jeans and raglan shirt with red sleeves he'd thought was festive enough. He even dressed Domino in a red bandana.

To his surprise, she embraces him and presses a warm kiss to his cheek. "You look great. Come on in."

Walking in, he takes in the smell of onions and garlic, and it makes his mouth water. "Something smells good."

"Is Domino good with kids?" she asks, crouched below him and receiving Domino's licks on her cheek.

"Yeah, he plays with Brody's kids all the time." He used to, anyway.

A group of men carry on a boisterous conversation in Spanish around a dining table.

"We were just getting ready to eat. The kids are in the game room if you want to let him run around in there."

"Yeah, sure." He hands her the container. "*Melomakarona*. They're Greek Christmas cookies. My mom's recipe."

Rosario gasps and gushes over the container. "I can't believe you baked." She lifts the lid off and takes a whiff. "Oh wow, they smell good. Can I eat one?"

"Yeah." He laughs. "That's why I brought them."

Before he can finish answering, she's already yanked one from the container and taken a bite. She makes a big show with her reaction, letting her eyes roll into her head. "Wow. Ulysses, these are so good."

"Glad you like them."

She sets the container on the elegant banquet table filled with food. Its scuffed plastic exterior stands out like trucks nuts dangling from a Rolls Royce. She looks at them and bites her lip in brief contemplation. "Would it be alright if I put these on a platter?"

"Yeah, of course."

After they let Domino loose to play with the kids, Rosario takes Ulysses by the forearm. "Let me introduce you to everyone," she says and pulls him into the kitchen, where five women mill around. One pulls what looks like packages wrapped in leaves from a steaming pot and sets them in a chafing dish.

"*Abuela, este es* Ulysses," Rosario says, leading him toward a small, tan, wrinkled woman with short gray hair and painted-on eyebrows. She wears a floral print dress and squints at him. Giving Rosario a confused look, she mumbles something in Spanish. "Ulysses," Rosario repeats, louder.

"Ah ha…Oo-Lissie," she says, extending a hand that shakes with a slight tremor. "Nice meet you."

"*Mucho gusto*, ma'am," he replies, feeling pretty impressed with himself.

She raises her painted eyebrows. "Ah, *hablas español?*"

"No. That's all I practiced."

She smiles at him with an expression that lets him know she didn't understand what he said. Rosario rubs her back. They speak to each other in Spanish, and from the way her grandmother looks at him, then gestures toward her neck, he suspects they're discussing his tattoos. He stands there awkwardly for a few moments before Rosario's grandmother nods at him and Rosario drags him away.

The noise of the apartment is relentless. Children playing. People talking, laughing. The sounds of the kitchen. Music playing. For so long, he's been living in silence. Even when it was just him and his mother, the house was always peaceful. Church-like. Here, he can't hear himself think.

"Mom," Rosario calls. A woman roughly Rosario's size turns to face her, a glass of wine in her hands. Beside her, leaning against the counter, are two other similarly aged women. "This is Ulysses. Ulysses, this is my mom, Mercedes."

The women look him up and down. Mercedes's eyes appear slightly glossy from intoxication. "Are you Italian?" she asks, each syllable perfectly pronounced.

"Greek, ma'am."

"Your name should be Odysseus."

He smiles at her, surprised. "Yes, ma'am. You're right. Ulysses is the Roman version. Not a lot of people know that."

"Well, I'm an English professor, so I'm not a lot of people."

"Mom," Rosario scolds.

"What? I'm being nice. Ulysses, why so many tattoos? You're very handsome. What's with all the tattoos?"

"Mom," Rosario scolds again.

"It's okay," he says. "I'm an artist. I designed these."

She looks him over again and hums pensively, as if she's still deciding whether she approves of him. "Has anyone ever told you you look like Jesus?"

The women around her begin to laugh.

Rosario covers her face with her hands to shield her apparent embarrassment.

"Yeah, actually. I get that a lot."

"Well, the long hair doesn't help if you're trying to combat that connection." She looks up at his hair, rolled into a bun atop his head. "Although," she says, reaching up and gently squeezing it while Ulysses holds perfectly still. "It is quite nice."

"Okay," Rosario says, pulling Ulysses away. As they leave, the women burst into laughter. "Those were my aunts. I'm not introducing you to them; I'm sure they'll introduce themselves later."

"Can't wait. Do they think we're…." He trails off, letting her pick up his meaning from context and the look in his eye.

She gives him a tense smile, almost pleading. "They kind of just assumed, and since they're always giving me crap about being single, I just kinda went with it. I'm sorry. That's weird, right?"

"Uh." It is weird, but it actually makes him feel a little less guilty for crashing her family celebration.

"Of course it is," she frets. "I'll tell them we're not—"

"Nah, it's okay. Glad I can be of service."

They enter the dining room, where one of the men appears to be telling the others a story. They watch him intently with wide grins. There's a punchline Ulysses doesn't understand but, based on the hand gestures, appears to be something sexual in nature. They explode with laughter and Rosario rolls her eyes. She waits for the laughter to dissipate before calling out, "Dad." The realization makes Ulysses's gut tighten. "This is Ulysses. Ulysses, this is my dad, Hector."

A burly man with dark features looks up at Ulysses from where he sits at the table. "Nice to meet you, Ulysses," he says, but his expression remains stern.

Ulysses clears his throat. "Nice to meet you, Mr. Martinez."

He nods in acknowledgement of this sign of respect. Ulysses finds himself wanting to make a good impression for Rosario's benefit.

"Titi Rosario," he hears a child's voice shout from behind them. They turn, and a little girl rushes up to them. Her hair is parted down the middle with Wednesday Addams braided pigtails. "The dog peed in the game room."

"Shit," Ulysses says, then quickly corrects himself, not meaning to cuss in front of the child. "I mean shoot. I'm sorry, I'll go clean it up."

"It's alright. I'll grab a mop. Wait here," Rosario says, leaving him standing there while she rushes off. He and the child look at each other, and he offers a tight smile and an awkward wave.

She looks at his arms. "Did you draw those on yourself?"

He's taken aback by the question, chuckling slightly at the innocence of it. "I did. I used really powerful ink so it doesn't wash off."

"Oh," she says. "Probably took a really long time, huh?"

"It did."

"So, Ulysses. What do you do?" Rosario's father asks.

Their plates are piled high with roast pork and rice with pigeon peas. Ulysses was watching one of Rosario's aunt's unwrapping one of the leaf-covered packages on her plate to see what was inside and how to eat it when he hears Hector's question. "I'm a mental health counselor, sir."

"Like a psychologist?"

Ulysses clears his throat, feeling a bit of heat creeping up his neck. "Uh, not exactly. I have a master's in psychology. Psychologists usually have a PhD."

"Uh huh," Hector says pensively before scooping a forkful of pork into his mouth. He nods and chews, seeming to contemplate the answer. Wiping his mouth, he leans back in his chair. "Do you plan to go back to school?"

Rosario's eyes widen, and she drops her napkin in her lap. "Dad."

"What?"

"I'd like to," Ulysses replies. "I planned on it. But things changed."

"What happened?" Hector presses.

Ulysses was told this was a more the merrier kind of crowd, and though everyone has seemed welcoming enough, he senses he's being judged. "Well, my mother's condition. Dementia."

Rosario's mother clicks her tongue and shakes her head with regret. "I'm so sorry."

"Thank you. Even with PhD programs in the evening, there was always something else to do. You know, looking after her after work. Eventually, it got to the point where she couldn't live alone. But even now, I'm tied up most evenings doing extra work to pay for her facility, so it's just not in the cards right now, unfortunately."

Rosario reaches over and places her hand on his, giving it a gentle squeeze before drawing it back. Hector nods, chin high, his eyes intense and fixed on Ulysses. "Family is everything. It says a lot about your character that you're taking care of your mother." He turns to Rosario's grandmother and says something to her in Spanish.

She looks up at him confused, as if she hasn't been paying attention. "Ah?" Hector seems to repeat himself, and Rosario's grandmother's eyes light up before she turns to him. "Ah, you good boy."

Hector and Rosario's uncle's eyes squeeze shut as they both start to crack up. Ulysses smiles at her. He wouldn't dream of laughing at her lack of mastery over the English language, but apparently everyone else at the table finds it hilarious. Rosario's uncle says something else in Spanish and he and *abuela* laugh together.

Rosario's fingers trace gentle circles against his back. She's so tactile. Never shying away from touching him, comforting him. He and Sofie took one of those love quizzes a while back. While she wanted to hear encouraging words, Ulysses craved touch. Kissing. Hugging. Holding hands. Cuddling on the couch, in bed. A smile creeps across his face and he relaxes into a comfortable warm feeling being there beside Rosario. They look at each other, and for a moment, he wishes this interrogation was part of a real courtship, not an awkward misunderstanding. Not Rosario taking pity on his loneliness on Christmas Eve.

After dinner, Rosario invites Ulysses to relax in the den where it's quiet. He unbuttons his pants to make room for the food baby protruding from his gut. He'd been drinking homemade sangria that was more powerful than he anticipated and eaten so much delicious food his belly feels like it might burst. He sits back and closes his eyes, drifting off.

He wakes on the couch. Rosario's father and uncle sleep in nearby lounge chairs, their heads rolled back identically with their hands clasped on their bellies. Getting up, he follows the sound of activity in the kitchen. When he enters, the women seem to be setting up dessert. Their eyes all turn to him in unison. It makes him freeze.

"Look who's up," one of Rosario's aunts says.

"I went into a little food coma," he says sheepishly.

"We'll take it as a compliment," she replies.

Rosario's mother is eating a *melomakarona*. "Ulysses made those," Rosario says with a smile, catching her mother mid-bite. Mercedes looks at Ulysses, then back at the cookie, seemingly evaluating it with a new level of scrutiny. "They're very good," she admits, and Ulysses feels a surge of pride.

"Thank you. It's my mom's recipe. I was worried; I've never made them on my own before."

Mercedes's brows draw together in a compassionate look, and she reaches out with both arms to pull him into a tight hug. When he's in her embrace, he inhales her scent—soap and some kind of floral perfume. Pulling back, Mercedes pats his cheek gently. "I like this one," she says, her voice carrying a teasing tone, then nods approvingly at Rosario. Mercedes warmly squeezes his bicep with a wink. Glancing at his arm, she hums curiously, then squeezes again.

"Mom," Rosario scolds through a laugh. Ulysses flushes at Mercedes's groping him, but Rosario intervenes, pulling him away with a bit of pink in her cheeks. "Dessert? I made *tres leches*."

He's had it before. Spongy yellow cake soaked in sweetened

condensed and other kinds of milks, topped with whipped cream. It's sinful. Rosario carefully unveils a large *tres leches* cake from its protective tin foil wrap.

"Oof," he says, holding his belly. "Maybe just a taste." He leans against the counter, catching a whiff of sweet milk and vanilla, and finds himself genuinely excited to try a piece. She cuts a slice and sets it on a plate, handing it to him. Taking a bite, the rich flavors melt on his tongue. He can't help but feel at home. There's something about Rosario's presence that's comforting, and despite the earlier chaos, he's grateful for the warmth and liveliness of the evening.

"You hear that? Your mom likes me." Ulysses raises an eyebrow.

"Does that surprise you?"

"Well, when I got here, your parents looked at me like I was some kind of gang leader."

She shoves playfully against his chest. "No they didn't. They just say what they think. They're honest people."

"I'm noticing that."

Smiling at him, her eyes glitter. His gaze lingers on her, a flutter in his chest. Taking his fork from his hand, she cuts off a corner of the cake from his plate and feeds it to herself. Holding his breath, he watches the metal prongs disappear into her mouth, knowing they'd just been in his. Her tongue slips out to collects the remnants of whipped cream, and he swallows hard.

"Mm," she hums. "So good."

He lets out a low chuckle as heat rises to his face. "I didn't realize we were sharing."

Her eyes hold him, her flirtation palpable. "Want more?" The question is met with her sectioning off another bite onto the fork and presenting it to him with a graceful swoop, the morsel of cake poised at his lips.

Locked in a heated gaze, he nods slightly and opens his mouth to receive it. She feeds it to him, and sparks of electricity propagate across his skin. The attraction is mutual. Licking his lips and taking in the contours of her face, the delicate curve of her lips, he imagines they'd feel so warm and soft against his. Wonders about the heat of her flesh beneath that dress.

"Alright you two," one aunt says, bumping into Rosario and breaking his trance. "Stop hogging the *tres leches*. I'm putting it out in the dining room for everyone."

As the night winds down, guests start to exchange gifts, and Ulysses takes his cue to head out. After retrieving Domino, he politely says his goodbyes, but before he can leave, Rosario stops him at the door with a box wrapped in gold paper. "Merry Christmas."

"What is this?"

"It's for you. I wanted you to have something to open tomorrow morning."

Ulysses hesitates in the hall, suddenly aware of his empty hands. It's such a sweet and thoughtful gesture. A pang of guilt aches in his chest for not having anything to offer in return. "You didn't have to get me anything. I feel awful. I didn't get you—"

Rosario leans in close. "Don't worry about it," she whispers, close enough to feel the sweet scented warmth of her breath. "Just being here is enough."

"Are you kidding? You saved me from a sad, lonely night alone in my motel room. That was a gift all by itself."

"Well, you saved me from intrusive questions about my love life. So we're even."

He wishes it wasn't a ruse. But even with their mutual attraction, what could he possibly offer her? He can't even ask her out on a date because he can't afford to take her out to dinner, a movie, anything she'd probably enjoy. But he wants to see her again.

"I guess there's Brody's party coming up, huh?"

"Oh, you're not getting out of that, mister. We had a deal."

He holds up his hands in defense. "I'm looking forward to it."

"Me too."

Leaning forward, he presses his lips to her cheek. "See you then."

When they pull apart, they exchange a charged glance and small smiles. Her dark eyes gleam at him.

"Goodnight, Ulysses."

"Goodnight, Rosario."

Returning to the bleak motel is a jarring downgrade, but the sensation of their tender goodbye is an analgesic that numbs his worries for the night. Wanting to honor her intentions, he waits until morning to unwrap his gift. Inside is a wooden box carved with a classic Greek key geometric spiral. The hardware is silver and embossed with olive branches. It's beautiful. Turning it over, it says *handmade in Greece*. Opening it, he finds a leather bracelet and a note inside. The bracelet has black leather cords with two entwined ropes forming a knot engraved in silver. He reads the note.

> *Ulysses,*
>
> *I'm told the engravings on this bracelet are made to represent Hercules. I know this holiday season has been difficult for you, and I wanted you to have a reminder of your strength.*
>
> *Merry Christmas,*
> *Rosario*

Later that day, he visits his mother at the memory care facility and finds her asleep, sitting up in a chair in a common area in front of a television stuck on the Lifetime network. An orderly mops the floor, and Ulysses breathes in the scent of lemons and piss. Eleni's mouth hangs open like a ghoul. It's a frightening sight.

"Did something happen?" he asks the nurse, who glances at his mother briefly before returning to her paperwork.

"She's on medication. It makes her drowsy, but she's okay." Scribbling a last thought, she gets up from the table and taps on Eleni's knee. "Ms. Eleni," she calls, and it stirs her awake. Her eyes fling open, then focus with recognition. "Uly," she says, and it shocks him.

Smiling, he sits on the ottoman in front of her. "Hi, Mom. Merry Christmas," It's rare she's clear this time of day. Her recognition makes him comfortable showing her all the affection he'd been holding back as to not frighten her. He was often a stranger to her, after all. But as her son, he could kiss her cheek, hug her, hold her hand.

Looking around the room, she seems distressed. "Where are all my things?"

"The nurses put them away," he lies, not wanting to upset her.

"Have I missed them?"

"Missed what, Momma?"

"The fireworks."

He strokes her arm to calm her. She's confused. "It's alright, Momma. There's no fireworks today."

"No fireworks today," she echoes back, half a question. "Mary will never sing in the choir with Calliope," she says, trembling. "Never!"

Ice runs through his veins. She's lost in a memory. Trapped there in the prison of her mind. A old man nearby lets out a high-pitched groan of distress at her outburst. Patients turn their heads with alarm. Hearing her shouts, the nurse motions for Ulysses to give her space, and Ulysses backs away.

Fireworks, he thinks. Maybe she remembered how much he disliked them. The very idea draws sweat from his pores. New Year's is approaching. Every year he does his best to avoid events that used them, a nearly impossible task. Most likely, he'll spend New Year's Eve in bed with his noise cancelling headphones in, holding Domino to calm their anxiety together.

The nurse whispers to Eleni, and it's only a few moments before she falls silent again. He's not sure if the nurse has given her something to calm her, or if she's freed herself from this moment of confusion, but soon after, she falls asleep. He leaves the visit shaken.

Chapter Twelve

SHAWNEE SITS with Rosario as she applies her makeup. It's an hour before the Randall party, and Ulysses is expected at any minute to pick them up. Shawnee picks a piece of lint from her leopard print sweater. "I've been tossing around ideas for the Calliope series. What do you think about *the trailer park vanishing*?"

"No," Rosario responds without hesitation and hopes the disbelieving glare she gives Shawnee sends a clear message. "Ulysses is never going to go for that."

"It's not up to him. Is it?"

"I promised he'd have a say in the narrative. That's the only way he was going to talk to us." Rosario stands in front of a long, dark marble vanity in her bathroom while smudging black eyeliner around her tear line. She finds her favorite red lipstick and leans in close to the mirror to glide the pointed red tip around her lips.

"You like him," Shawnee accuses, and Rosario's eyes shoot at her in the reflection. "Have you forgotten he's a suspect?"

"He's not a suspect."

"He gives off a weird vibe."

Rosario swats her makeup drawer shut and fluffs up her blonde hair to awaken the soft curls she'd unraveled earlier. "You're just pissed he stood up to you."

"He didn't stand up to me." Shawnee frowns and pushes her glasses up the bridge of her nose.

"Well he didn't answer your rude, intrusive, personal questions."

"We're *supposed* to ask questions. You're losing your objectivity here."

A row of perfume bottles line a shelf. Crossing the room, Rosario picks a dark, wintery fragrance by Yves Saint Laurent. Spritzing it into the air, she forms a cloud of mist and walks through it. "You should have seen him here on Christmas Eve. *Yes ma'am*, this and *no sir*, that. It was adorable. He's a southern gentleman. He takes care of his mother. He's a counselor. His literal job is helping people through the worst times of their lives. What's the matter with you?"

"Do you know how much counselors like him actually make?"

"I don't care."

"No, I mean they make a decent living. Especially at a bougie place like Palms. You mean to tell me a guy like that ends up living in a motel?"

"Sofie screwed him over."

"And he has no savings? No retirement to borrow from? Can't he just take out a loan?"

"He pays for his mother's care. He has student loans. Maybe he didn't want to get into more debt over this. Seriously, what is it you think he's doing with his money that's so suspicious?"

Shawnee shrugs. "I don't know. But he's a suspect for a reason."

The sound of the doorbell interrupts their conversation, and Rosario quickly checks her appearance in the mirror one last time. "That's probably him." She narrows her eyes at Shawnee in warning. "Behave yourself, okay? We need him on board, and I promised we'd treat him fairly."

With a sigh, Shawnee puts on a contrived smile in silent acquiescence. On the way out, Rosario grabs her purse and switches off the light.

Opening the door, she notices he's worn his hair down. It falls in thick waves and ends in curls that rest against his chest. His scruffy beard has been tamed, combed through and neatly straightened. "It's cold out there," he says, his hands tucked into the pockets of his black and brown flannel shirt jacket. "Bring a coat. It's even colder where we're going."

Pulling her leather jacket out from the entry hall closet, she overhears Shawnee commenting on Ulysses's hair.

"Wow, I almost didn't recognize you."

Rosario rolls her eyes to herself, slipping into her jacket before remerging into the foyer. "I like it," she says.

He combs his fingers through it self-consciously. "Thought I'd switch it up. Keep my ears warm. Ready to go?"

Shawnee insists on riding in the back seat together, despite the fact her long legs make it a less than ideal choice. Rosario quickly learns it's so Shawnee can continue to whisper her cockamamie theories on the long drive.

"Maybe he's covering for his friends. Or paying for their silence."

"Keep your voice down," Rosario says, briefly catching Ulysses's piercing eyes in the rearview mirror. This isn't how she envisioned their night—him riding alone up front like a chauffeur.

"Y'all warm enough back there?" he asks.

"We're good," Shawnee says.

He lowers the volume of the radio. Rosario finds it endearing he listens to the actual radio. An alternative rock station. Sitting in the back seat of a car in the dark, on the way to a party with the music playing, a wave of nostalgia passes through her thinking of nights like this on her way to a party, nights she'd miraculously avoided trouble despite being patently up to no good. It makes her wonder.

"So, what kind of party is this? Family friendly or…"

"Family friendly, I guess you could say. But they're an interesting bunch."

"What's that mean?" Shawnee asks.

"You'll see."

A twinge of unease tightens her stomach. Soon, they're far out of the city, deep in the rural town of Parrish, where streetlights are few and far between. The air smells cleaner, the night sky clearer. When they finally arrive, Rosario is grateful Ulysses agreed to take them. She never would have found this place on her own. They turn into a wall of darkness and hear the crunch of gravel under the tires. The change in sound, the jerk and bounce as they traverse the uneven terrain the only indicators they've arrived. Staring through the windshield at the beams of light as they illuminate the feet ahead, she can make out a narrow dirt road lined with oaks covered in kudzu vines that climb up their base. Spanish moss hangs in snaggy wisps. They create strange shadowed shapes that sway in the wind. In the distance, she can make out string lights. After a moment, the air smells of charred wood.

"Is this all their property?"

"Yeah, they've got a few acres. The house is set back a ways."

"It's fucking creepy out here," Shawnee whispers.

As they approach the house, Rosario can make out the silhouettes of many guests—standing, sitting in congregation around the fire. Ulysses pulls up to a gravel lot where several pickup trucks and Jeeps sit in a neat grid. Country music carries on the air, and Rosario feels out of place. This isn't usually her scene.

"Here we are," he says and shifts the Jeep into park. He looks through the passenger window toward the party, draws in a deep breath and exhales slowly.

"Thanks for doing this," Rosario says. Reaching over, she squeezes his bicep.

Holy hell. It's hard as stone. It makes her wonder what he's got going on under that jacket, under that shirt. She'd planned on saying something reassuring like *you're going to do great*, or *you got this*, but then he yanks up his sleeve and shows her that he's wearing the leather Hercules bracelet she got him, and a small smile turns up the corner of his mouth. She can't say anything at all because her throat closes up, and by the time it calms, he's halfway out of the driver's side door.

He helps them out, and they walk through the cold. Rosario

clutches her jacket close as a wind sweeps through. They make it to the fire and she's grateful for the warmth.

"Oh my lord, look who rose from the dead," a man shouts. His stocky silhouette slowly emerges from the dark. An intricate mandala tattoo wraps around his thick neck, partially hidden behind a short beard. The perked up apples of his cheeks give his broad smile a boyish quality. Once he's close, he doesn't hesitate to grab Ulysses and give him a hard slap on the back.

"Brody, this is Rosario and Shawnee, the ladies from the podcast I was telling you about."

"Alright," Brody says enthusiastically. "So glad you could make it. We've got coolers of beer all around here. Warm food's in the house."

"Actually, it's a little noisy out here. Maybe we could head in there for a talk?" Shawnee immediately suggests. The woman has no finesse whatsoever.

"Whenever you're ready," Rosario adds.

Brody's grin glints in his dark eyes. "Yeah, I'm sure we can find a quiet spot inside." Turning back to Ulysses, he says, "I got your money."

"Really?"

"Told you I would."

Ulysses shakes his head, seeming to fight his better judgment. "I don't know, man. I appreciate it, but it's not right. You shouldn't have to pay for your sister's bullshit."

"Don't worry. I'm handling it my own way."

A confused stitch forms in Ulysses's brow, and Brody chuckles. "That's four months' worth of daycare she's working off. We got a live in-nanny for the foreseeable future."

"She's been living here? I thought she was living in a van down by the river."

"Didn't agree with her just like I knew it wouldn't."

A tall, lanky man approaches Brody from behind, his head shaved to a low buzz cut, complexion ghast and pallid. Rosario recognizes him from his mugshot as Warren. It's been ten years since he was sent to prison on an armed robbery conviction, and he's aged poorly. The sharp angles of his stubbled face make dark shadows in the hollow of his cheeks. Deep lines mar his forehead, and the skin of his eyebrows droops slightly over his deep-set blue eyes. They widen as they lock in on Ulysses.

"Holy shit, dude." His mouth falls open. "Uly actually showed up."

He's missing a few teeth, and it gives his speech a swishy quality. Warren glances over at Rosario and Shawnee, his demeanor becoming noticeably excited in a way that unsettles Rosario. "My goodness, ladies. I apologize for the strong language. I had no idea you beauties were standing there."

"What strong language?" Shawnee replies, her voice husky as ever.

Warren chuckles and says something, but Rosario is drawn to Ulysses's face, suddenly hardened. His jaw twitches, and she suspects he must have just seen Sofie. Something protective in her rises. She closes the space between them, takes his arm, and hooks her own around it to claim him. Just then, Rosario sees her too. No introduction is required from the way she and Ulysses look at each other, the glow of the fire lighting them in flickering shades of gold.

She's beautiful—big doe eyes with thick lashes and a button nose. Everything in perfect symmetry. The realization twists Rosario's heart, and it tightens further as Sofie approaches them.

"Hey," she says with an innocent expression.

Hey? The audacity is strong with this one. Ulysses faces her, blinking as if he's confused. But he doesn't speak. Instead, he turns back to Rosario, his arm wrapping around her waist. The sense of protectiveness grows to something possessive, territorial. She tugs on the lapel of his jacket. "Why don't we go inside, get our conversation out of the way, and afterward we can just enjoy the party?"

"Good with me," Shawnee says. Rosario closes her eyes, remembering their chaperone.

He glances down at her, his expression softened. "Good with me too."

Chapter Thirteen

IT'S BEEN ALMOST a year since Ulysses has been to Brody's house. For a relatively young couple, Brody and Ashley's home decor screamed baby boomer, with floral valances, sponge painted walls and tufted polyester upholstered reclining sofas. Slate-blue walls contrast against the gold oak hues of the floors and kitchen cabinets. Rosario and Shawnee set up two mics on either side of a low oak and glass coffee table. Sofie joins them, sitting in an easy chair opposite them at glaring distance. Ulysses won't look directly at her, but from what he can see from the corner of his eye, she's scowling at them.

Rosario taps a few keys on her laptop and sits beside Ulysses. Rubbing his thigh affectionately, she turns to him. "Ready?"

"Yeah, let's get this over with."

"That's the spirit," she says, squeezing him above his knee. Since they've arrived, she's hardly kept her hands off him and all he can think about is getting her alone.

"What's all this about anyhow?" Warren asks just as Rosario signals to Shawnee that they're recording.

"It's been twenty years since Calliope disappeared," Shawnee starts. "Now, the only people that we know from the police reports were present at the Water Oak park that day were you—Ulysses, Brody, Warren and Sofie."

The sound of her name, the thought of her sitting just feet away, makes Ulysses grind his teeth. Rosario's hand passes gentle strokes over his thigh again, and he wonders if the mic would pick up the obscene things he wants to whisper in her ear. She's the only reason he's holding it together.

"We all talked to the cops. We ain't suspects no more," Warren says, a hint of irritation in his voice.

"This isn't an interrogation," Rosario interjects, leaning over Ulysses slightly. She smells nice, like perfume. "Think of it like a conversation. The hope is that by talking together about the things you remember, we might spark new memories that could lead us to finding Calliope."

Warren nods agreeably. It's so strange sitting here with him after all these years. Graying in his beard, crow's-feet deepening every time he smiles. Yet his demeanor is just as it always was. Like he's still sixteen—excitable, playful and easy to laugh. "It was the summer. I was fixin' to play football with a couple of friends. Mom and Dad was fighting at that time about God only knows what. Mom went on to work, Dad went out on the road, and then Brody come out and said Uly's comin' over to play on the PlayStation. I wasn't gonna babysit, so I said y'all are on your own. I left right after Uly showed up. I was gone the whole rest of the afternoon with my friends. By the time I came back, it was gettin' dark and Calliope was already gone. It was summertime so that musta been like damn near eight o'clock when I finally get home."

He shrugs and shakes his head, as if to say that's all he's got, then turns to Brody.

Brody agrees. "Yeah, basically that was it. Uly came by. We played a video game. We got bored and wrestled each other around like we were wrestlers. Got him good one time, you remember that?"

"Gave me a shiner screwin' around."

"His mom lost it."

"Yeah," Sofie chimes in. "Remember she told Mom you were a

little demon child who needed to be baptized again because the first time didn't take?"

Ulysses scoffs. "My mom didn't call him a demon child."

"The baptism part was true though," Brody insists, raising his eyebrows. "Made me dig a hole as punishment. Dug till my hands bled. Then she made me fill it back up again."

Warren chuckles. "Yeah, she did. Made me dig one too. I can't even remember what for."

Ulysses hardly remembers any of that. "My mom is very religious," he explains. "Old school. But what's that have to do with Calliope?"

Shawnee crosses her legs and folds her hands over her knee. "Did you ever…" she starts, trailing off. "Was Calliope ever injured from your wrestling?"

"We ain't doin' that," Warren says, raising his voice. "I already warned you once. Nobody here hurt that little girl."

Holding up her hands, she backtracks. "I'm not suggesting anyone hurt her intentionally."

"Nobody hurt her, period," Warren says. This time, his eyes hold a crazed threatening look.

Ulysses gets a small thrill watching Warren's brand of crazy winning out over Shawnee's pushiness.

"Okay," Shawnee concedes. "Let's move on."

"I'm surprised Uly's even doing this," Sofie says. Just the sound of her voice grates on him.

"What do you mean?" Shawnee asks.

"Uly hated Calliope."

"Fucking liar." The words fly out of Ulysses's mouth, and before he can stop himself, he's shouting at her. "Why are you even here?"

"I live here," she shouts back. "And I'm not a liar. You said you hated her because your mom worshiped that little girl. Don't you remember?"

Rosario's arm is around his, holding him back. "Relax," she whispers. "She wants to set you off, don't give her what she wants."

"He might not remember because he'd had a few that night. Does your new girlfriend know about your little drinking problem?"

"Alright, that's enough," Brody says, rising to his feet. He quickly closes the distance between him and Sofie and grabs her by the arm.

"Hey!" she cries.

"You're a goddamn troublemaker," Brody grumbles.

The sound of their shouts summons Nadine, whose sagging cheeks fix her face in a perpetual frown. Her brow stitched, Nadine strides toward Sofie, who struggles to yank her arm free from Brody's grip. The fear of his mother's wrath is evident in Brody's widened eyes as he lets go and backs away.

Nadine approaches and slaps Sofie hard across the face. It invites low gasps from Shawnee and Rosario and makes Ulysses stomach sink. As much as he hates Sofie right now, watching her take Nadine's abuse is difficult.

"I told you to behave yourself, didn't I? Now you apologize to everybody here."

"Momma," Sofie whines, gripping her cheek.

"You stole from this man, and we all had to clean up your mess. Now you apologize."

She's silent. Her face a red, twisted and tear-streaked mess.

"Ms. Randall, please," Ulysses says. The thought of the family having to scrape together the money to pay him back weighs him with guilt. Sofie's humiliation is palpable, and he takes no pleasure in it. "The debt's been paid. I don't need anything else."

"I'm sorry," Sofie says, if only to spite him one more time. "I'm sorry I stayed as long as I did. I'm sorry I didn't save up longer to find a way out."

Find a way out? Months without an explanation and now she decides to finally tell him why she left in front of an audience. "You want to do this here in front of everyone?" he asks.

"You should have thought about that before showing up here."

"I was invited!" he shouts, rising to his feet, yanking free from Rosario's attempt to stop him. His blood pressure rises, heartbeat thumping in his temple. Taking a breath, he tries to calm himself. His voice steadies. "You've got a complaint? I'd love to hear it, because I was good to you, Sofie. You weren't a prisoner. Hell, if you'd have told me you wanted out, I'd have found a way to get you the money myself. You blindsided me."

"When was I supposed to tell you? I never saw you. And when you were home, you were drinking all the time and feeling sorry for yourself."

"Alright," Brody interjects, turning to Sofie. "We're not doing this here."

Sofie looks at Brody and Nadine before storming off. Nadine goes after her, and Brody sighs, the apples of his round cheeks bright red. He addresses the group. "Sorry about that, y'all. She's got her feelings hurt is all. Now she's acting out." He addresses Shawnee. "Are we done? Cause I don't remember nothing else."

Ulysses can't seem to pull in air fast enough. His pulse races as he takes a deep breath. Who the fuck does she think she is going off on him like that? She left *him*, not the other way around. Now, suddenly he's being attacked. It's not fair. He clenches his fists and expels a hard breath through his nose.

Rosario takes his wrist. "Hey," she says softly. "You want to take a break? Get some air?"

"I'm done," he says, yanking his hand back. He never wanted to do this in the first place. "You get what you wanted?"

Her expression falls and her shoulders sink. Stepping back, Brody fills the space between them and squeezes Ulysses's shoulder. Somehow, his show of support makes the knot in his heart tighten further. A sting rises to his eyes, and he's practically suffocating just as Warren appears, a bottle of Jack Daniel's in his grip.

"I don't know if you heard, but this is a party," he says. "Let's get fucked up."

Chapter Fourteen

IT'S FREEZING COLD, but near the fire, the flames dance tall amid a spire of charred oak branches. It flickers in the dark, casting strange shadows against the trees and post-and-rail fences. Rosario fights the bile rising in her throat, the twist of regret in her belly, alone in a sea of strangers. Shawnee has disappeared into the crowd, trying to salvage the night with an interesting story. Ulysses and his friends howl with laughter across the party as they drink themselves stupid, and Rosario wonders what she ever saw in him. All that misplaced anger directed right at her. She'd thought he was better than that, that he was emotionally mature. She doesn't know him at all.

"Hey," she hears a voice say against the music and crackling fire. Sofie, with the same innocent look she shot Ulysses earlier. Rosario doesn't buy it. She looks around, hoping to summon Shawnee over for protection, but she's gone. "What do you want?" Rosario says.

"Can we talk?"

Already nearing her max bullshit tolerance for the night, Rosario debates whether she wants to take the bait. She doesn't know this woman. "What do you want to talk about?"

"Calliope."

The unshed tears in Sofie's eyes glisten against the warm glow of the bonfire. Why should Rosario believe anything this woman says? The jealous side of her wants to tell her to piss off. And yet, this is what they came here for. Sofie was there that day, after all. Whatever she says, fact or fiction, will become part of the story. Rosario takes a moment to put her personal feelings aside, then motions for Sofie to follow her toward the house. "Let's go somewhere quiet."

Sofie nods in agreement, and they make their way across the lawn. Returning into the house, Sofie guides Rosario to a bedroom with two twin beds and a trundle bed made up on the floor. The room smells earthy, like the sweat of children who'd been playing outside all day. Is this where she's been sleeping? Ulysses called her manic. Maybe so. Though, how bad does a relationship have to be to prefer sharing a bedroom with two little girls and sleeping on the floor?

Closing the door, Sofie clicks on a small bedside lamp and sits on the bed. "Sorry about earlier," she says. "I thought y'all were seeing each other, and it just felt like he brought you here to rub it in my face."

"What do you care?" Rosario says, digging into her bag. She pulls her mic out and sets it on the end table. "You broke up with him. You want him to stay single forever?"

"I want him to get his shit together's what I want."

"I'm recording."

"Wait," she says. "Let me say something first. I do love him, you know. And that stuff about stealing from him, that's not all true."

"He's living in a motel for fun?"

"Ask him where his money goes."

Rosario stays fixed on her eyes, looking for a hint of deceit. Her gut tenses at the words. She hates it when Shawnee's right. "I really need to get this on the record if we're talking about the case."

"Fine, do what you need to do. But I'm telling you, ask him yourself."

"I will," Rosario says, then presses record. "I'm recording now. I'm here with Sofie Randall. Sofie, when you invited me in here, it was because you told me you wanted to talk about Calliope. Let's hear it."

Chapter Fifteen

A STEADY STREAM of piss patters against the base of an oak, the heat of it steaming up in the frigid air in swirling tendrils. Ulysses is unsteady on his feet, uncomfortably holding his dick with cold fingers. "You seen Rosario?" he hears Shawnee's husky voice sneak up behind him, and he stumbles back in the dark, his stream veering left and sprinkling onto his boots.

"Holy fucking hell, woman," Ulysses slurs. "Can't you see I'm taking a piss? You can't just sneak up on me like that." He wipes his hands on his jeans and tucks himself away, zipping up his fly.

"Where are your keys?"

"In my pocket. I'm not driving anywhere right now."

"Damn right, you're not. Give me your keys."

"Whoa, hold on a sec there, chief. You're always running that mouth of yours like —" He's mid insult when she grabs him by the belt and yanks him forward, throwing him off balance. He grunts, tripping forward as her hand shoves into his pocket. "The fuck are you doing?"

Searching his other pocket, she finds his keys and fishes them out. "I'm taking Rosario home. Have a good night."

"Hey," he calls, but she's already walking away. "You're stealing my car!" He follows behind her, barely keeping pace. "Hey," he protests again.

Brody and Warren, having taken shelter in an open side garage, notice the commotion and rush out as Shawnee strides toward the front yard. The smell of marijuana and beer carry on the air. "Whoa," Warren says, staggering toward her, throwing up his hands to stop her. "Hold up." The hollow of his gaunt face gives him a ghoulish appearance under bright floodlights. She laughs, stepping around him, and continues toward the bonfire where the party guests still gather.

"Rosario," she shouts.

Just then, as if the mention of her name caused her to appear, Rosario emerges from the house with Sofie. Seeing them together makes Ulysses's nerves flare. "You've got to be fucking kidding me," he says slowly, his attention shifting to the pair of them. He lumbers toward them, boots scraping on the concrete path bridging the front porch to the driveway. His glare shifts between them, eyes straining to focus. Isn't this what women do? Come together around a common enemy. *Unbelievable.* "Look at this. Just fucking great."

"Go home, Uly," Sofie barks back.

"Home? You wanna know what home is cause of you, you horrible fucking bitch?"

"Hey," Brody yells. "You don't talk to my sister like that."

"Oh, okay," Ulysses says, stepping back. He addresses Brody. "You know what? Fuck you too. I didn't even want to come to this shit."

Beads of sweat speckle Brody's greasy face as he rocks from one foot to the other, eyes drooping with intoxication. "Fuck me?" He charges toward Ulysses.

It's a blur, his shoulder quickly making contact with Ulysses's chest. In a weak attempt to hold his footing, Ulysses grabs Brody around his barrel waist. Their clumsy tussle, a combination of falling and wrestling to the ground, sends them both tumbling onto the dirt. Ulysses lands hard on his back, and the air is driven out of his lungs. While dazed by his forceful collision with the frozen earth, Brody crawls on top of him, his thighs straddling Ulysses's waist.

Shirt forced up, Brody's bare belly spills over the top of his jeans. Ulysses covers his face with his forearms as Brody pummels him with his fists. The icy air and the whiskey work to slightly dull the pain of each heavy blow, but Ulysses can barely breathe with the bastard sitting on his chest.

"Get off of me, you fat fuck," he groans.

"You gonna hit him or kiss him?" Warren shouts.

"Stop it!" Sofie cries. "You're hurting him!"

Brody rests back on his heels, breathing hard, and wriggles off of Ulysses before struggling to his feet. The metallic taste of blood spreads across his tongue as Warren helps Ulysses off the ground.

"Alright, time to go," Shawnee says, tugging Ulysses by his arm.

He struggles, but she's strong, and he's dragged against his will to his Jeep, where she shoves him into the back seat. He stews there in the silence, reeking of piss, whiskey and grass. His hands are stained with dirt, head spinning. The inside of his lip stings and bleeds. Closing his eyes for a moment, he's startled by the abrupt sound of the driver and passenger doors opening almost simultaneously, the cabin filling with sound.

"Are you okay?" Rosario asks.

"Peachy." He wouldn't even be here if it wasn't for her. But he'd bought that little act of hers. She's lied to him from the start, why would she change now? He lies back with a huff, then closes his eyes, tucking his hands into his armpits for warmth.

Falling asleep, he's aware of the murmur of voices. His eyes flutter open from time to time, and he feels as if he's been abducted by aliens. The glow of the streetlights above them gleam through the windshield, and he catches glimpses of Shawnee and Rosario looking over their shoulders at him as they whisper to each other unintelligibly.

At some point, the car stops, and he's not sure if they've parked or they're at a red light. But after a few moments, he hears the door click open and Shawnee reaches for him.

When he wakes in his motel room to the sound of Domino's whines, he's still in his jeans, drenched in sweat. Sitting up with an ache pounding in his temples, he notices the layer of dirt on his hands, under his nails. His memory is distorted. Despite his struggle to pull up an image, he finds only blackness, and a bitter taste fills his mouth. His phone is charging on an end table. Opening the curtains, the sun pours in and blinds him. What time is it? What day is it? Sunday. It must be.

Quenching his thirst with a bottled water from the fridge, he sits in the hard dining chair and thinks. Wrestling Brody to the ground. Rosario. He'd been mean to her. Letting out a long sigh, he curses himself. Sofie's button pushing worked as she'd intended, and he blew it. Made an ass of himself. He rakes his hands through his hair. Just perfect.

Despite his desire to smooth things over with Rosario and apologize, he can't bring himself to text or call her. He waits in hopes she'll make the first move, let him know there aren't any hard feelings. But as time passes, he hears her silence loud and clear.

After a few days, he breaks, texting her from bed around ten o'clock at night on a workday.

> Hey. Sorry about last weekend. I'm an idiot.

The next morning while taking Domino for a jog, she texts back.

> All good.

Her cool brevity sends an ache of disappointment through his chest. Whatever romantic feelings might have been budding between them are dead, and he killed them.

* * *

IN FEBRUARY, he finds a nice place. It's a smaller one-bedroom, but it has new appliances and a washer and dryer. It's in a good neighborhood close to work, and by extension, close to Rosario. Though he hasn't seen her since the night of the party, he's made a point to keep in touch. They text often. Not just about Calliope's case. He asks about her day. Tells her he's sold all his paintings. Or, how Dr. Okafor's long-winded stories always seem to come just as Ulysses is trying to leave work for the day.

After taking Domino for a walk, he sits at his small dining table over a homemade tomato sandwich and texts Rosario.

> My mom remembered me today. But then she started saying odd things again. Made herself upset.

HE DROPS a lemon-scented pod into his garbage disposal just as his phone vibrates on the counter. Drying his damp hands on a towel, he looks at it.

> Glad she remembered you. You okay?

Smiling to himself, he's pleased she asked.

> I'm okay. Thank you. How was your day?

Chapter Sixteen

SOMETHING IS TERRIBLY WRONG. It's been three days since Shawnee stormed out. It seemed like a minor disagreement at that time, and their spats tended to settle within twenty-four hours at most. But Rosario is starting to wonder if Shawnee has done something stupid and gotten herself hurt.

For weeks after the Randall party, Rosario and Shawnee tried to make sense of Sofie's interview—The Church of the Ninth Order, Calliope's father and how they might be connected to Calliope's disappearance. They got the sense she was holding something back. Shawnee paced the dim living room of Rosario's apartment, headphones on, replaying their interviews over and over again.

One day, when she quickly pulled the headset from her ears, hooking them around her neck with wide eyes, Rosario knew she'd found something. "Listen to this," Shawnee said, playing the audio through her phone's speaker. It's Warren's voice, recounting the morning of Calliope's disappearance. "He said '*Dad went out on the road.*' As in, he wasn't already out on the road like we thought. He was home that morning."

"Oh shit. Nadine lied to the police," Rosario realized. Why would she lie to the police about Lang Randall's whereabouts the day of Calliope's disappearance? Was that what Sofie was trying to tell them? *It's all connected*, she said.

It was overcast, and the floor-to-ceiling windows in Rosario's office took in the impending storm outside. They sat with their laptops open, intently searching for any information on Lang Randall. Finding him was easy. Rosario spun her laptop around to show Shawnee her screen, where an aerial satellite photo of his property—8619 Running Horse Road, Whispering Hope, Florida—was pulled up in her browser. A Zillow photo with a bleak-looking white plantation mansion in the center of over one hundred acres of flat green was surrounded by white post-and-rail fencing and large travel trailers, suggesting others might be taking residence on the property as well.

"Whispering Hope? Where the hell is that?" Shawnee asked.

"About an hour and a half south of here."

"When are we going?" Shawnee glowed with an excitement that made Rosario's stomach drop. Shawnee was always ready to drive head-on into a tornado, while Rosario held firm on the brakes.

"What? You're joking." Rosario slammed her laptop shut. "We're not going."

Pressing her hands to her temples, Shawnee squeezed her eyes closed, as if Rosario's resistance gave her a migraine. "Why bother finding him then?"

"Two women show up uninvited to a man's house in the middle of nowhere to ask him about a missing little girl? He clearly doesn't want to be found, and if we did find something serious, he'd kill us. No way."

Shawnee leaned back, her expression a mix of frustration and contemplation. With a shake of her head, she froze and bore into Rosario. "This is the job. It's dangerous. You have to take risks. Why are you so scared to do anything all the time?"

"That's not fair."

"The Candy Bandit?" she mocked, throwing up her hands. "Come on, Rosario. We could be so much more than that. You're holding us back. You might be content with mediocrity, but I'm not."

"Whoa, fuck you," Rosario shouted. "You're being unfair. What happened to the Belladonna case?"

"We don't have the budget to fly across the country on a hunch. This guy's within driving distance, and if we found Calliope, we'd be launched into the stratosphere. I mean, sponsors would be falling all over themselves to get featured."

"This is about money?"

"Yes, most people care about money. I know you've never had to, but I'm trying to make a living. And your scaredy-cat ass is making it impossible."

"Excuse me for not wanting to get murdered."

Shawnee got up and started to pace, a deep stitch in her brow. "What if we made up a story. We ran out of gas. Ask to use their phone because we can't get a signal. Then we snoop around a little, check out the property. If we catch a whiff of something, then we call the cops. In and out."

An uneasy feeling sunk into her belly thinking about the risks. Reflecting on her conversation with Deputy Beau Harris after their diner meet-up on the Carla Whitman murder investigation, he'd nearly burst with excitement at the mention of possibly working with the podcast again. "Maybe Deputy Harris can help."

"Deputy Dimples?" she teased, referring to the adorable dints in his stubbled cheeks that emerged whenever he smiled. "If we get the police involved now, any potential witnesses are gonna clam up. We want them to let their guard down."

"There has to be another way."

Shawnee threw up her hands and picked up her backpack. "I can't just sit on my ass and do nothing. We have a lead. It's a good lead. You're not being very solutions oriented."

Rosario hated it when Shawnee threw that corporate buzzword bullshit at her. Maybe she was being overly cautious. But there's something about that place that didn't feel right, and she wasn't going against her gut. "I'm sorry. I'm not going."

That was three days ago, and not a word since. Rosario's calls and texts have gone unanswered, and Shawnee's social media accounts haven't been updated. Rosario even stood outside

Shawnee's door listening to her neighbor's birds screech and squawk for thirty minutes before walking away empty-handed. It's making Rosario worry. Had Shawnee gone out there alone? Why wouldn't she say something? Tell someone? If she was going on a date with a new person, she'd turn on location services, text Rosario their dating profile picture and set a time after which, if she hadn't heard from her, she'd call the police. *Location services.*

Opening the Find My app on her iPhone, she waits for Shawnee's picture to load. Shawnee was eighty-seven miles away yesterday, and her location hasn't updated since. She texts Ulysses.

Are you home?

She changes in her closet and, finding a weekend bag, packs a change of clothes and toiletries just in case. She's already on her way out the door when Ulysses texts back.

Yes, everything okay?

In her car, she sends a quick response before hitting the ignition.

On my way!

It's the first time she's visited him at his new place. It's not far from where she lives, and she arrives just minutes later on the dark, cold winter evening. When he opens the door, he's still dressed in his work clothes; a crisp white button-down shirt tucked into his khakis. It's a sharp contrast to the tattoos that peek from his cuffs and collar. His long hair is worn down and falls in a dense blanket of ringlets that rest on his chest and shoulders. He lets her in, and she takes in the space. "Sorry to show up like this."

"Had I known you were coming over sooner, I'd have taken more time to clean up," he says, picking up a hoodie and a pair of socks from the arm of a chair and shoving them into a hamper behind a shuttered sliding door. It's a small apartment. A candle flickers on an open shelving unit near the front door that divides the cozy living space from his sleeping quarters and fills the room with the scent of sandalwood. Domino, still on his leash, struggles toward her, but Ulysses holds him taut. He lets out quick, desperate pants as his paws click and scratch against the wood floors.

"I'm sorry. I know it was last minute. You can let him go."

"Don't apologize," Ulysses says, then crouches and untethers Domino like releasing a coiled spring. Rushing toward her, she finds a bit of comfort in his excited licks and tail wags. "I'm glad you're here," he says.

Rising from her crouched position, she straightens out and shoves her hands into her coat pockets. "Nice place."

"You're very kind. Would you like a tour?"

"Sure."

He takes a step backward, then extends his left arm. "Living room." Extending his right arm, he adds, "Bedroom. Behind me is the kitchen slash dining room. And that door," he says, pointing at it, "is the bathroom."

"Cozy."

"I don't know. It's kind of a lot for me. Thinking about getting a roommate," he jokes.

It's nice to see him in good spirits. The last time she saw him, his life was falling apart and he had a gloom over him. It seems the clouds have parted. She doesn't want to ruin it, but she's not sure how to ask for help without dredging up bad feelings.

"You okay?" he asks, clearly sensing her anxiety.

She hesitates, torn between her need for help and not wanting to burden Ulysses with her problems. But the urgency of the situation wins out. Taking a deep breath, she begins. "Actually, I'm here because I need your help."

Ulysses gestures toward the couch. "Sit down, tell me what's going on."

As they settle onto the cushions, Domino curls up at their feet. Rosario takes a moment, collecting her thoughts. "It's Shawnee. I think she's missing."

The relaxed set of his shoulders shifts, and his casual smile presses into a thin line. He leans in. "What do you mean you think she's missing? When was the last time you spoke to her?"

"A few days ago, but her cell phone stopped updating her location yesterday. It's not like her to go this long without responding. No updates online. I've been to her place. No answer. I think she might be in trouble."

"Have the police done a wellness check?"

"No. I'm worried she might have gone to find Lang Randall."

His eyes glint with humor and the corners of his mouth turn up. Hesitating, he lets out a soft chuckle. "I'm sorry, I don't mean to laugh it's just..." Observing her failing to get the joke, he shakes off any amusement and takes her hand. "Lang Randall is like Ned Flanders. He's a nice guy."

"Are you sure?" His response loosens the vise around her heart. It's a reserved moment of relief, and she wants it to be true, but the things Sofie said suggested otherwise.

"Yes," he says, emphatic and reassuring. "Why would she track down Lang anyway?"

"We were just listening to the interviews again and, well, Warren said something about Lang going out on the road that day. Police reports said he was already gone."

"Warren's a little touched in the head if you didn't notice. Guy's been a heavy meth user for years. I wouldn't be surprised if he mixed up a few facts. Lang was gone that day, I told you myself."

"Maybe so, but would you come with me? Maybe it's nothing, but I need to look for her. She'd do the same for me. I need to know she's safe."

Ulysses rubs a hand through his hair. "Okay. If it'll put your mind at ease, I'll come with you. But I think you'll see it's all a big misunderstanding."

"Thank you." Rosario exhales, a wave of relief washing over her. "I just can't ignore this feeling."

"It's late. If we leave now, it'll be after midnight before we get there. I think it's better we wait until morning."

Her gut turns with worry. She knows he's right. Showing up in the middle of the night would only complicate things further. But the thought of waiting, the uncertainty lingering through the night, seems unbearable.

"Okay," Rosario finally agrees, albeit reluctantly. "First thing in the morning then."

Ulysses gives her wrist a reassuring squeeze. "I promise, we'll leave at dawn. In the meantime, try to get some rest."

The offer of rest feels hollow to Rosario, her mind racing with scenarios and possibilities. But Ulysses is right. They need to be prepared and clearheaded for whatever they might encounter at Lang Randall's place.

"Do you want to stay here tonight?" Ulysses asks, seeming to pick up on her unease.

Rosario considers the offer, a flash of heat creeping up her neck. She'd decided at the Randall party that he wasn't right for her. He's moody, immature. But looking at him now in his work clothes looking so professional, his expression so compassionate and touch so gentle, she wonders if that was just a rough patch. Being alone in her apartment, waiting and worrying, isn't an appealing prospect.

"I'll take the couch," he clarifies.

"I don't know, it's weird popping up like this and invading your space. I'll just come back in the morning."

"You sure? It's not a big deal." Ulysses stands up. "I'll warn you, though, Domino is a bed hog."

Rosario manages a faint smile at the mention of Domino. "I think I can handle him," she replies as she scratches behind his ears.

"Have you eaten?" Ulysses asks.

She hadn't, having worked herself sick trying to figure out where Shawnee might have gone. They order takeout and eat together at his coffee table. It's strange being there with him, letting him comfort her after not seeing him for weeks, making lighthearted conversation while somewhere in the back of her mind Shawnee is in danger.

Ulysses gets a few things ready for her, making sure she has enough pillows and blankets for the night. "If you need anything, just holler. I'm right out here on the couch," he says, pointing toward the living area.

"Thanks. For everything," Rosario says, feeling a bit more reassured not being alone.

As Rosario settles into the bed, taking in Ulysses's scent in his sheets, the events of the past few days replay in her mind. Despite the comfort of the bed and the safety of Ulysses' home, her thoughts are restless. Every so often, she hears the soft rustle of Domino shifting his position, his presence a small comfort in the otherwise tense night.

The next day, Ulysses stands in the kitchen in boxer briefs, sipping coffee. His thighs and calves are muscular and defined. His back is bare, and she learns the tattoos on his arms stretch up to his shoulders. When he turns to say good morning, she can see the colors and patterns continue under the hair on his sculpted chest. *Holy hell.* She thought he'd be decently fit, but she did not expect him to look this good under his clothes. The flyaways from his pulled back hair catch the morning light.

"How'd you sleep?" he asks as she creeps out from behind the bookshelf dividing the space, green eyes serene and welcoming.

"In and out."

"Coffee?"

"Sure."

Chapter Seventeen

OUTSIDE THE CITY LIMITS, past the suburbs and country towns, are two-lane highways lined with dense vegetation, green and wild. Tall sabal palms topped with bulbs of fanning spiked leaves wear gray petticoats of decay. Between these lush places are miles of flatness, interrupted by an occasional farmhouse, a billboard promoting legal services or Jesus.

Ulysses takes his eyes off the road to glance at Rosario, whose eyes have been fixed on her phone. "Any word?"

"Not yet. But the signal is spotty out here." She sets her phone back into the cup holder, returning her tense stare to the road. There's little traffic at this time, just after eight-thirty in the morning. The GPS tells them they should arrive within the hour.

"What are we going to say?" Rosario asks.

It's a question he's been asking himself, playing the various scenarios in his mind, anticipating how Lang will react in each hypothetical scene. But nothing has inspired much confidence as of yet. "Well, I'll ask him if anyone has been this way to talk to him."

"And when he denies it?"

"If he hasn't seen her, then he hasn't seen her. We can get the police involved at that point. God forbid she's been in some kind of an accident."

Rosario wraps her arms around her midsection, her face stricken with worry.

"It's going to be fine," he assures her. His memories of Lang are mostly benign. There are a few memories of his loud arguments with Nadine, he knows the man isn't perfect. But Sofie would visit him at least once a month and report back on the state of things—he'd sold a cow, added a few pigs, nothing earth-shattering.

Even so, what lies ahead is unknown, and he decides to address the matter weighing on his heart while he still can. "Look. I'm really sorry about how I treated you that night at Brody's. I had my feelings hurt, and I took it out on you. I behaved like an idiot."

"Don't worry about it. I'm over it."

"I'm not," he says, taking his eyes off the road to glance at her. "I know you said we're better as friends, but there was a minute there you wanted to try for something more, and I ruined it. And I can't stop thinking about what could have been if I wasn't a moron."

She laughs softly and looks out the window.

"I'm serious," he says. "I haven't had a drink since that night."

"Really?"

"Yeah," he says. How many relationships was he going to ruin? Sofie ended things and then he spoiled things before they ever started with Rosario. "I didn't want to lose anything else. Here I thought you and me…" He trails off, a wave of embarrassment tightening his throat. "Tell me you didn't feel the same way, and I'll never bring it up again."

The wheels whir against the smooth asphalt as they travel on the narrow road, a blur of green beyond the window. She looks at him, sweeping a lock of platinum hair behind her ear. "Of course I did."

Their eyes meet and a smile creeps across his face. He knew it. His pulse races with excitement. Maybe this was his way back to her. Maybe once this was all over, Shawnee was found safe, they'd return home together with the hope of something new. "Well, I'd like to try again, if that's alright with you."

She grins at him, a sparkle in her dark eyes. "Okay."

"Okay, then," he says. Extending his hand, he slips his fingers into the space between her index finger and thumb, claiming it. Their clasped hands come to rest on the center console, and his heart beats a little harder, the sensation of an irresistible smile creeping across his lips.

When they arrive, a primitive-looking archway reads *Songs of Angels* in faded black hand-painted letters. A crucifix mounted at the center points toward the sky like a lightning rod. Rosario sits up in her seat, her expression tense, limbs rigid.

He squeezes her hand. "It's okay."

A dirt road winds through a thicket of pines and oaks where Spanish moss hangs and billows like lace curtains. The trees thin out, opening up to a clearing. At its center is an old Queen Anne style mansion. Its white paint is weathered. A wraparound porch and second floor balcony are both enclosed with intricate ginger-bread scrollwork. Tall, narrow windows are shuttered. The steeply pitched roofs, clad in rusted corrugated metal, are adorned with decorative trim. The home is set between large oaks and travel trailers. Ulysses counts six.

As they drive up, there's activity on the lawn. People at work in plain, unassuming clothing. Three women wear aprons and toil in the dirt of a garden. Children gather near a chicken coop, chasing each other. Domino lets out a high-pitched, anxious whine.

"Who are these people?" Rosario mutters.

"Members of the church, if I had to guess." But not any church; The Church of the Ninth Order. He'd wondered what had become of them once their leader went on the lamb. It seems they've set up a congregation of their own out here. Why hadn't Sofie ever told him about this place?

A tall, wiry man watches them approach while tugging on a wooly beard before motioning for them to stop. The wheels crunch against the earth, and Ulysses rolls his window down.

"You lost?" the man calls.

"No, I'm here to see Lang Randall. Is he here?"

The man looks at them curiously, as if offended. Before he can respond, a woman emerges from behind the screen door of the main house, pregnant and with a toddler on her hip. "Everything alright, Jeremiah?" She quickly closes the distance and peers at them with sharp accessing eyes.

"Yes, ma'am, we're just here to see Lang Randall."

Her eyes widen. "Are you friends of his?"

"Yes, ma'am. Well, I grew up with his son Brody. I'm Ulysses."

"Ulysses," the man echoes back. "Why don't you park over there by the stable." He motions toward a dilapidated structure with a flat metal roof, rusted metal railings and rotting wood pillars. Jeremiah and the woman back away from the Jeep as he pulls around.

As they park, Ulysses draws in a deep breath.

"What the fuck," Rosario says. It's not a question. "Is it just me, or were they a little intense?"

"No, they were definitely weird. Let's just say hello, find out if Shawnee was here, then go."

"Don't leave me alone with them."

"I'm not leaving you anywhere. Stay close. And before we go in there, Lang doesn't know about Sofie and me."

"What? I thought you dated for years."

"We did, but he never would have approved. Let's just say I was not an impressive teenager. I got into a lot of trouble back then, and Lang thinks I'm a fuckup. If he knew we were living together, he would have probably disowned her. So just don't say anything about Sofie, okay?"

"Of course."

They exit the car, and he takes in the smell of manure as the distant wail of a cow carries on the breeze. Domino struggles against his leash. "Come on, bud," Ulysses urges. Each step toward the house is met with a reluctant tug backward. Domino, who fires like a bullet from a pistol toward any new life form he encounters, digs his back paws into the earth.

"The animal cannot come inside," the woman says, the toddler on her hip bouncing slightly. "You can tie it up out here."

Though his heart aches for Domino, clearly nervous about his new surroundings, he'll be okay out here for just a few minutes.

Ulysses gets permission to tie his leash around a wooden pillar. Children, noticing him, start to rush in their direction.

"Get back, children," the woman warns. "It'll bite you."

"He doesn't bite," Rosario says defensively.

"He's a sweetheart," Ulysses says. "But he's a little nervous right now I think. Best to give him some space."

The children, a little boy no older than five and two little girls with dirty knees beneath their tan cotton dresses, peer up at him with quiet curiosity.

"We'll be right back," Rosario says, scratching behind Domino's ears. Standing, she gives Jeremiah and the woman another look before reluctantly backing away from Domino.

"I'm Esther," the woman says. "Come. I'll take you to him."

Pulling open the screen door with a creak, Ulysses gets a glimpse into the dimly lit house, which upon entering, doesn't appear to have any lights. No sconces on the ceiling or on the walls. The only light is from standing lamps in every corner, lit with oil.

"Dude," Rosario whispers, only loud enough for Ulysses to hear.

"We weren't expecting visitors today," Ester says, confidently hustling down the narrow hall. In the back of the home is a large office with French doors. Men stand on either side with straps across their chests. It takes another look to realize they're armed with rifles on their backs. Why would Lang need armed guards? The moment Rosario has the same realization, she grabs on to his arm. His stomach sinks. This isn't anything like what he imagined.

"Uly," Lang says jovially, arms outstretched. He pulls Ulysses into an unexpected hug and squeezes him tightly. "God bless you, son. It's been too long." Pulling back, he gives him a warm, loving look. For a man protected by security guards, he's casually dressed in a denim collared shirt and tan slacks. His leathery forehead is marked with deep horizontal lines. Deep-set eyes glitter behind a heavy brow, set above wide and prominent cheekbones. "To what do I owe this special visit?"

"Mr. Randall, this… Well, I uh…" Ulysses stammers, the presence of the armed guards flanking him making him tense.

Lang picks up on it and waves them out. He scratches his short salt and pepper beard. "Sorry about that, son. We've had to increase security around here. One of the kids posted about this place on TikTok, and we started getting strange visitors."

"What is this place?"

"It's a place where people want to live simply and worship God, free of government oppression. That's all. I guess that kind of lifestyle is becoming more attractive now that the world's gone to heck in a handbasket."

"We're looking for my friend. Shawnee. We think she might have come here," Rosario says, her nervous grip on Ulysses's arm betraying her fear, though her voice carries an impressive firmness.

Lang glances at her for a moment before responding to Ulysses. "Uly, who's this?"

He smiles and his mouth opens to speak, but before any words can escape, Rosario jumps in. "I'm his wife. Nice to meet you."

Ulysses clears his throat. Things have progressed quickly. "How rude of me," Ulysses says. "Lang, this is my wife, Rosario." Hooking his arm around Rosario's waist, Ulysses draws her close.

"Oh my, Ulysses. You've done well for yourself. She's lovely."

"Thank you," she says brusquely, annoyed by him speaking to Ulysses as if she's not there.

Lang nods at her politely before returning his attention to Ulysses. "I've not had anyone come through by that name."

"A tall woman, kind of...athletic," he says.

"Nope. Can't say that I've seen anyone like that."

"That's strange," Rosario chimes in firmly, "because her phone showed her location near here before it stopped updating."

Lang doesn't look at her when he shrugs and pats Ulysses on the arm. "Strange," he says. "Sorry, wish I could help you."

"Bullshit." Her voice takes on an irritated edge.

Ulysses's gut goes rigid. He pulls Rosario back, wondering if she's already forgotten about the men with guns just outside the door. "What's gotten into you?" he asks, his voice a low hiss.

Lang smiles and lets out a humorless laugh. "Your wife's got some mouth on her. I'd appreciate it if she'd honor God's presence in this place."

"I'm sorry," Ulysses says. "It was a long drive. She hasn't eaten. I think her blood sugar must be low because she's speaking nonsense."

"I know what I'm saying. Where is she?"

The men return, grabbing each of them by their arms and pulling them from the room.

"It was nice seeing you, Uly. Thanks for the visit. You take care now," Lang says as they're forced from the room, dragged down the hall and indelicately shoved outside onto the porch.

He's relieved to see Domino still tethered to the pole. What was that about? He takes Domino's leash and starts toward his Jeep before realizing he's walking alone. Rosario is still on the porch, shouting through the screen. Ulysses rushes back, grabbing her around the waist and lifting her over his shoulder. She kicks and shouts as he struggles to maintain his balance. Holding his grip on her and Domino's leash, he struggles to return them both to the Jeep.

"Let me go!" she cries. "He knows where Shawnee is."

Setting her on her feet beside the vehicle, he squares his shoulders to make his posture intimidating and brings his face close to hers. "You're going to get us killed if you don't relax."

Tear stream down her face. "They've got her. I can feel it."

"Please. Relax." He draws in a deep breath, motioning for her to do the same. She swallows hard, choking on tears, and her long exhale trembles. She's terrified. He passes a comforting hand across her hair, coming to rest at the back of her head. "It's okay. We'll find her."

Chapter Eighteen

THE NEAREST HOTEL is in a historical district of Whispering Hope that was a sliver of the 1800s. The Venus Inn looked like it could have been lifted from New Orleans' Bourbon Street and dropped into an otherwise unassuming main road. Brick buildings with striped awnings had been converted into antique shops, a coffee house and a single restaurant with a bar. Despite its small-town feel, this street and nearby businesses were flooded with people. It was the only oasis of civilization for miles in every direction.

In the last available room at the hotel, the footboard of the queen-sized bed curved up tall like the bow of a ship with absurdly ornate Louis XVI styled gold and ivory designs, with an equally ridiculous headboard that was mounted to the ceiling with a custom chandelier. It was a strange fixture in an otherwise drab room. The only other seating in the room are two wood and cushion baroque chairs upholstered with red brocade fabric.

Finding themselves famished, they discover the lone restaurant in town has an hour wait to be seated, so they take their fried chicken and cornbread to go, eating at a wrought iron table and chairs in a courtyard outside the hotel shaded with oaks. A curved plastic take-out container lid doubles as a water bowl for Domino on the ground beneath their table. The weather is mild, sixty-degrees and sunny despite the darkness looming in Rosario's mind.

"He's got Shawnee. Why else would he have us dragged out like that?"

"You were accusing him of holding a woman captive. Aggressively, I might add." He wipes chicken grease from his mouth with a crumpled paper napkin. "Why'd you tell him we were married?"

"Just in case things got weird. Figured they wouldn't separate us."

His expression softens. He sets down his sweet tea, fingers gently tracing the side of his Styrofoam cup. "I wouldn't let anything bad happen to you, you know that right?"

She wants to believe him, and while she's sure he'd try, he's just one man. This is an organization, an ideology. He can't stand against them all. "Listen," he begins, his voice firm but gentle. "I think I should go back there alone."

Rosario's head snaps up from where she'd been staring down at her cell phone, "Alone? Uly, no. It's too dangerous. We don't know what we're dealing with. I don't think Lang is the man you think he is."

He reaches across the table, placing his hand over hers. "I know it's risky, but think about it. If I go alone, try to smooth things over, they might let their guard down."

The thought of finding herself alone in this strange place, of Ulysses getting hurt, makes her sick to her stomach.

He gives her hand a reassuring squeeze. "You stay here and look after Domino."

Once he's set his mind to it, there's no talking him out of it. She's filled with nervous energy on their walk to his car, her heart fluttering in her chest. What if something happens to him? What if she never sees him again? In her heart, she'll know it was her fault. She dragged him into this, convinced him to do this, asked him to help. "I never should have forced you to come here."

Facing her, his green eyes flash with intensity. His hand brushes against her hair, cradles her head affectionately. "You didn't force anything, okay? I chose to come here. And I'm glad you're persistent, because now that I know you, the thought of not having you in my life feels kind of tragic. And I know I blew it, but I like you. That's why I'm here. God, I just wish I was good enough for you."

"Stop that." She grabs a hold of the fabric of his T-shirt at his chest with both hands and tugs at it. "You are wonderful. You're kind and you're a good man."

Ulysses looks at her with a deep affection, something vulnerable. Wetting his lips with his tongue, he leans toward her, tentatively at first. Her fingers dig into his hair and she draws him closer. When their lips meet, the heat of his mouth makes her knees buckle. Throwing her arms around his neck for support, their kiss deepens. His tongue softly brushes hers, and he moans gently against her mouth, his hands gripping her hips. He presses her back firmly against the car door. His kiss is hungry, urgent. Her blood rushes through her veins, pulsing in molten bursts.

When they finally pull apart, their breaths mingle in the short space between them. Rosario's eyes search his. There's a silent understanding there, a promise. "Come back to me. Please."

Ulysses rests his forehead against hers, his breath still heavy. He gives her a small, determined smile. "I will. I promise." With one last look, Ulysses turns and gets into the car.

Domino's leash wrapped around her wrist, she watches Ulysses drive away, the Jeep disappearing down the road.

* * *

UNABLE TO SETTLE HER NERVES, Rosario wanders down the main road past the inn and into each open shop. She presents a picture of Shawnee on her phone to anyone who will look. "Have you see this woman?" All she gets in response are sympathetic looks but no clues. Watching the time, she imagines Ulysses has already made it back to Lang's.

She can't keep her mind from traveling to dark places. The longer she thinks about the potential for danger, the more she regrets not getting the police involved sooner. But what was she going to tell them? *These anti-government church people have guns and are a little sketchy.* This is Florida. None of this is unusual here, really. But she can't fight the sick feeling in her gut.

Running through her phone contacts, her eye stops on Deputy Harris. It's a different city, but maybe he knows someone who could help. The line trills just once before he answers. "Ms. Martinez," he says, a hint of amusement in his voice mixed with his smooth southern twang.

"Deputy Harris, hi. How are you?"

"I can't complain. But it's Detective Harris now."

"Oh, congratulations on the promotion. Well deserved."

"Thank you, darlin'. And how are you? Chasing down another story?"

"Yes, actually. I was hoping you could help. It's Shawnee. I think she might be in some trouble."

He clears his throat, the sound of a police radio in the background trails off, and his usual affable tone turns somber, his voice dropping a note lower. "Tell me what's going on."

She recounts the events of the last few days, against the backdrop of the past few months and the Calliope Katsaros case. "Wish you'd have called me sooner. I'd have made some phone calls, could have gone with you. You really shouldn't go out to places like that on your own."

His concern for her is endearing, hinting at his fondness of her since their coffee "date" during the Vernon case. Despite his charm —adorable dimples, vivid blue eyes and chiseled jawline—his jokes were dorky, he was relentlessly optimistic, and far too straightlaced for Rosario's 'down with the establishment' rebellious edge. His personality was basically *Ted Lasso* with a badge. Not really her type.

"I know. I brought a friend with me."

"Alright, good. I have a contact in that office. I'll reach out. Make introductions."

"Thank you. That would be perfect."

"You bet. But do me a favor. I'm sure everything will be fine, but could you give me a call when you're back home so I know you're alright? Please."

She finds herself smiling into the phone. "You betcha."

There's a brief pause on the line, a moment of charged silence. Then Detective Harris chuckles, the sound warm and intimate over the distance. "Alright then. You stay safe now."

Within the hour, Rosario's phone buzzes and Harris's name appears on her screen.

"Strangest thing," he says. "My contact's not there anymore, but I was able to get some information."

It felt a little dirty that her first thought was to record their conversation. This was about finding her friend, not entertaining their listeners. But Shawnee would want it this way. In fact, when Shawnee returns home safe and sound, she'll be pissed if Rosario hadn't recorded this. "Can I record this?"

"You know I love the show and all, but I think this is going to have to be off the record."

Her heart sinks. That's not a good sign. "Alright. What'd they say?"

Letting out a pensive sigh, he seems to organize his thoughts. "They left the city. Apparently the Order's gotten a little big for their britches. Did you see or hear mention of a John Russell Thorne?"

"Only what Sofie told me. That he was Calliope's father. I didn't see him or hear about it while I was there."

"Well, he was wanted on murder charges. My friend suspected he was hiding there, but they were never able to gain access to the property, and any focus on the Order or their little commune was strongly discouraged by leadership."

"Murder?"

"Twenty years ago. A member of the church by the name of Orson Roy. My contact said Thorne executed him in front of the entire congregation."

A cold chill runs through Rosario. What had she done letting Ulysses return there on his own? "If there were witnesses, why aren't you allowed to search the property?"

"The murder happened when the congregation was outside of Tampa. Before they relocated to Whispering Hope in 2004."

Calliope disappeared in 2004. Hearing that there's serious money involved takes Rosario by surprise. Aside from the main mansion, everything out there looked run down. And how is it possible she wouldn't have read about this murder? This story was probably buried in some internet news archive. Rosario thinks out loud. "Calliope disappeared that summer. I wonder if the events were related somehow."

"Anything is possible. Please, Rosario. Stay safe out there."

Chapter Nineteen

THE GUARDS WERE ready for him this time, already waiting along the fence line as Ulysses's car slowly rolled onto the property. Three men with rifles intercept him, guns in their grip and at the ready. Holding up his hands, he shouts from the open window. "I don't want any trouble. I just came back to apologize to Lang. Left the wife at home this time. Please. We're practically family."

The guards, their faces set in hard lines, don't release their guns, but their posture relaxes ever so slightly at his words. The apparent leader, a stocky man with a youthful face, squints at him suspiciously. "Stay in the car and keep your hands where we can see them," he barks.

Ulysses nods, his hands raised in a gesture of peace.

The guards circle around the Jeep, keeping a cautious distance. The leader, maintaining his grip on his rifle, gesture toward the main house with a nod. "We'll take you to Lang, but any funny business, and it won't end well for you."

Ulysses swallows hard, his throat dry. "Understood. I'm not here to cause any problems. Just want to clear the air with Lang."

The walk to the house feels longer than last time. The crunch of gravel underfoot mixes with the chirping of birds in the nearby trees. As they approach the house, Ulysses catches a glimpse of movement behind a curtain on the second floor. Someone is watching.

Finally, reaching the front porch, the wooden boards creak under their collective weight. The leader knocks on the door, a code-like rhythm, and after a moment, it swings open. Out glides Lang, his weathered face bearing a mixture of surprise and apprehension as he meets Ulysses on the porch. He's not getting inside easily his time.

"Ulysses," Lang says, his voice cautious. "Didn't expect to see you back so soon. Left the little lady at home I see."

"I'm sorry about that. She was pretty emotional about her friend. I tried to tell her you're good people. You were like the father I never had growing up," Ulysses says, laying the reverence on thick. "I know it got heated, and I didn't want to leave things on a bad note."

Lang studies him for a long moment, then nods to the guards. "Let him in."

As the guards step aside, Ulysses enters the house, the door closing with a definitive thud behind him. Now inside, face-to-face with Lang, Ulysses knows this is his chance to find out more about the Order, and possibly about Shawnee's whereabouts. He has to tread carefully, though. One wrong move could be fatal.

They sit in a parlor adjacent to Lang's office in comfortable leather chairs. "Tell me," Lang says, striking a match to light up a cigarette. "How's your mother doing?"

"Not well, unfortunately. She's been struggling with cognitive decline the last few years. It's been difficult."

"Oh my," Lang responds, extinguishing the match with a sharp back and forth whip of his wrist until thin tendrils of smoke dissipate in the air smelling of charcoal and sulfur, a look of genuine shock on his face. "I'm so sorry to hear that. She was such a wonderful, devoted woman."

"Thank you," Ulysses replies. Looking around the room, he takes in the antique Americana decor mixed with rustic flair. A faded American flag hangs near a mounted deer head. "And you? I take it you're not driving a truck anymore."

"No. The Lord saw fit for me to retire, fortunately. I've devote my days to His work now, looking after the people here."

"This place, it's like a commune?"

"You could call it that, though, it's not one of those hippie free love places." He chuckles to himself. "No, we follow God's law here. Live off the land. It's a pure, honest life. Suppose that's why you really came back. I reckon something about this place piqued your curiosity."

"You might be right about that."

Lang smiles wide, his eyes gleaming with charm. "Ah, I knew it. Young people are surprisingly interested in this place. We're removed from the pressures of modern society. We do our best to live without technology."

"How'd you end up on TikTok?"

With a nod and a disappointed shake of his head, Lang sighs. "We asked ourselves the same question. But we have families here. All ages. And some of them are still assimilating from the world outside, you know. Some have an easier time letting go than others. But it's been dealt with," he says, turning his body around sharply and pointing toward a row of boxes mounted to a beam across the ceiling. Each has a series of antennae. "Jammers. You could bring outside technology here if you want, but the signal won't go out."

Hearing the words leave Lang's mouth make Ulysses's heart sink into his belly. It's the technological equivalent of telling him no one will hear him scream.

"That's great. I, um, I'm a counselor. Work with youth battling addiction and the like. I think a lot of the pressure kids feel these days has to do with how connected everything is, how every minor thing can be amplified and broadcast to an audience. It's like you don't get the grace to grow anymore."

Lang gives him an approving look. "I'm proud to hear it, son. Truth be told, there was a time I was worried about the kind of man you'd become. I'm happy to hear you've chosen the path of helping others."

"Thank you."

"You know, we could use a man like you around here. We've got plenty of people who need an understanding ear. Heck, I know I could use a sounding board from time to time."

Ulysses nods, but says, "I'm not sure I'd fit in here."

Lang leans back in his chair, the wood beneath the leather creaking under his weight. He takes a long drag from his cigarette, eyeing Ulysses thoughtfully through the smoke. "You'd be surprised. People here come from all walks of life. You've seen the world out there. You know it's no good for the soul."

"You're right about that," Ulysses says, pausing to gauge Lang's reaction. "Actually, if it's not too much trouble, could I take a look around?"

Lang eyes him for a moment, the smoke curling from his cigarette forming a hazy veil. "Of course," he replies, his voice smooth. "We pride ourselves on being an open and welcoming community. I think you'll find everyone here has their own unique story to tell."

Ulysses must have missed the open and welcome part of the community as he was being dragged out earlier. As Lang rises to his feet, the guards, still watching, perk up their attention. He leads Ulysses through the large house, the many footsteps of security following close behind. Walking through a communal kitchen where women are busy preparing vegetables—peeling, washing, chopping —the atmosphere feels subdued. The women work diligently, but there's an undercurrent of tension.

"This is where the women of the congregation prepare meals. We share all our meals together—breakfast, lunch and dinner."

The women look up over their workstations, their smiles seeming forced as the men stroll by on tour.

Outside, they pass children playing. Elders sitting enjoying the nice weather. Passing a pen, pigs stomp through the mud, letting out shrill squeals and basking in the stink of their shit. A coop enclosed with chicken wire houses several chickens that cluck and peck at grass. No signs of Shawnee.

In the distance, the sounds of heavy equipment rumble and the sound of chainsaws rip through the air. "What's all that?" Ulysses asks.

"We're expanding. Bought the plot of land behind us to build a church."

Their current property is already massive and as they trek further, at least a dozen more trailers Ulysses hadn't noticed before come into view. They're nestled in the woods, nearly invisible from the main house. They walk past them where men work outside. Looping around a cul-de-sac style curve of trailers, they double back toward the mansion. As they approach, Lang stops to talk to a man repairing fence.

He's young, maybe in his early twenties, engrossed in his work, and doesn't seem notice their approach until Lang clears his throat. He's short and petite, with an intensity to his movements as he measures and cuts the wood.

"This is Thomas," Lang introduces. "One of our skilled carpenters. Thomas, this is Ulysses, an old friend."

Thomas nods politely, wiping sawdust from his hands onto his pants. "Nice to meet you," he says, his voice tinged with a cautious curiosity. He extends a hand, and Ulysses shakes it.

"No wedding ring?" Lang asks, his attention on Ulysses's hand pulling away from his handshake and shoving it into his jean pocket.

"We're saving up to buy a house. Tough out there these days."

Lang clicks his tongue. "Another tragedy of modern society."

Just then, a woman creeps out of the door of a nearby trailer. She wears a long skirt to her ankles and a thick sweater. Her big brown eyes study Ulysses with curiosity. "Thomas," she calls, her eyes fixed on Ulysses.

"Get inside," Thomas says wearily. It's not threatening, but it still unsettles Ulysses at its casual dismissiveness. Without saying another word, she obeys and reverses back through the door before closing it.

"Sorry about her. Always got to be involved in everything," Thomas says, lining up a hammer with a nail. "What brings you to the Order?"

"Ulysses's mother was one the original members of our congregation," Lang answers for him. "We spent many a Sunday together you and I, didn't we, son?"

"Yes we did," he says. He'd hardly remembered it. But being here, the fog in his mind is gradually being lifted. His heart starts to race. A pit forms in his stomach, but he's not sure why. It feels like worry, like dread.

"Beautiful place you've made here, Lang. You should be very proud." He casts his eyes around, taking in the vastness, looking for potential threats. The world seems to slow and blur with panic. *Breathe*. His gaze stops at a row of second-floor windows of the main house, where a ghostly figure stands. A curtain swings closed after a moment, concealing what he might have seen. *Who is that watching from upstairs?* A metallic tang coats his tongue. He has to get out of here.

Then, a gunshot. It cracks through the air in the distance and gives Ulysses a jolt that makes his knees weaken. He fortifies himself as the shock of the sound dissipates. "What was that?"

"Dinner, probably," Thomas says, then swings his hammer. "Fresh meat."

"That's right. We're self-reliant here," Lang says. "Spend enough time out in God's land, find yourself hungry, you'll remember the real order of things mighty quick."

"Amen," Thomas says. "You staying for dinner?"

"I, uh." Ulysses hesitates. "My wife is expecting me back soon. Maybe another time."

Lang and Thomas look at each other with smirks. "Wouldn't want to upset the boss," Lang jokes, inviting a chuckle to burst from Thomas's lips.

"Here, men are men, women are women," Thomas says. "You start to give up your power, it's a slippery slope. That's how you end up with a whore for a wife, makin' a cuck out of you cause she don't respect you. I'd nip that in the bud right now, if you don't mind me sayin' so."

"You should listen to him," Lang adds. "That wife of yours has quite a mouth on her."

"Like I said, I'm sorry about that, she just —"

"No need to apologize again. I'm sure you'll see to it she learns."

"Sir," a young guard approaches Lang. "Turner's here to see you. Had 'em wait in your office."

Lang gives the man a quick nod before turning to Ulysses. "Busy day," he says, and pats his arm, inviting him to follow him back toward the main house. Ulysses gets the sense this is the conclusion of their visit. "Well, what do you think? Could you see yourself being a part of our family?"

"It's an impressive place. I've really been looking for a chance to get back to my roots. It's been too long."

"It has. You've returned for a reason, I believe that. I know things were sometimes challenging. It was a time of reflection for the church. Many of us were tested. But I can assure you, things are different now. God brought you back to us, and I hope you'll consider staying."

Ulysses takes a pause. What's he talking about? All of it was challenging, but trying to imagine what Lang could be referring to is met with a blank. "I'm grateful for the invitation," he replies.

"I'd like it if you and your wife came back sometime. See if it suits you. Just make sure you straighten her out first. We don't tolerate smart-mouths around here, and we take a community approach to discipline. I held my hand back, but I can't promise another man in this congregation would do the same."

Ulysses clenches his jaw at the suggestion. If anyone laid a hand on Rosario, Ulysses would make sure they regretted it. Although, Rosario would probably beat him to it. "I'll let you know. Thank you for the invitation, but I've got a few things to sort out with work first before we can plan another visit."

"Think about it," he says with a wink. He puts a hand on Ulysses shoulder. "It's been nice seeing you again, son."

"Nice seeing you."

The armed guards walk Ulysses twenty or so yards from the porch, letting him make the rest of the trail to his Jeep alone as the sun begins to set. Beside his Jeep is a Ford Explorer and Dodge Charger, both gleaming new models with red and blue lights mounted to the top. A uniformed officer shoots the shit with a group of men, a mix of armed guards and congregants. They appraise Ulysses as he passes, and he offers an amiable nod which they each return almost in unison. Orange and pink streaks break through deep cobalt bands in the winter sky. The temperature has cooled.

Climbing into his Jeep, he looks at his cell phone. No signal. The Order's jammers must be powerful. He starts the car and slowly pulls toward the long driveway leading to the main road, waving at the guards as he goes. Rosario will be disappointed he's returning empty-handed.

He makes it half a mile down the main road before the reception bars on his cell phone return, and he decides to call her. Balancing the phone in one hand, his left hand on the steering wheel, his thumb hovers over the call button. He hears a sound, then sees movement in his rearview mirror. A figure sits up in his backseat, hidden underneath a blanket he'd kept back there for Domino's shedding fur. His heart leaps into his throat and he slams on the brakes.

The figure jerks forward, and a pair of glasses fly past Ulysses, landing near his feet. "Please," a raspy voice pleads. "Please drive."

* * *

SPEEDING BACK INTO TOWN, Ulysses's mind races. Being at the Order's compound had knocked something loose. A room in his memory that had been locked, a key intentionally chucked into a ravine. His mind travels back to memories from before.

Years earlier, visiting Mom's quaint single-story house lined with teal lap siding and a yellow porch swing he'd sometimes sit in as he'd wait for her.

"Oh, Ulysses," her muffled voice called through the door. It swung open.

"Hey, Mom."

His mother's blonde hair was usually pulled back into an elegant bun. She'd kiss his cheek. The television was always on, marked by a laugh track. She watched old sitcoms. A wall of bookcases filled with books—mostly religious texts, but also classic poetry, Greek mythology, and studies of the cosmos. Warm ambient light reflected off the polished dark wood floors. It smelled like home, with a light peppery tang in the air.

"Did you cook?" Ulysses asked.

"You want me to make you a plate?"

"Yes, please."

The living and dining rooms combined into one open space. Every white wall featured a piece of Ulysses's art—modern takes on Greek renaissance works. Save for one wall. The Calliope wall, adorned with photos of his little sister. Beneath it, a narrow table held rows of flickering candles.

He sat at a round glass table supported by a fluted column in the center. Eleni set a plate down in front of him. Pan-fried meatballs, salad and rice. "What's wrong?"

"Rough day, that's all."

She stood over him while he ate, observing him. Prodding him. Playing with his hair. "You want to tell me about it?"

He chewed, the flavor so comforting and delicious he had to make a conscious effort to slow down. He set down his fork. "I just feel like I don't think I'm meant to do this work. I don't think I have the right disposition."

Eleni pulled out a chair and sat next to him. "Have you prayed about it?"

"Yes, Mom."

"And what did God tell you?"

He sighed, tired of her pulling his string so he could spout off the same answer. "Nothing."

She shook her head and rose from her chair. "What is it that you want to do? Quit? I hope not," she said, rubbing his shoulders. She kissed the top of his head, and he reached his limit of affection.

"Mom, please. I'm eating."

She playfully nudged his head and disappeared to the kitchen. She spoke loudly from the other room. "When you were getting help with the drinking, how did you treat your counselors?"

"With respect," he said, knowing it wasn't the whole truth.

It was a problem that had been brewing for years. Getting into fights at school. Skipping classes. Drinking every day to excess. Until one day he found himself an unemployed, directionless grown man sleeping in a hammock in his mother's yard, a bottle of whiskey clutched to his chest. He was angry, bitter. Life had shortchanged him, and this was his form of rejecting it. It was an act of protest.

"How has life cheated you, Uly?" Dr. Okafor had asked him.

The faith-based facility the doctor worked at then wasn't nearly as nice as Palms Waterside, but Ulysses recalled the food being good. Ulysses had hated it when Dr. Okafor asked him those kinds of questions. Before his trouble with alcohol, he wasn't an honor student, but he'd done well enough. He showed an aptitude for art. Ran track.

Boys weren't supposed to know the weight of the things he'd carried. The point was avoidance. Being specific about the things that disrupted his life meant facing them and acknowledging the truth, instead of the lies that made his life bearable. The burden of his sister's disappearance, the trauma of watching a man die. The screams, the smell of gunpowder and copper, all the blood. Digging until his hands bled. The things that kept him awake at night. But most of all, the fear that he was next to die for his sins. How could he have forgotten?

Now, speeding back from the Order's compound, memories spinning in his mind, it all comes into focus, refusing to be ignored. The things he'd seen. The awful truths. Looking into his rearview mirror, he takes in Shawnee's sunken eyes , cracked lips, bruised face.

"We're almost there," he assures her.

"I saw her," she rasps.

"Who?"

"Calliope."

Chapter Twenty

AT THIRTEEN YEARS OLD, sitting in the front pew at Sunday mass was torture. Posture perfectly upright and at attention, no yawns or sleepy eyes permitted. Ulysses was required to receive the prophet's words enthusiastically beside his mother and little sister, who, despite being just eight years old, was enthralled by everything that came out of John Russell Thorne's mouth.

It was Easter Sunday, but there were no baskets stuffed with plastic grass or egg hunts. Pagan rituals, Thorne called them. Maybe it was true, but all Ulysses wanted was a peanut butter egg at the end of a long sermon. His mother had made a ham at least, he thought. The kind with the sugary glaze he liked. Bright, plump maraschino cherries and pineapples on toothpicks punctured through the thick leathery flesh and made his mouth water.

"You know ham's not real," he told his sister.

"Liar."

"It's not. You don't cut a ham off a pig. I learned it in school."

"Mom, is ham from a pig?"

"Yes, angel."

"See," she said, sticking out her tongue.

Stupid brat. That's not what he meant, but he wasn't going to argue with them. He knew where ham came from. He was responsible for holding it in place in the back seat on the way to church, to keep the sweet-smelling juices in the pan from spilling everywhere. It was a job he took seriously. With every hard stop, his fingers gripped a little tighter on the aluminum pan.

"You still got it?"

"Yes, Mom."

They arrived a few minutes late and the energy was different inside that day. After setting up in the kitchen, they went into the church. It was eerily quiet. People shuffled around, sitting in pews with worried expressions. Speaking from the pulpit, Prophet Thorne scanned the room in his seersucker suit, salt and pepper hair neatly combed and styled. "Today we celebrate the ultimate victory over sin and death and rejoice in the promise of eternal life. That was the theme of the homily I'd prepared today. But I've received some troubling news that threatens the sanctity of this Holy Order, and I must address it with all of you. Brother Orson, could you please join me in the sanctuary?"

Whispers scattered around the small chapel. Ulysses turned to glance over his shoulder. Men from the congregation with hardened expressions approached the exit door, blocking it. Orson, a middle-aged man with glasses and arms that were covered in a blanket of thick black hair and a matching mustache, cautiously approached, adjusting the tuck of his golf polo into his dress slacks as he rose.

"Orson Roy, please join the rest of the congregation by kneeling." The kneelers thudded to the ground and creaked under their weight in unison. The sounds echoed through the room as Orson looked around, anxious, standing firmly on his feet. "Please," Thorne insisted.

Orson reluctantly obeyed. "Let us pray," Thorne said, his voice commanding. "Prophets are entrusted with messages for humanity from God. Thus, when prophets such as myself speak by divine inspiration, it is as if we are part of the celestial order, and our words resonate throughout the heavens. I understand that some of you have come to question my place on this divine ladder. To those with doubt in their hearts, I warn hold fast to your faith. For those who do not believe will atone, then face a second death through the eternal separation from God. Orson Roy is one such disbeliever. He has rejected God's messenger and, in doing so, has rejected God Himself."

"I haven't rejected God. I —" Orson protested from on his knees.

"Silence," Thorne ordered, stifling him. "I will not stain this Holy institution by repeating the allegations you've raised, the purely malicious gossip that has pervaded this sanctum like a cancer. You seek to divide our Order, and you will be reminded of God's instruction. I am His messenger, and you will atone." His voice dripped with distain as he held up his hand, reading from the Bible. *"There is a judge for the one who rejects me and does not accept my words; the very words I have spoken will condemn them at the last day."*

Ulysses lowered his head down in prayer, his heart racing fast as the tense dispute played out before him. The sounds of the men's voices were amplified by the cathedral ceiling. Then a collective gasp brought his eyes upward. Thorne held a gun. Studying it as best he could from five feet away, Ulysses's mind refused to believe it was real. Why would Thorne have a gun? No sooner than he asked himself the question, it went off. Orson's body collapsed on his side as the congregants screamed.

"Silence!" Thorne boomed.

Eleni pulled Ulysses and Calliope close to her. He was numb. What had just happened? Could it be that this man was just murdered right before his eyes? He returned his focus to his clasped hands, where specks of Orson's blood had traveled from the blast. "Mom," he whispered, terrified.

In those moments, he ran through a mental inventory of his sins. The dirty pictures with naked ladies he'd seen on Brody's computer. How he'd thought about them at night. He'd copied Brandon Dudley's algebra homework. Stole an extra chocolate milk in the school cafeteria. Took the Lord's name in vain and cussed a bunch when his mom wasn't around. He'd smoked one of Warren's cigarettes.

"Brothers and sisters, please," Thorne calls, a hint of jest in his voice. "We as a community have been called to uphold our Order's moral and spiritual integrity by not condoning serious sin." Thorne's voice, now chillingly calm, filled the silent chapel. "Let this be a lesson to us all. Disobedience, disbelief, dissent within these hallowed walls…these are not mere misdemeanors. They are direct affronts to our covenant with the Almighty. To question His appointed is to question His authority."

Orson's body bled out onto the mauve carpeting, pooling and dripping down the short stage steps. "Now," Thorne started in an impossible attempt to redirect the day's focus to his sermon. He paced slowly and set the revolver on the pulpit before clearing his throat. "We are reminded today that just as Christ faced betrayal, suffering, and death, we too are called to confront the trials and tribulations of our faith."

A hatred brewed in Ulysses's heart. He knew better. The lessons he'd learned of peace and forgiveness were the truth. This man was no messenger of God, but possibly the devil himself.

Now, twenty years later, Ulysses stares out into the dark street through the window of their room at the Venus Inn still pondering it. It's still wet outside from a heavy band of rain that passed, and the lights of the bar across the road glow from the asphalt like neon watercolors.

His training had taught him about repressed memories, how it's a survival mechanism his brain relied on to protect him while he was forced to continue that day, and every day after, like nothing happened. Eventually, forgetting it had ever happened had become his truth. But being there again, among them, hearing their vitriol, that gunshot, it triggered something. Activated an acid that threatens to burn a hole through his gut as he struggles to discern what is real and what he'd invented to survive.

Nearby, Shawnee and Rosario sleep. They'd stayed to let her rest and weather the storm before returning home to Tampa. After Shawnee filled them in on what happened—she'd driven out to the compound yesterday morning. Once they realized she was there for information on Calliope, they beat her, held her captive. She escaped in the middle of the night and, not wanting to wander a rural road in the dark, she camped out until morning. It's a good thing he got to her when he did, the rain and wind outside would have been a nightmare to suffer out in the woods.

Rosario had called the police almost the moment she'd laid eyes on Shawnee. They waited patiently in their hotel room for what would come next. But then, instead of an officer arriving for an interview, a call came in, which Rosario answered on speakerphone.

"We're deferring action pending further investigation."

"What the hell does that mean?" Rosario asked, pacing the scuffed wooden floors of their room.

"We understand your friend trespassed on their property. They asked her to leave but she refused, is that correct?"

"Are you serious? They beat her up, kept her captive."

"Ma'am, please calm down," the officer said. "Look, I'm sorry to be blunt, but we don't find your friend's story credible. We've talked to over half a dozen people out there, all of whom we know to be upstanding citizens in this county. All of them swear your friend was trespassing, refused to leave when politely asked, then became physically combative when residents tried to escort her from the property. Last anyone out there saw of your friend was her running off into the woods after fighting with them. Frankly, your friend is lucky no one out there wants to press charges against her."

"Just, forget it," Rosario said, hanging up. "Can you believe that?" she asked Ulysses, her face twisting in disgust.

Ulysses leaned against the heavy, ornate footboard. "They were chumming it up with a few officers while I was out there. Bet they got the force wrapped around their finger in this Podunk town."

Shawnee sat up in bed, still wrapped in a towel after her bath. "I told you, I'm fine. We'll handle this our way." By that point, they all just wanted to get out of there, but a strong wind shook the old walls of the inn and a curtain of rain flooded the roads, blurring anything further than a few feet in the distance. Despite their apprehension, they decided to wait until daylight before braving the return home.

Now, he waits for dawn and to leave this place, staring at the street beyond the window. Rain cleared, patrons shuffle across the road between the hotel and the restaurant bar. The itch for a reprieve tickles somewhere deep in his brain—neurochemical, structural, and functional changes that began at thirteen when his habit started. Ulysses had drunk two six-packs of beer shortly after Calliope disappeared, purchased from Warren in exchange for a fifty lifted from his mother's purse. He chugged each bitter, sudsy gulp until he blacked out. The next morning, he came to with urine-soaked sheets, which he changed quickly before dragging a garbage bag of beer cans out of his bedroom once his mother had left for work.

Apart from the mild embarrassment of having pissed himself, he marveled at alcohol's ability to prevent him from giving a fuck about anything. About his sister, and how everyone believed it was all his fault for not watching her that day. How everyone would think he failed at being a big brother, at being a son. Especially the fact that every day after he lived in the Church of Calliope, faced her photos, his mother's tear-streaked face and incessant prayers as she lit candles. And now, he wonders how he could have ever forgiven her.

What kind of mother enlists her children in a cult? Exposes them to horrors and violence, and instead of running, takes them back to mass the following Sunday. *She was probably frightened,* he reminds himself. He swipes a hand down his face, exhausted. Rising to his feet, he creeps toward the door, past the bed where Rosario and Shawnee sleep.

Chapter Twenty-One

A CRASH. Domino's loud barks blare and ring in her eardrums. Shocked awake, Rosario's heart seizes up and she silences a gasp. *They've found us*. It's dark, but a beam of moonlight shoots through the curtains and she can make out the outline of a figure. A man. She slowly tilts her head ever so slightly to where she'd remembered Ulysses setting a spare pillow and blanket on the floor. He's gone.

She takes a closer look just as another clamor breaks out. He's bumped into a chair and it screeches. "Shhh," he whispers, and she recognizes Ulysses's voice. Domino quiets except for his excited pants.

With a relieved sigh, she flips on the lamp. "Uly?"

Falling into a chair, he leans back and closes his eyes. "Go back to sleep," he mutters. His clothes are slightly askew and there's a certain looseness to his posture that she recognizes. Shawnee, now fully awake, sits up and rubs her eyes. "You okay?"

"Just needed some air," he slurs. "Sorry I woke you." Sitting in a hard wooden chair, he rests the back of his head against the wall, arms crossed over his chest.

Rosario doesn't want to be insensitive to his situation, but less than twenty-four hours ago, he was convincing her to give their non-relationship a chance under the guise of sobriety. Shawnee squints through the dimness, then rests her head on her pillow again, pulling up the blanket to settle back to sleep. But now Rosario is wide awake. She can't help but feel a twinge of disappointment. "You gonna sleep in your boots?

"Mm," he hums in confirmation.

A few moments pass before she slips out of bed and her bare feet touch the cold floor. The gentle creaks cause Ulysses to peek at her through one half cracked open eye. "You don't ever listen," he says, devoid of any bitterness.

"Nope," she says, kneeling on the floor in front of him. Bathed in twilight, the corners of his mouth perk up. She grabs a boot and unlaces it. Not wanting to disturb Shawnee, she keeps her voice low. "Where'd you go?"

His smile vanishes. "Where do you think?"

Sliding off his boot, she sets it against the wall. Domino sniffs around, his snout disappearing into it. The smells of sweat and whisky waft together. "I thought you were done with that," she says, reaching for the left.

"I know," he says. Opening his eyes, he looks down at her in a silent plea. "You done with me?"

Having loosened the thick nylon laces, she yanks the boot off and sets it beside the other. More than disappointment, a sense of pity rises. Will she regret it if she lets this go? She can't help but wonder if, one awful day after he's broken her heart, she'll look back at this moment as the red flag she ignored.

But if anyone was ever due a mulligan, Ulysses had more than earned his extra chance by saving Shawnee. She slides her hands up his denim-clad thighs. "No, but I'm worried about you."

"I know." Taking a beat, he looks off toward the window, eyes caught in the silvery light.

Since they met, she's been taken with him. Not just his good looks; he fascinated her. Despite all of the things he's been through, he had a natural serenity to him. At least when he was sober. At the Randall party, she'd seen another side of him. A side that gives her an uneasy feeling and now makes her want to be extra delicate to avoid setting him off. But she's also grown to care for him. Their daily text conversations, although just friendly, gave her insight into the kind of man he was. Caring, thoughtful. There's potential here, and it's too good to let go over a set of circumstances that would break most people.

Getting up, she pulls a blanket from the closet and lays it next to the pile of sheets, blankets and pillows Ulysses laid out to sleep on. "Come on," she says, inviting him over. He crawls over and rests on his back, and she rests her head on his chest. Domino, not wanting to be left out, fits his fluffy body between their legs. His warmth is a welcome comfort against the cold.

"If the woman Shawnee saw really was Calliope, I don't want to see her," he says softly. "That's horrible, isn't it?"

"No, it's not."

"I'm mad at her. Isn't that dumb? To be mad at a kidnapped little girl."

"You can't help how you feel."

"I know. But it still feels pretty shitty. And I don't want to see my mother again either. I'll pay for her care, I'm not gonna let anything bad happen to her, but I'm not going there again. She knew. She knew I was convinced my sister was dead. Let the world believe it was my fault for not looking after her. And she just let it happen. Let me destroy myself with it."

"You really think she'd do that?"

"There's a lot I can't remember, but you were right when you said I'd always remember how I was made to feel. There's a feeling in my gut. I know she'd put the church before me, no matter what. If the Order wanted Calliope, told her to keep it a secret, best believe she'd take it to her grave even if it killed me."

The sound of his voice cracking raises her gaze to see his face, where his eyes well with unshed tears. She can't imagine the immense pain he must feel, but she does her best to comfort him, the little boy he once was, crushed under the weight of an unfathomable guilt.

"If she's been living there, then Sofie probably knew too. How can I trust anyone? Brody? My best friend. This is fucked."

It seems a little far-fetched that everyone in Ulysses's life would know the truth and keep it from him. She tries to reassure him. "We're jumping to a lot of conclusions. Sure, Shawnee said that woman looked like Calliope. But that doesn't mean it's her. It's been twenty years after all."

"I don't know what to believe anymore."

Chapter Twenty-Two

PODCAST: **Mysteries of the Southern Gothic; Episode 51: Calliope and the Church of the Ninth Order Part I**

[INTRO MUSIC FADES **out**]

Rosario Martinez (Narrator): Welcome back to Mysteries of the Southern Gothic. I'm your host, Rosario Martinez. This episode is called "Calliope and the Church of the Ninth Order Part I.

I was just a little girl twenty years ago when Calliope Katsaros went missing. If you grew up in the Bay Area or anywhere in the State of Florida in the 2000s, then you may remember her face, because it was everywhere. An eight-year-old girl playing outside her home in the Water Oak mobile home community in Tampa, Florida, disappeared without a trace and was feared dead.

[A series of newscaster voices reading headlines of

Calliope's disappearance. Fade into soft mysterious music.]

Rosario: Her face haunted me for years. Of all the cases we've covered, this case always lingered in the back of my mind as the mystery we were meant to solve.

[Ulysses's audio clip]

Ulysses Katsaros: Brody, my best friend, lived next door. He'd just gotten a new PlayStation. I was supposed to watch Calliope that day. She played outside, and I could see her from Brody's window. We were playing SmackDown vs. Raw. Edge versus Bubba Ray Dudley in the WWE Championship.

Rosario: That's Ulysses Katsaros, Calliope's older brother. A substance abuse therapist and talented artist, who designed all of the tattoos that adorn his arms and neck, including a piece dedicated to Calliope. I met with him in an extended-stay motel where he'd been living alone with his Poodle Collie mix Domino.

[Sound effect: children playing]

Ulysses: She was out there hopping around on her little skip-it thing. She never screamed. Cried. Whoever took her probably led her away somewhere.

Rosario: The day of Calliope's disappearance, there was another little girl around her age named Sofie playing nearby. I asked Ulysses whether she and Calliope ever played together.

Ulysses: She's always been a little…manic. Running around from thing to thing. We couldn't keep track of her. Brody didn't even try.

[Audio cuts off with a click. Eerie music starts softly and continues under Rosario's narration]

The only people at the Water Oak mobile home community the day of Calliope's disappearance were Ulysses and the Randall children—Warren, Brody and Sofie. What did they know?

[Sound effect: fire crackling, outdoor night sounds]

We met the Randalls at their home in the remote town of Parrish. It was winter, and guests gathered around a large bonfire on the lawn, gripping beer cans and celebrating Warren Randall's release from prison. He'd just completed a ten-year sentence for armed robbery after holding up a gas station attendant at gunpoint in 2013. When we spoke, their stories all lined up perfectly.

[Music fades out]

Brody Randall: Uly came by. We played a video game. We got bored and threw each other around like we were wrestlers. Got him good one time, you remember that?

Sofie Randall: Remember she told Mom you were a demon child who needed to be baptized again because the first time didn't take?

Rosario: That's the voice of Sofie Randall, Brody's younger sister and Ulysses's ex girlfriend. It was the first time she and Ulysses had seen each other since their breakup. According to Ulysses, she was the reason he was living in a motel, having pocketed two months' rent money before leaving him without warning. Needless to say, their exchanges were contentious.

Ulysses: I'm living in a motel so Sofie could start a fucking travel blog? I'm hallucinating. This can't be real life.

Sofie: Uly hated Calliope.

Ulysses: Fucking liar! Why are you even here?

Sofie: I live here! And I'm not a liar. You said you hated her because your mom worshiped that little girl. Don't you remember? He might not remember because he'd had a few that night. Does your new girlfriend know about your little drinking problem?

Ulysses: You've got a complaint? I'd love to hear it. Because I was good to you, Sofie. You weren't a prisoner. Hell, if you'd have told me you wanted out, I'd have found a way to get you the money myself. You blindsided me.

Brody: Alright. We're not doing this here.

[Audio cuts off with a click. Eerie music starts softly and continues under Rosario's narration]

Rosario: We took a break to let tensions calm. Ulysses disappeared with Brody and Warren for a night of drinking. To my surprise, Sofie quietly approached me near the fire.

[Dramatized voiceover: "I know what happened to Calliope."]

[Sound effect: a door closing]

Rosario: I'm recording now. I'm here with Sofie Randall. Sofie, when you invited me in here, it was because you told me you know what happened to Calliope. Let's hear it.

[Sofie Randall's audio clip]

Sofie Randall (whispering): Remember how Uly said his mother was religious? Well, she was deeply religious. I mean the kind of woman who went to church a buncha times a week. Just before she got pregnant with Calliope, Eleni found this new church. The Church of the Ninth Order. Now, at that time, Eleni wanted a little girl so bad. I mean, Uly's got long hair his whole life. You know why? Cause his mother never let him cut it. I mean, she really wanted a little girl. She told him all the time, she wished she'd had a girl instead of a boy. He hated it.

So then one day, she gets pregnant. Meanwhile, Uly's daddy's been out of the picture a long time. I mean, like he was never *in* the picture. He's never met him. Doesn't know what the man looks like, nothing. Well, it raised the question—who's this baby's daddy?

Rosario: Wait. You're Calliope's age, how would you even know any of this?

Sofie: My momma and Uly's momma used to be good friends. She even got my momma to go to that new church with her a few times. Brought my daddy, too, but momma didn't like it. Said they were creepy. Called it a cult. But my daddy stayed, became a leader in the church and all. The man that ran it, John Russell Thorne, was this charmer. Handsome. A slick talker. The women of the congregation were all over him.

Now, when Eleni comes up pregnant, everybody knew he was the father. But she swore up and down she'd been abstinent. Didn't want anyone to know this Thorne guy was the father. Nobody believed her because she and Thorne were real close, but it was a scandal. He was the head of the church, and she's an unmarried woman with a child. So naturally the women who worshipped him were up in arms about the whole thing. Eleni took a step back because she didn't want to cause any trouble for Thorne. And even though he was supposedly not the baby's father, he came around all the time. Drove Uly crazy.

He's always had a sore spot on his heart about not having a daddy. Now, here comes this little girl, a surprise, and a man who's over there all the time playing daddy. And it's not like he's playing catch with him, he's being ignored. His momma's finally got the little girl she'd always wanted, and he felt all alone. It wasn't right to make a child feel that way. But Uly loves his momma, and he's always gonna forgive her even if she messed him up something good.

Rosario: Do you know what happened to Calliope?

[Soft audio hiss continues in the background]

Sofie: All I know is there's more to this. Thorne. The Order. It's all connected.

[Mysterious outro music fades in]

Rosario: Check out the Mysteries of the Southern Gothic website for a recap on the facts of this case and hit up our forums to share your theories. Stay tuned for the next episode, where we'll dive deeper into the mystery of Calliope and the Ninth Order. This has been Mysteries of the Southern Gothic. I'm Rosario Martinez, reminding you to sleep with one eye open. Until next time.

[Outro music fades out]

* * *

Mysteries of the Southern Gothic Forum

Subject: Episode 51: Calliope and the Church of the Ninth Order Part I

—

Bishasspoppy *3 hours ago*

did you see Uly's picture on the website? might start drinking so he could be my rehab counselor

⬆ 10 ⬇

—

Overtheline *3 hour ago*

Right? Sofie dropped the ball on this one. I want to lick that neck tattoo.

⬆ 7 ⬇

—

ForensicGuy92 *2 hours ago*

you're in the wrong forum. this is for case theories not gushing over boys. go braid each other's hair somewhere else.

⬆ -3 ⬇

———

Rosario4ever *1 hour ago*

found the incel.

⬆ 2 ⬇

———

HerbertsHole *1 hour ago*

I wouldn't believe a word Sofie says.

⬆ ⬇

———

ForensicGuy92 *45 minutes ago*

I don't know. If this Thorne guy is real, what if he took his kid and ran off? They could be living in Argentina for all anyone knows.

⬆ ⬇

———

DeadGirl *30 minutes ago*

Calliope is probably with the Order.

⬆ ⬇

——

AlwaysBees *25 minutes ago*

I've been to the order. I'd bet money she's there too.

——

Scrawny_eric_ *15 minutes ago*

I lived across the street from the Katsaros family. There's definitely something wrong there.

Chapter Twenty-Three

THEY'D RECORDED SO MUCH. He knew they had, but he must have been naive to think they'd have the decency to paint him in a favorable light. Rosario broadcasted it all. He'd been played. Christmas Eve, her little gift and all the little complements, batting her eyelashes at him. She only pretended to want a relationship when she needed something, but after they returned home with Shawnee, she went right into production mode.

"How about that date?" he'd asked.

"Hmm. Can we plan for next week? We've been working on the first Calliope episode and then I promised my mom I'd help her with my cousin's quinceañera. We're making a million party favors. Maybe you can be my date? Or would it be weird that our first date is a fifteen-year-old girl's birthday party?"

"I would love to go to a fifteen-year-old girl's birthday party with you," he said with a chuckle. She told him it was formal, and he'd planned to rent a tux. But then the episode dropped. All he could think about was how he'd done everything she'd ever asked of him, and she made him look like an idiot for their thousands of listeners. That night, he blocked her number, deleted her contact card from his phone, and drank his body weight in whiskey.

He'd known the Randall interview led them to the Order. When Shawnee insisted she'd seen Calliope there, he didn't think it could be possible. Sofie said it was all connected. If Calliope had been living there, Sofie would have known about it. Had everyone lied to him? Was Lang the bastard who took her?

* * *

THE HORRORS he's seen in his lifetime, the struggles, the lies. *This would be a fitting end*, he thinks, weaving over the solid yellow line of the darkened road with his shotgun in his lap. The path reveals itself beyond his headlamps in ten-foot increments at sixty miles per hour. He charges up to the property, accelerating through the uneven terrain until he reaches a gate. It wasn't closed the last time, perhaps because he and Rosario arrived during daylight hours then. Now, Ulysses decides the best way to get Lang Randall's attention is by firing his gun in the air and screaming at the top of his lungs.

"Come out and face me!" The shot cracks through the sky and echoes into the night.

It's no surprise that the guards and residents mobilize, armed and ready to greet him from the ends of their guns. He can make out their militant figures in various states of nightwear and undress, their many weapons pointed in his direction, illuminated by the headlamps of Ulysses's Jeep. He drops his shotgun, and it falls with a *thunk* in the grass at his feet. Raising his hands, he closes his eyes, ready for their imminent gunfire. He's all but written his own obituary in his mind when he hears Lang's voice.

"Lower your weapons! Don't harm this young man."

The surprise forces Ulysses's eyes open. He watches as their guns lower and breathes a momentary sigh of relief. The night isn't over, but at least for now he's still alive. Lang Randall, dressed in his night robe and slippers, cuts through the row of armed guards and approaches the gate. With the lift of an iron bar, he unlatches it and begins to draw it open.

Lowering his arms, Ulysses watches as Lang, an unexpected savior in this moment, slips through to meet him on the other side.

Lang holds up a hand to his eyes to shield them against the glare of the lights. "What's gotten into you, son? It's the middle of the night."

Ulysses, his heartbeat still erratic from the adrenaline and the near certainty of death he'd just faced, struggles to find his voice. "Why'd you do it? Why'd you take my sister?"

Lang's expression shifts subtly, a flicker of pain passing over his features. "Calliope," he says, the name hanging between them like a ghost. For a moment, the night holds its breath, the only sounds the idling engine of Ulysses's Jeep and the cries of nocturnal creatures. Lang stares at Ulysses, measuring him, calculating. "You've been drinking again?"

"This isn't about me. This is about you and what you did."

Then, surprisingly, Lang steps back, gesturing for Ulysses to follow. "Come inside," he says, picking Ulysses's shotgun off the ground. "Let's talk."

Ulysses, caught off guard by the invitation, hesitates only for a moment before turning off the Jeep and following Lang through the gate on foot. The sea of armed guards and residents parts to let them pass.

They enter the home, and Lang starts up the stairs, holding a lamp to light their path. The floors creak under his footing. Ulysses doesn't know where he's being led to, but he asks no questions. The room Lang shows Ulysses into is dimly lit by moonlight filtering through thin curtains. The air is thick with the scent of old wood. Ulysses stands in the doorway, swaying slightly, the effects of the alcohol and the adrenaline crash turning his legs to rubber. He glances around the room, taking in a narrow canopied bed, the antique dresser.

Lang sets the shotgun against the wall near the door, then turns to Ulysses, his expression inscrutable in the low light. "You'll find everything you need here. We'll sort this out in the morning." There's a finality in his voice, a command that allows no argument.

The door closes, and Ulysses is stunned silent, staring at his gun. What just happened? What's to stop him from picking up this gun, walking down the hall and blowing Lang's head off?

Answers, he supposes. The long drive and the alcohol have made his eyes heavy. Picking the shotgun up from against the wall, he carries it to bed, where he removes his boots and lies on his back. The length of the deadly weapon rests across his chest as he dozes off.

A rooster crows, jarring Ulysses awake. From the window, a ball of fire cracks over the horizon. He's drenched in sweat, and a surge of fear send his fingers fumbling around the cold steel of the shotgun. He's alone. Memories of the night before blur as he awakens, returning to his ongoing nightmare.

Floorboards creak under his weight as he approaches the door, one hand around the firearm's wooden grip. The other reaches for the handle when he hears footsteps outside it. Cracking the door open an inch, he peeks to find a young woman standing there, her hand poised in a tentative knock. She quickly draws it back as the door opens.

"Oh," she says. "Good. You're awake."

Her familiar eyes give him pause. The shape of them, the color. Shawnee's story playing out in his mind, he recalls the woman she saw. Could this really be her? "Calliope?"

"Mary," she says, then notices the gun. Her body goes rigid.

"I'm not gonna hurt you." He studies her for another beat. "You look like her." Though, she seems younger. Her pretty face is plump in her cheeks. She couldn't be older than twenty.

Raising her gaze back up at him, she tilts her head in acknowledgment. "Like Calliope?"

"Do you know her?"

She nods, her hands clasped and wrists twisting nervously. "Well, I know she's my sister, but I never met her."

"Your sister?"

Before she can answer, heavy footsteps creak on the stairs and he can make out the top of Lang's head as he lurches upward. "I sent you for him half an hour ago," he says bitterly.

"I didn't want to wake him." Mary sulks, her voice softening before addressing Ulysses again. "There's breakfast downstairs."

"I didn't come here to eat," he says, then faces Lang, his finger hooking into place to fire if needed. "I came here for answers. I want to know what kind of sick games you're playing."

Lang looks him up and down, then shakes his head with disappointment. He waves dismissively and turns his back, walking away. "We can talk and eat. But put that gun away, 'cause if you point that thing at me again, I'm not going to give you a chance to change your mind."

Ulysses hesitates, glancing over at Mary, who's frozen in a cautious stance. He sets the shotgun down and watches the tension leave her body. He follows Lang downstairs to a large table, where a little boy kicks his legs on a bench and gnaws on a long strip of bacon. Ulysses feels a wave of shame thinking about how he'd almost fired that gun with this child nearby. Lord knows what this boy has already seen in his lifetime growing up in this place. Lang drags out a chair and commands Ulysses to sit. Arching over the table, Mary tips a porcelain carafe over a coffee cup, her hands trembling. From her point of view, Ulysses is the threat.

"Thank you," he says softly, offering her an apologetic look he hopes will help her see he's not a madman. The hot coffee she pours smells like chicory and awakens Ulysses's senses.

Lang addresses the little boy. "Go play outside, grownups have business to attend to."

The slice of bacon tight in his fist, he eyes Ulysses suspiciously before sliding off the bench. Lang slathers butter on a roll, humming to himself. With a nod of his head, he instructs Mary to leave. "So," he says casually. He groans a little reaching for a jar of what looks like strawberry jam. "You're here because you think I'm the boogie man."

Drawing in a breath, Ulysses tries to calm his rising temper, gritting his teeth at Lang's relaxed demeanor. His words are measured. "When I was thirteen, I was in the church bathroom picking brain matter out of my hair. You came in and told me I should be helping with the Easter puppet show. You remember that?"

Lang's teeth sink into the bread, and his mouth smacks as he chews. A bit of jam stains the corner of his lips, and he slips out his tongue to lick it clean. "Those were dark times. If you look at the Order's history, you'll see there was a fracture. You can trace that jagged line right back to that year. What you remember as callous indifference, I remember as maintaining composure in the face of fear. We weren't going to win that war in one day, son. If we'd have stood up then, we'd have all perished."

Ulysses can't help but let out a sardonic laugh. "Paint it however you want, but I'm just saying I know what you people are capable of."

Lang's expression hardens. Swiping his hands of crumbs, he seems to decide what to say next. "Let me get you up to speed here, son. My little girl," he says, his voice wavering. "She never did have a kind word for the Order, did she." It's a question stated as fact. "Now, I don't know what possessed her to bring up John Russell Thorne being Calliope's father. But I know that to be a fact because there was a time when we had to make decisions for the church and there was a paternity test involved."

He pauses and sips his coffee. To Ulysses, having always assumed that to be true, it's not much of a surprise. Thorne was a constant presence in his mother's life, until he wasn't. Lang continues. "Son, I did what I could for you kids. For Calliope. For Mary. I warned Eleni about Thorne, but she was too far gone I guess. You'd have to be to love a man like him. It destroyed us. Like I said. There was a fracture. Thorne went his way, and the Order returned to its founding principles, which we embody here. We're peaceful people."

Ulysses must have overlooked that when armed guards dragged him out after his first visit. "You had Shawnee beaten. Held her captive."

"Now, that's a bit of an exaggeration. Hold on here," he says, then cocks his head back and shouts. "Mary!"

After a moment, her bare feet patter into the kitchen. When she returns to the table, her hands are clasped at her belly, eyes wide. "Yes, sir?"

"Tell Ulysses what you told me about that butch woman coming up here and making a mess of things."

Wiping her hands on her apron, she swallows hard. "Well, she came here saying her car broke down and she wanted to call for help. I told her we don't have a phone, but then she said she had to walk a long way and asked for a drink of water. Whatever's done for the needy is done for the Lord, so I brought her in. I didn't think anything of it.

The men were in the Chapel and the girls were preparing lunch for prayer group. Sir told me to hurry things along, so I went in there to check, and she started saying things. She called me Calliope. I asked her who she was, and she told me she was working for some kind of radio program. I told her I don't even own a radio, and even if I did, there's no reception here anyhow.

But I remembered what you'd said, sir, about those TikTok people coming around, and I thought she was being nosey. I asked her to please leave, and when she didn't listen, I called the guards. But she was rough with them, kicking and carrying on. They knocked her around pretty good before she finally left."

Ulysses narrows his eyes at her. As skeptical as he should be, this girl doesn't look like she's capable of telling a lie. He tests her story, asking Lang, "Why did you say you hadn't seen her?"

Mary flushes, shooting Lang a guilty glance, then looks down at her hands as she twists her fingers. "I didn't tell him."

"And why not?" Lang asks chidingly, suggesting he already knows.

"Because I was afraid you'd be upset."

Lang shakes his head regretfully and clicks his tongue, "Had to let those guards go. Pretty girl like Mary begs them to keep secrets just so she can stay out of trouble and they lose their better judgment. But she learned her lesson. Didn't you, Mary?"

"Yes, Sir," she says softly. The sudden flush in her cheeks makes Ulysses contemplate the punishment she must have received for the lie of omission.

"You didn't hold her captive?"

Lang chuckles as if the idea is ridiculous. "Captive? I think the point here is we couldn't get rid of her fast enough. We didn't harm her for the heck of it, we defended ourselves."

It was a farce. He'd known he wasn't a hero, but even less so now. Shawnee wasn't really a victim. What was Shawnee up to? "What about her car? She said you stole her keys."

Mary's lips tighten into a thin line. "Oh, I don't like that one bit. She said she walked here. That's what started the whole thing to begin with."

What else was Shawnee lying about? None of this makes sense.

"You said Calliope's your sister."

"Yes, sir," Mary says. "Well, my half-sister."

"Thorne," Ulysses says, making the connection.

She flinches, as if the name causes her distress.

"Ulysses, this is Erma Roy's daughter," Lang clarifies. "I've been taking care of her and her mother as if they were my own flesh and blood since that terrible Easter."

Erma Roy. Orson Roy's wife. Mary is the child born from the scandal that ended on that awful Sunday. "Nice to meet you, Mary. I hope you'll forgive me for all the trouble."

She offers a small smile. "Of course. Can I get you more coffee?"

Chapter Twenty-Four

AFTER ULYSSES DRANK himself half to death and woke up in Lang Randall's house, he knew he'd hit a new low. It was the violence that frightened him most. The complete loss of control. The wanting to die. It was time to get help.

Ulysses finds himself in Dr. Okafor's office one evening after work. "Relapses happen. You know this. But it's different when it's personal, isn't it?" Dr. Okafor says. "Just like you'd tell one of your clients, it's what we do after a relapse that counts most."

"I know."

"So, let's unpack it. What's been going on?"

"Sofie and I broke up. Few months ago."

The doctor wears a pensive, solemn expression, not articulating the thing Ulysses knows he's thinking but won't say—he's disappointed Ulysses kept the breakup a secret.

"I just didn't want anyone feeling sorry for me."

"It's okay to need support. Your friends want to give you that support."

Since Shawnee told him what she saw, Ulysses had kept his distance from the Randalls. Stopped visiting his mother. He was confused, not knowing now what was true or fiction. He felt like he was losing his grip on reality. Since the podcast aired his dirty laundry, he's cut Rosario out of his life. Ulysses doesn't have the heart to tell Okafor there's no one left standing in his corner. It hurts enough just to admit it to himself.

"I thought you and I had a solid bond," Dr. Okafor continues. "A long history of communication."

"We do. That's why I came to you now."

Dr. Okafor leans forward, his clasped hands sliding across the leather writing mat on his desk, giving Ulysses his undivided attention.

"Lately, I've been getting these images. Not just at night, but during the day. Flashes of things. Feelings."

"Such as?"

"Well, that man they executed. I keep seeing him. The way he looked, how he was afraid. All the blood. And when it happens, I feel like I can't breathe, I start to sweat. My heart races."

"Panic attacks," Dr. Okafor says, half a question.

"Yeah. They don't last long, but they've been happening more often. During sessions. While I'm driving." Ulysses wipes his sweaty palms on his khakis. "I'd forgotten it, but now these memories are starting to resurface," he says, his voice cracking. "I thought I understood all this. But realizing I've repressed significant parts of my own past…How could I not see it?"

"Ulysses, the phenomenon of repressed memories, especially in the context of trauma, is incredibly complex. The brain has its mechanisms for self-preservation, often shielding us from memories that could otherwise incapacitate us emotionally and psychologically. Your work has given you insight into how substances can affect memory. Alcohol, as you know, can disrupt the hippocampus's function, the part of the brain essential for creating and storing memories. But Uly, at this phase, I wouldn't invest too much time in trying to decipher your memories. You're not approaching this with a clear head. I would, however, suggest you return to treatment on an outpatient basis."

Ulysses hesitates. He's not sure it's gotten to that point yet, but maybe Dr. Okafor's right. "What about my clients?"

"Don't be silly, Uly. You're a member of this family. We'll see to it that your clients are taken care of. God loves you, Ulysses. We love you. Let's get you back on track."

After work, Ulysses takes Domino for a run, the anxiety of starting treatment again gnawing at him. Upon their return, he starts dinner. His post-run endorphins help dull the nervous edge, but he's famished. Still dressed in his running shorts and tank, he boils pasta. There's a knock at the door. Domino barks defensively, the kind of shrill sound that makes the inside of Ulysses's head vibrate. "Shhh," he scolds, quickly turning off the stove. He dashes to the door. Leaning in close, he finds the peephole obscured. Opening the door a crack, he sees Rosario, arms crossed.

"You stood me up."

"What happened to not popping up unannounced?"

"Well when you're ignoring my texts, how else am I supposed to talk to you?"

He scoffs, stepping out into the colonnade. "You're supposed to take the hint and respect the boundary."

"The episode didn't even paint you in a bad light."

"Oh right, I sound like a real fucking winner. Uly lives in a motel. Uly hated Calliope. Uly's an alcoholic. Right, those were awesome points." His jaw clenches as he draws in a hard breath, remembering all the awful things Sofie said that Rosario broadcast to the world.

"The forums are very positive. Listeners really like you. They can hear the pain in your voice. They empathize with you. And episode two drops tonight. They'll all know you're a hero."

She's talking about him like he's not even a real person. "I'm glad my suffering is working for you and your listeners. Please leave."

"You don't mean that."

He raises his voice. "Why don't you ever listen?"

"Just hear me out. Let me play you the next episode. If you hate it and you hate me after, then I promise I'll never bother you again."

Against his better judgment, he lets her inside.

* * *

Podcast: Mysteries of the Southern Gothic
Episode 52: Calliope and the Church of the Ninth Order Part II

[Intro music fades out]

Shawnee Lewis (Narrator): Welcome back to Mysteries of the Southern Gothic. I'm your host, Shawnee Lewis. Today, we delve into my chilling encounter at a place frozen in time, where the modern world blurs with the past.

[Sound effect: Gravel crunching]

Shawnee: Sofie Randall's statement led me to a sprawling property in Whispering Hope, a rural town in central Florida, where an imposing house reminiscent of an old plantation mansion stands. I found myself at its doorstep, undercover. My story? My car betrayed me miles back, and I was in desperate need of help.

[Eerie music starts softly and continues under Shawnee's narration]

The lady who answered, dressed as though she'd stepped out of The Handmaids Tale offered me water—a gesture of kindness, or so I thought. Inside, the dimly lit interior revealed the absence of electricity.

[Sound effect: Footsteps leading into ambient kitchen sounds]

In the kitchen, I encountered three women, their nervous

glances revealing an unease that went beyond my unexpected presence. As I looked on, one whispered they were preparing lunch for a men's prayer meeting.

"Are women allowed at these prayer meetings?" I inquired. They have their own meetings, she explained. To which I asked, "Who makes their lunch?" A question so absurd to their sensibilities, they all laughed out loud.

[Laughter track fades in and out]
[Sound effect: Door flying open, heavy footsteps and unintelligible yelling in a woman's voice]

Suddenly, the atmosphere shifted. The sound of laughter must have summoned their leader.

[Audio clip: Shawnee's interview at Venus Inn, slightly lower quality]

Rosario (co-host): Who stormed in?

Shawnee: I'd bet every cent I have that the woman was Calliope Katsaros.

Ulysses: She's alive?

Shawnee: I know in my gut it was her. And she was less than pleased to find an outsider standing in her home. She accused me of disrespecting their holy day, and before I knew it, guards were trying to drag me out. I tried to fight them off but there were too many of them.

[Sound effect: Scuffle, punches, grunts]

Shawnee: I awoke in a shed, handcuffed, abandoned. The escape that followed was nothing short of a miracle, driven solely by my will to survive. I slid a bobby pin out of my hair and shimmied it into my cuffs. The shed was old. The wood rotted. I kicked my way out in the middle of the night and went looking for my keys.

[Sound effects: Metal clinking, wood breaking, night sounds]

They'd moved my car onto the property. My phone was inside, dead. But I couldn't find my keys to escape. Hiding until dawn, I weighed my chances of survival.

[Sound effect: Footsteps in leaves, distant gunshots]

I hid out in the woods until daylight, waiting on an opportunity. When I finally saw Rosario and Ulysses arrive, hope flickered briefly. I wanted to run then, but all the guards were out there with their guns. I wanted to scream when Rosario and Ulysses drove off, tried to run into the road where they'd find me, but I wasn't fast enough. I was too weak. Thank God, Ulysses came back to save me.

[Ulysses's audio clip, voice filled with despair]

Ulysses: I'd been paying her tithes to the Order. My mom. A not insignificant amount of money, every month. What if she knew?

Rosario: Your mom?

Ulysses: Yeah. What if she knew all along?

[Mysterious outro music fades in]

Shawnee: Check out the Mysteries of the Southern Gothic website for a recap on the facts of this case and hit up our forums to share your theories. Stay tuned for the next episode, where we'll dive deeper into the mystery of Calliope and the Ninth Order.

This has been Mysteries of the Southern Gothic. I'm Shawnee Lewis, reminding you to sleep with one eye open. Until next time.

[Outro music fades out]

Chapter Twenty-Five

WHATEVER REVELATION she expected him to have doesn't happen. Their eyes meet.

"It was thirty minutes of Shawnee's bullshit lies," he says. "They didn't lock her up, and she didn't *MacGyver* herself free from being handcuffed in some shed. She didn't see Calliope either. It was Mary Roy, Thorne's daughter."

"What? What are you talking about?"

"I went back to the Order. I thought the congregation would kill me. Lang Randall *could* have killed me. It was a fucking suicide mission. But they didn't. I met Mary Roy and honestly I don't think the girl would know how to lie if she needed to save her life. She's not even old enough to be Calliope, which is obvious. Shawnee wasn't ever in danger."

She's stunned silent, stuck in a confused expression.

He's even angrier than he was when she arrived. "I trusted you. I felt things for you. You used me."

"Is that really what you think? I used you?"

"Yes." He's sweaty from his run, hungry from never getting to make his dinner. He's certain he smells bad, and he's a little sick to his stomach. "I need to shower and eat something. You said what you needed to say. You can go now."

She rises to her feet, looking over toward the kitchen. "What were you making?"

"Half boiled spaghetti thanks to you."

"Let me make you something."

"I don't need you to make me anything."

"Just go take a shower, let me take care of it. Please. I already ruined your dinner."

"Seriously. You never listen."

"No, I don't. I'm sorry. You're hungry. You're grouchy. Take a shower, I'll make dinner, then we can talk. Please?" Her pretty brown eyes gleam at him through thick lashes and he hates how it makes him lose his nerve.

Giving up, he huffs into the bathroom. Ulysses turns on the shower, letting the water heat up as he stands in front of the mirror, examining his reflection. The stress of the last few months has taken its toll, evident in the weariness of his eyes. He strips off his clothes, slides the curtain open and steps inside. The hot water washing off the grime makes him feel a measure more human.

He's lathering up when the door clicks open. Sliding the curtain a skosh, he peeks out to find Rosario sliding down her jeans. Once undressed, her eyes fix on his before grabbing the curtain and joining him inside.

"Whoa," he says.

"Do you want me to go?" she asks.

She knows exactly what she's doing. *God she's beautiful.* He expected she would be and yet she's nothing like he expected. The shade of her skin is like the meaty part of an almond, her nipples the almond's brown papery skin. Reaching out to touch his chest, she traces a tattoo with her finger. The sensation of her hands on him in the confines of his shower in this vulnerable state trigger something instinctive, and his arms encircle her waist, pulling her close.

They kiss, the warm water cascading down their bodies. His mouth dips down to feel her tender breast against his lips, his tongue. Her moans echo in the small space as the steam and rhythmic patter of water weave around them in a serene moment of undistracted intimacy. Kissing her mouth, her chin, her neck, all he can think about is how furious he was with her, and yet being with her feels so good.

Washing each other, her soapy affectionate hands traverse his body, rubbing, gripping, stroking, and setting off a series of explosions in his brain. Pressing a palm against the cold tile, he supports himself from the threat of his weakening knees. Rinsing away the last traces of soap, they share a lingering look, a silent acknowledgment of what's to come that sends a pulse of electricity through him. He shuts off the water, and they reach for towels to dry off just enough. Before he can wrap the towel around himself, she's taken control again, pushing him backward so his ass presses against the edge of bathroom vanity.

Dropping to her knees, she takes him into her mouth. The intensity of the pleasure stuns him; it's been a long while. Toward the end with Sofie, their sex life had become dry toast. It was better than nothing to a starving man, but certainly nothing to get excited about. And oral sex was always out of the question, giving or receiving. Despite not being a member of the Order herself, she was raised with the fear of Lang Randall and God in her. She was clear her mouth was off limits.

Looking down at Rosario, gorgeous dark eyes glitter up at him, her blonde hair falling over them in wet strands. She has no idea the magnitude of the power she wields over him right now. As she continues her magic, the pressure builds fast, starting in his thighs.

"I'm gonna come," he says, almost a moment too late. The words leave his mouth just as the waves of pleasure pull him under and he falls apart. The sounds leaving his mouth are unrecognizable to him, involuntary. His mind goes blank. After a moment, the details of the bathroom—the sound of the vent, the damp in the air—return and he catches his breath with trembling legs. "Oh no," he says. "I'm so sorry."

Grinning at him, she teases him with her hands, her lips. "Don't be."

Her smile, along with the lack of tension anywhere in his body, make him light. He helps her to her feet. When they're face-to-face, she grips his neck and kisses him deeply. It's all-consuming, erotic. It's been a long time since he's been with anyone like this, someone who's confident in their sexuality, who knows what they want. Someone assertive. There's an underlying primal challenge to it, to his dominance, and it incites him.

"Get your ass in my bed. Now."

She lights up with surprise, and for the first time ever, she does as instructed, scurrying from the room. With a quick peek over her shoulder to be sure he's watching, she climbs up and crawls on all fours toward the edge of the covers and shoves them down. She squirms against the sheets where she'd once slept alone. It feels like an eternity has passed since that chaste night he'd slept on the couch. Now, he's positioning his mouth between her thighs, parting her with his tongue, tasting her sweet flesh. She writhes and moans against his bed.

Humming against her, he revels in the moment, taking his time. Feeling her struggle to maintain control as her thighs tighten around his head. He waits until she's ready, until she's begging. *Condoms*, he thinks. A full box in his end table. Purchased when newly single and never opened. He'd struggled with the prospect of casual sex. It was much more thrilling to indulge in the one he's been fantasizing about. Lunging toward the table, he jerks open the drawer and retrieves the box. Domino looks on curiously from beside the bed. "Get. Go lay down," he orders, then returns to Rosario. She watches him as he resists the temptation to tear the box of condoms to shreds. He rips one open and puts it on, slowly rolling it into place.

When he's ready, poised to enter her, they lock eyes, hearts beating fast. For all the quiet confidence she exhibited earlier, there's a vulnerability to her now. "Is this okay?" he confirms.

"Fuck me," she says, then gently kicks her heel against his ass, like spurring a horse into trot. They kiss, and as he sinks into her, she gasps against his mouth. Now connected, they take another look at each other. It's different this time. Affected. As if they've just acti-vated something beyond their control.

The first time he got drunk, there was a distinct feeling of sitting in the back seat while someone else drove. His better judgment would sometimes shout directions, but whether the driver followed that instruction wasn't up to him. He liked the sense of losing control, the buoyancy of it, the feeling of invincibility. It's a feeling he chased with every drink that came after, and it became more and more elusive. But now, he's found it in Rosario. The feeling of their bodies connected, of their rhythm together. Whatever it is, it was in the driver's seat, and he was just along for the ride.

Changing positions, she climbs on top, pinning his hands above his head. She wants him powerless, and he's happy to give in as she eagerly takes everything she needs from him. He watches her, works with her as her hips rock and he thrusts up to meet her, crashing over and over again until her head rolls back and she cries out. Hands free, he grips her hips before returning to their cadence. Accelerating each swing with punishing force until he brings himself over the edge.

When he does, he's spent. Refusing to break their connection, she lies on top of him, pressed chest to chest. Her body rises and falls with each of his labored breaths as they recover together and let the involuntary trembling stop, wait for his muscle control to return.

After, they lie together. She seems content, but his mind travels back to the podcast, to her showing up unannounced, to her manip-ulation.

"I don't get you," he says. "One minute you're the sweetest person in the world, and the next, you're hanging me out to dry."

"It's not as bad as you think it is. It just feels that way because it's still raw. I think people are going to see who you really are. See you the way I do."

"And how's that?"

"Wonderful, flawed, loving, wounded, empathetic, brave," she says, her fingers tracing a line from the middle of his chest to above his navel, traveling up and down again. He lets out a bitter laugh at the word brave. It's a fine line between being brave and being stupid. Rosario presses a gentle kiss to his shoulder. "I mean it. You're really special, and I promise by the time we've told the whole story, everyone's going to know it."

Domino barks and there's a knock at the door. "That's dinner," she says. "Ordered takeout."

He slips into a pair of shorts and opens for the delivery woman holding a plastic bag with two containers. He grins to himself at Rosario's cockiness. She knew well enough he wasn't going to throw her out of his shower and ordered herself a victory meal to enjoy after their little romp. She meets him in the kitchen wearing the button-down shirt he'd taken off after work. It looks perfect on her.

They have dinner together on his couch, and Domino begs nearby, allured by the aroma of human food while ignoring his kibble. Ulysses tells Rosario about his art classes and his talk with Dr. Okafor. How he's back in treatment now and doing administrative work in between. She tells him about Shawnee's search for their next explosive story. He feels a bit of relief at the idea that soon their focus on him and his family will end. That soon, he can forget about the secrets they'd all kept and move on, having excised the last remnants of the Orders' influence in his life.

After dinner, Rosario cuddles with him on the couch under a blanket with Domino nuzzled beside them. Cozy and relaxed, it seems as if she has no intention of leaving. Ulysses decides he's fine with it. More than fine. He likes that she challenges him, always pushes back when she thinks he's being unreasonable. He's glad she didn't listen when he told her to go.

After their evening walk with Domino, they climb into bed. Holding her close, his mind wanders to a conversation on her balcony they once had. The one about her not giving long-term relationships a chance. He wonders if that's their fate. If there was some test he's passed, or failed. Some threshold crossed that will force her to examine where they stand. He hates how it makes him feel a twinge of insecurity. Was their sex good enough? Is he good enough? He wants to ask what she's thinking, how she feels, but can't imagine anything worse than coming off as needy, especially in this landmark moment together. He lies back, tucking his arm underneath the pillow behind his head.

"You know, when I was out there and I had a bunch of guns pointed at me," he whispers, "I closed my eyes, and I swear to God I saw your face."

The sentiment lights her up from the inside and she takes his face in her hands, pressing a tender kiss to his lips. "I can't believe you went back."

"I wasn't in my right mind. It was stupid."

"I'm proud of you for getting help." Her fingers comb through his hair. It feels nice.

"I feel so blessed. This place where I work, it's faith based, you know? Dr. Okafor, he's a good Christian. I don't think there's another place in the world that would help me the way he is."

She trails her fingertips up and down his torso, through the blanket of hair on his chest and down the muscular ridges of his abdomen. Rolling onto her side, she looks up at him and asks, "Are you still pretty religious?"

"I still have faith, but I definitely don't follow the Order's way of things anymore."

"What's the Order's way?"

He's a little surprised she doesn't already know this as in-depth as their research has been thus far. "It's a hierarchy. They say that mortal men and women who enter this life and live it purely will ascend to the Order of Angels. The Ninth Order. That's the level on the ladder that's closest to humans. They get mixed up in humanity's drama. Well, the Order believes the world is immoral, impure, and the angels will form kind of like an army. A celestial force that will ultimately save humanity from itself. When Thorne was in charge, he framed it like a war. You put it like that, and any act, no matter how violent or extreme, can be justified as long as it's meant to protect the sanctity of the Order." His mind goes back there—to Thorne, to Orson Roy's blood dripping down the stairs, and the words return to him. "'*Purify your hands with the blood of sinners,*' he'd say. It's a fucked and dangerous ideology, and I'm glad I'm not in it anymore."

"Wow. I thought it was just an offshoot of Christianity."

"They pretend to be," he says softly. "But it's not, not at all. Lang says they've turned it all around but, I still felt it while I was there. It's a different energy."

"Do you think they know what happened to Calliope?"

Despite how disturbing it was being back there, looking into Mary's eyes when she spoke about Calliope, how Lang spoke about that time—it felt like they were telling the truth. "No. I think they care more about separating people from their money and creating their own twisted vision of what the world should be."

"I'm glad you got out," she says. Her touch is so gentle, so sweet.

"I love how affectionate you are," he says without even thinking. The words bring a heat to his face. He didn't say he loved *her*. Even if he did, any use of the L-word could be dangerous at this juncture. He clears his throat. "Physical touch is my favorite way to express love," he adds, unintentionally saying it again.

"I'm glad. Mine is acts of service. You being a part of this, showing up when I needed you. It meant the world to me."

"Well, if this was my reward, I'd do anything legal and several illegal things to serve you again."

Her body shakes against him with laughter. Turning on his side to face her, he whispers, "Thanks for not letting me push you away."

"I'm very persistent."

"I'm grateful."

* * *

WATCHING THE CLOCK, it's just after four thirty in the afternoon, and Ulysses counts down the minutes. His work arrangement with Dr. Okafor allowed for Ulysses to take private sessions throughout the day, and although he wasn't seeing clients, he was helping the doctor keep up with his paperwork.

Rosario is waiting at home for him, and when he pushes his key into the lock of his front door, he'll open it to find her there smiling at him, Domino wagging his tail beside her. He'll kiss her, and if the last few days together are any indicator, they'll fool around and have a quick dinner before his next job. Maybe he'll convince her to come with him. After, they'll take Domino for a walk around the neighborhood, get back and then fool around some more. When they've exhausted themselves, they'll watch television in bed together. She'll stroke his hair or tickle his arm or some other kind of sweet affectionate thing she does before they fall asleep. None of this would be possible if Sofie hadn't walked out on him. He's suffered long enough, and being with Rosario feels like his reward.

After a deep session with Father Caden, Ulysses returns to his office, hoping to quickly pack up so he can rush home to her. Sitting at his desk, his phone vibrates in his pocket. *Rosario*, he thinks. Pulling it from his pocket, he glances at it and finds Brody's name instead.

> Sofie dipped. I'm screwed on the daycare situation. Any chance you could loan me a few bones until payday?

Surprise surprise. You got Sofie'd. Ulysses lets out a discontent hiss as he clicks through the client notation system where he enters Dr. Okafor's handwritten notes. But the longer he sits with it, Ulysses realizes that taking money from Brody to repay Sofie's debt never quite sat right with him in the first place. It wasn't Brody's debt to pay. Ulysses might have needed it then, but now that he's back on his feet, returning it feels like a gesture of closure. Since he's downsized and stopped paying his mother's tithes, he's been able to put himself in a pretty comfortable financial situation. If he returns the money Brody gave him, he can move on with his life knowing he's not indebted to the Randalls in any way.

Without texting back, he simply opens Venmo and sends Brody twelve hundred bucks to tide him over, planning to return the rest over the next couple of paydays.

Chapter Twenty-Six

Mysteries of the Southern Gothic Forum

SUBJECT: **Episode 52: Calliope and the Church of the Ninth Order Part II**

———

ForensicGuy92 *5 hours ago*

Shawnee is a badass! Seriously, she makes this show what it is. She's the only one that really does anything. I knew Calliope was still out there.

⬆ 3 ⬇

———

Second_Chances *5 hour ago*

Hell yeah! Have you seen those videos from the order on TikTok? Those people are unhinged. I can't believe she made it out alive.

⬆ ⬇

———

StartsNSparks *3 hours ago*

Ulysses is a national hero. I want to have his babies.

⬆ ⬇

A_hole_for_uly *2 hour ago*

It's cute you think I'll share my husband with you

⬆ -2 ⬇

—

ForensicGuy92 *2 hours ago*

You people disgust me

⬆ -3 ⬇

—

LaurenListener *2 hours ago*

I was at the order once and everything Shawnee said is true.

⬆ ⬇

—

Chaos_at_Home *1 hour ago*

Single handedly solved the case. Someone give Shawnee a raise

⬆ ⬇

—

MagicDad *43 minutes ago*

Yeah but if it wasn't for Ulysses she would have died out in the woods. He saved her

ForensicGuy92 *5 minutes ago*

Shawnee would have found a way

Chapter Twenty-Seven

ROSARIO RETURNS to her apartment for the afternoon. If she didn't need to meet with Shawnee for the show, she'd have gladly stayed at Ulysses's place. It's cozy and romantic. No matter where they went in the space, they had eyes on each other. Even when he had to leave to work, there was something magical about being home when he returned and catching that glint of happiness in his eyes. It was their little nest. Thinking of the days spent with him there brings a smile to her face. *Is this what it feels like to be in love?* The thought brings a mix of excitement and apprehension.

"What's got you all dreamy-eyed?" Shawnee asks.

Rosario hesitates for a moment, caught off guard by the question. But the genuine curiosity in Shawnee's gaze encourages her to open up. "Ulysses," she admits. "I've been staying at his place."

Shawnee grins, leaning back in her chair. "Sounds like things are getting pretty serious."

It does feel serious. She's never felt this way about someone before. It's all so new and terrifying. But she quickly remembers the conversation she'd planned to have with Shawnee, and her smile vanishes. "Why'd you lie about the Order?"

"Excuse me?"

"Your story about being held captive."

Shawnee's eyes light up with amusement, a gesture Rosario recognizes as her being caught in a lie. "I suppose the infallible Ulysses told you that?"

"Is it true?"

With a deep breath and a sigh, she rolls her eyes. "So I exaggerated a little bit. Do you think it was easy camping out in those woods overnight? I wasn't planning on being out there that long. My fucking car got towed. It's not like it was all peaches and cream. Anyway, that episode got half a million downloads."

"Your car got towed?"

"Apparently Whispering Hope doesn't like it when you park illegally on a county road."

Rosario holds back a laugh, not wanting to relish in Shawnee's self-inflicted misfortune even now that she knows she's safe. But, she can't help but find a little humor in it. She showed up there, confronted the Order, fought off the guards then camped out in the woods to stalk them, witnessed nothing of interest, only to discover her car was gone. Shawnee must see the glee in Rosario's eyes.

"See, this is why I didn't tell you. I knew you'd look at me with your *I told you* so face."

"I'm sorry. You're right. You said you had new intel on Belladonna?"

The confrontational moment passes, and Shawnee's professional demeanor returns. She pulls out her laptop. "The family attorney sent me a case file. Gruesome stuff. This chick was not fucking around. Young male victim: dead. His mother: dead. Two different forms of asphyxiation. It's a goldmine."

"Sounds promising. But what about Calliope?"

"What about her? We found her. She's alive in a cuckoo for Cocoa Puffs cult. The end."

"No, not the end. The woman you saw was Mary Roy. Thorne and Erma Roy's kid."

Shawnee's mouth falls open, her eyes wide. "Oh fuck," she says, bringing her hand to her lips. "That makes a lot of sense actually. She did seem a little on the young side."

"Apparently, the Order split the year Calliope went missing. They went on their way with Erma and Mary, and John Russell Thorne rode off into the sunset. Supposedly, they don't do any of the murder-y stuff anymore. Just misogyny. I don't think they're at the center of this."

"Why would a power-hungry, homicidal maniac like Thorne leave peacefully?"

Rosario leans forward. "That's exactly why we need to keep digging. Find out what happened to Thorne."

Shawnee slides the thick, green Calliope binder across the desk and flips it open. "I've looked at these pages a bazillion times."

"Start from the beginning."

With a hiss, Shawnee flips a page and crosses her arms. "Water Oak Mobile Home Community LLC," she announces unenthusiastically. "Home of the Katsaros family, the Randall family, and the McNichols."

"Have we talked to the McNichols?"

"They had alibis."

"So what? There weren't there the day she went missing, but that doesn't mean they don't have any helpful information."

Shawnee flips quickly to another page, deep within the binder. "Chelsea McNichol, high school dropout and Dairy Curl cashier. Debra McNichol, young mother and an associate at commercial printing company. They were both at work all day. Said they didn't interact with the families much."

"Wasn't Warren in high school around that time?"

"Yeah."

"Well, two high school aged kids in the same neighborhood. They didn't interact at all? Warren seems like the kind of guy who would know about a girl around his age living in the neighborhood. I'd bet he'd talked to her once or twice."

Shawnee opens her laptop and starts to type. Rosario looks over her shoulder as she pulls up Facebook and types in *Chelsea McNichol*. A few clicks on her laptop and a list of Chelseas come up. There's only one McNicol in Tampa. Her profile photo looks aged. She's giving the classic duck face pose, and her black emo bangs are strewn across her pale forehead. As they silently judge, Shawnee's email sets off a high pitched *ting*. An email notification briefly flashes on the screen. The sender's address catches their attention:

'dearsoutherngothicmysteries@gmail.com' "That's weird. It's like they created an email address just to send this." Shawnee clicks into the email to reveal nothing but a single link, stark against the backdrop of the otherwise empty message. No greeting, no explanation—just a solitary hyperlink inviting them to click.

"Don't click it," Rosario warns. Shawnee shoots her an annoyed look that says '*I know more than you.*'

"I'm not clicking it," she says, toggling to another screen. "Not yet, anyway. I'll use a virtual machine to open it. That way, if it's something malicious, it won't affect the actual system."

Rosario nods, impressed. "You're so hot when you're smart."

"I'm hot all the time," she says, as a series of windows and scripts load on the screen. "Environment secured." With a deep breath, Shawnee clicks the link.

The screen flickers momentarily before a video starts to play. It looks like an old VHS tape the way horizontal waves seem to scroll down the screen. A home movie of some kind. There's a date in the lower right corner in a boxy camcorder font: March 15, 2004. The camera pans across the exterior of a house; a sign reads M&B Homes. A woman holds up a thick folder as she smiles wide, one eye closed against the sun. There's no audio.

"What is this?" Rosario asks. The video cuts to black, then the image returns, except now the woman is standing in a small plot of land and the date reads March 23, 2004. A boy stands beside her in too-long denim shorts, an unwilling participant in the film. She wraps an arm around him. The image quality is fuzzy, but squinting at it for a moment, she can see the boy's hair is pulled back into a ponytail.

"That's Uly and his mom."

Shawnee brings her face closer to the screen. "Is that Calliope back there?"

Rosario had missed her, but in the background is a figure spinning. A little girl. She throws her arms out to steady herself, then frolics through the grassy patch. "Could be."

The film ends, and Rosario and Shawnee stare at the screen for a moment, perplexed. Someone went through the trouble of transferring this relic into digital format and setting up an email account to send this to them. It's Ulysses's family, so it must be related to their case. Who would even have access to a personal home movie like that one?

"M&B Homes," Shawnee says aloud, then pulls up a browser and searches *M&B Homes communities Tampa Bay*. "If the woman holding the folder was Eleni, it was probably her house."

"But Calliope is in the video. They lived in the trailer park then."

"M&B homes is one of those cookie-cutter builders. You buy the land, and they throw together a cheap little house. You get to customize the countertops and carpet color and shit."

Hmm. Rosario spins in her chair slowly, back and forth. Who sent this? And why? New home purchase. A glimmer of a brighter future. A short, happy moment for the family, captured for posterity. Ulysses seemed a little annoyed, but he was a teenage boy being coddled by his mother. Calliope was behaving just as children do—entertaining herself in the absence of toys or playground equipment, she spun in a circle. Rosario did that too as a child, spinning again and again outside her father's office. Hoping to get a moment of his attention in between meetings, she'd lurk outside, spinning until she'd fall down from dizziness, rendering herself immobilized by the world whipping around her even as she sat still.

"Well, that's interesting."

"What's interesting?"

"Checked out the property records site."

Rosario rolls over in her chair to get a closer look at Shawnee's laptop screen. There's a photo of the house, the legal plot specifications, tax history and owner: *Eleni Katsaros, 1082 101st Ave S.*

"She owns a house?"

"Yup. It hasn't been on the market for sale or rent. Who do you think lives there?"

"I have no idea. Someone must live there, otherwise why would Ulysses stay in a motel all that time?"

An odd feeling settles in her gut. She's being paranoid, she tells herself. There's probably a logical explanation for why he wouldn't have brought it up. It's not like Rosario goes around talking about her parents' real estate portfolio. It's just never come up.

THAT NIGHT, she lets herself into Ulysses's apartment with the key he gave her. She's greeted by an enthusiastic Domino. After a brief walk around the pond in his apartment complex, they return inside. She'd left the bed a mess earlier. Ambling over to it, she smooths out the flat sheet and pulls up the comforter. There's a knock at the door. Opening it, she's surprised to see Sofie standing there, her neutral expression instantly turning cold.

"What are you doing here?" she asks, scrunching up her little nose. Rosario should be asking her the same question. How does she even know where his new place is?

"I live here," Rosario lies. "Can I help you with something?"

"I came here to see Uly."

"He's not here."

Sofie scowls at her and shakes her head. "So he moved you in here, huh? That was fast."

Rosario shrugs and stays silent. She doesn't have to explain anything to this woman.

Sofie continues, voice strained. "You know it started out nice with us too. But one of these days, something's going to ruin his day. A difficult client, something with his mom, and the real Uly will come out."

"If he's so awful, why are you here?"

"I've known him all my life and I love him."

Rosario tightens her grip on the doorknob, ready to slam the door in her face. "Sorry, but you made your choice. It's time to move on."

Sofie forces a grin, then takes a deep breath before starting to leave. An afterthought seems to strike her and she turns back. "Does he still talk in his sleep?"

"What?"

"Oh, you'll see."

Having heard enough of Sofie's nonsense, Rosario shuts the door and locks it. Leaning against it, she waits for her nerves to calm before resuming her task of tidying up the apartment to make it welcoming for Ulysses's return.

She's lighting a scented candle when she hears the click of the lock and the door swings open. She and Domino both perk up. She never thought she'd find herself here, eagerly awaiting her beau's return from the workforce. It's so domestic. His tired expression brightens once he sees her. She stands to greet him, the tension from Sofie's visit momentarily forgotten in the warmth of their reunion.

Chapter Twenty-Eight

"A VHS TAPE?" he asks, twirling fettuccine around the prongs of his fork. He wonders when was the last time he ever laid eyes on a VHS tape, or a VCR for that matter.

"It was digitized, uploaded to a shared drive and sent to us via link. No audio, just a few minutes of you, your mom and Calliope at M&B Homes."

"I don't even remember a video like that existing." For the first time in ages, he remembers how exciting a time that was. They'd only known life in a cramped trailer. He and Calliope were each going to get their own rooms. He'd almost forgotten it because it wasn't long after that everything fell apart. "March?" he confirms.

"March 15th and the 23rd 2004. Hold on a second," she says, pushing out her chair with her legs. "I'll show you." She gets up, leaving him and her bowl of pasta behind. That was the year Orson Roy was murdered. The videos must have been made just a few weeks before.

Setting the laptop on the table, she lifts it open and retrieves the video. Once it starts, it's as if the oxygen is sucked from the room. His mother, smiling and hopeful. Then, a flash of fear. A distorted memory. *Blood on his hands.*

"You okay?"

"Yeah. I don't remember anything about that day." Whatever he did remember makes him lose his appetite. He pushes his bowl away.

"I'm sorry. Probably should have waited until after dinner."

His mother once had milk crates of VHS tapes in her closet. When he moved her to memory care, he'd packed it all up. Tossed most of it away and donated whatever furniture and extra clothing was salvageable. He kept a few things for himself of sentimental value, but he doesn't remember taking a video tape. The notion that a stranger might possess something so intimately connected to those days sends a sharp twinge through him.

Rosario puts on a smile that's too deliberate, her body language rigid with forced neutrality. "So, whatever happened to your mom's house?"

The question makes Ulysses recoil slightly, igniting a flare of shame that sends warmth to his cheeks. "What do you mean?" he deflects.

"Well she's in a nursing home now, right?"

"Yeah," he acknowledges, his response clipped.

"So…" She leaves it hanging, an invitation to fill in the gap.

Crossing his arms over his chest with an irritated hiss, he fortifies himself. She's still picking apart his life. All this time together is about gathering intel for her little investigation. "What business is it of yours?"

The air between them thickens, charged with a sudden shift in their dynamic. She jerks back. "I'm sorry, but obviously someone wants us to know about that house. Why are you being so defensive about it?"

He raises his voice. "Because I'm tired of not knowing when I'm talking to my girlfriend or an investigative journalist." It's not until she cracks a smile that he realizes what he's said.

"Girlfriend, huh?" she teases.

He's unamused. "I'm being serious. I want to be able to trust you, but I can't deal with a repeat of what happened last time. It's personal. It's embarrassing."

"What's embarrassing?"

Instead of providing assurance, she's asking more questions. Closing his eyes, he runs his fingers through his hair and takes a breath to calm himself. "Am I talking to my girlfriend?"

"Yes."

"It's bad," he says. "She was a single mom. We never had much, so she did everything on her own, including home repairs. Plumbing. Electrical. It was a new house, but cheaply built so it was only a few years before shit started falling apart. I learned a lot from watching her actually. But when her mind started to go, she started fixing problems that weren't there. I'd stop by after work and find the floor covered in an inch of water because she dismantled a pipe in the wall without shutting off the supply. Once, she started a fire trying to rewire the air conditioning in the middle of the summer. It was a nightmare.

"But you don't just snap your fingers and get someone out of the home they've lived in for years. That's not how it works. Even if it is for their own safety. Trust me, we tried everything. But she was stubborn, and by the time I was able to get her into memory care, the house was basically unlivable. I kept planning to fix it, but it's difficult to go there. There's so many bad feelings in that place, I just avoided it. I'm not proud of it, but it's just sitting there ready to collapse on itself any day."

Leaning forward, she rubs his hand. "I'm so sorry. I don't mean to upset you, babe. I just wonder what the significance of that place is to whoever sent this video to us."

"I have no clue."

"You keep saying you want to remember." The tone of her voice suggests she's ramping up to something.

"No," he preempts. "Not going there."

"But what if it triggers a memory?"

Her voice is so sweet, maternal. It's a technique she's used before, and he's not falling for it again. "You are so manipulative," he says through a humorless laugh. "Seriously. You're unbelievable. I said no."

Throwing up her hands, she shoves her plate aside and stands up in a huff. "You know what? You're right. This is too complicated." She wipes her hands together as is she's brushing off crumbs. "How about we make the lines super clear—I'm not your girlfriend. How's that?"

"Will you stop it and sit down."

"Why, so I can keep *manipulating* you? How does Sofie know where you live?"

The question comes out of nowhere, a verbal sucker punch. "What?"

"She came looking for you before you got home. Warned me about you."

He scoffs. "I bet she did."

"Answer the question."

He closes his eyes, his chest heavy with remorse. It was the whisky. Weeks ago, before Rosario reentered his life, he'd found himself alone and lonely, nursing his rejection. Sofie came by, the result of a drunken late-night text. It was one night, and he regretted it in the morning. They both did.

"Because she's been here before. Big deal. I'm not putting myself up for sainthood, okay? You'd turned me down."

"Ew, really?" she says, lip curled up with disgust. "You've really turned out to be a disappointment." She blazes a trail around the apartment, gathering her things, and his heart races at the thought of her storming out on him.

"It was before you and I started seeing each other," he reasons. "It didn't mean anything. You're being ridiculous."

She stops long enough to glare at him. "Dude, you're not over your ex. You want a rebound? Well I'm not the one, okay? Fuck off."

"Listen to me." He grabs her arm and yanks her toward him. A yelp escapes her lips as he reels her in. Bringing his face close to her, his voice low, he says, "You're the only one for me."

"Do you still love her?"

He loosens his grip. "Not even a little bit. It was dumb. I'd been drinking."

"It's always the drinking with you."

His hands find her waist and he draws her close. "I'm sober. Twenty-one days. I told you, I'm back in outpatient treatment."

She softens. "I know, and that's good."

Chapter Twenty-Nine

"THIS IS GOOD," Ulysses says, kissing her cheek, her jaw, beneath her ear. He whispers in it. "You and me are good."

"What if we're not?" The weight of it all bears down on her. Sofie's presence looming over their relationship. The fact her asking questions clearly upsets him. But she needs answers—for the show, for Ulysses, for her own deep need to solve this puzzle. This isn't going to work. "It's too complicated. You said so yourself."

He presses forward, walking her backward until the back of her knees find the bed. "It's simple," he says, his thumbs going to work on the button of her jeans. He tugs them down and nudges her backward so she collapses on the bed, jeans tangled around her thighs.

"Babe," she cries.

Taking the denim fabric into his hands, he pulls them down and climbs on top of her, pushing her legs apart with his knee. Grinding his hips, she can feel his hardness against the spot where she needs him. She runs her hands down his back, pulling up his shirt at the hem and inching it up until he raises his arms and helps her lift it over his head, his long hair spilling over her. She digs her fingers into it and melts when his gaze lingers on her, a small smile creeping up the corners of his lips. It makes her mind go blank, and all she knows is the heat of his mouth on hers, the weight of his body.

"Did you miss me today?"

"Yes," she whispers. She did, desperately, and it's clear he missed her too. He's ravenous. It's as if he's been sick all his life and her mouth contains the cure for his illness. The way he looks at her makes her heart swell with an emotion so profound it scares her. How has she fallen so deeply for him? He's brooding, there's a sadness in him that never fully recedes, even in the brightest moments. But as he brushes his lips against her neck, her collarbone, tears of relief spill from the corners of her eyes knowing that he wants her to be his. They charge ahead, shedding their clothes so that they're skin to skin. He enters her with a low groan.

"Don't we feel good together?" he whispers and presses against her with a thrust of his hips to bury himself deep. It sends a shiver through her. He draws his head back to look into her eyes as they move together, learning her. The light catches his, shining through them like peridot. They flicker with concern. "Are you crying?"

"I don't know."

"Do you want to stop?"

"No," she says. "Please. Don't stop."

He makes that face, a mix of compassion and reverence. The one she imagines him making at his clients after they've gone through a particularly emotional talk.

"Okay," he says softly. Moving slow, gentle, he presses a kiss to her shoulder. "You're the only one for me. I mean it."

After, he holds her and they're quiet. "Do you really want to see the house?" he asks. It takes her a moment to make the connection of what he's talking about, their makeup sex having wiped her mind of the reason they'd started arguing to begin with.

"Only if you're comfortable with it. I don't want to manipulate you."

He sighs. "I didn't mean it like that. I want to trust you, but I'm scared that thousands of people are going to know how I failed so miserably at being a son."

"Is that really what you think?"

"Feelings don't have to make sense." His fingers draw shapes on her arm. "If you want to go, we can go. But I'll warn you, it's a fucking disaster."

Deep in her soul, she wants to ask if Shawnee can come too. She has such an eye for these things. But she knows suggesting it will only stoke the flames. This is girlfriend material, not meant for the Mysteries of the Southern Gothic audience.

As they pull in the gravel driveway and park, she can almost hear herself narrating the scene. They walk up the rock lined path to the quaint single-story house with teal lap siding and a yellow porch swing. Reaching the front door, Ulysses uses his key to unlock it.

Her heart races with anticipation as he flips on the light. It reflects off jagged pieces of wood floor, bowing and curling from water damage, patterned with nebulous patches of black mold. Kicking a scrap of it aside, he mutters, "Plumbing repair." It smells like damp. The floors creak under their weight as they walk into a living space. Calliope's photos still hang above peeling sections of drywall. She takes a closer look. A kindergarten-aged photo, her thick blonde hair pulled away from her face with a headband slightly askew. First grade, pigtails. Second grade, a French braid. Third, she's missing her two front teeth. It's a visual timeline of her life, abruptly stopping at eight years old.

He points to a charred section nearby. "A/C repair." As he walks away, Rosario covertly snaps a photo of the Calliope wall with her cell phone. *Just in case he changes his mind*, she thinks.

She follows him to the kitchen, where the evidence of his mother's deteriorating condition is even more pronounced. The stainless steel sink is partially dismantled, a likely unnecessary repair left unfinished. The floor tiles are upturned in places, creating a hazardous maze.

As Ulysses guides Rosario through the kitchen's chaos, his steps become hesitant, his usual confident demeanor replaced by an uneasy tension that tightens his shoulders. She notices a flicker of something dark crossing his face. He picks up a large photograph on the kitchen counter. It's of Calliope. She's standing in front of her bicycle, hot pink streamers on the handle bars. Her bright smile shows off the space of rigid gums where her front teeth were missing.

"You okay?" Rosario asks, her voice tinged with concern as she watches him closely, sensing a shift in his mood. Ulysses doesn't respond immediately. His gaze is fixed on the photo, his breaths becoming shallow and rapid. Rosario can almost see the wheels turning in his mind. Swallowing hard, his Adam's apple bobs visibly.

"It's nothing," he finally mutters, but the tremor in his voice betrays him.

Whatever happened, whatever that picture of Calliope made him remember, makes Ulysses shut down completely. He's quiet the entire ride home. While he's in the shower, she examines the picture. Kodak photo paper, eight by ten, with a yellowing piece of scotch tape on the back as if it had been in a frame. It seems to have been taken at the trailer park, and based on the progression of photos she'd seen on the wall at Eleni's house, it was taken the year Calliope disappeared. Rosario takes a photo of it with her phone, front and back.

Steam mixes with the air once Ulysses emerges from the bathroom, a towel wrapped low around his hips. Rosario decides to press him a little. "Talk to me."

"There's nothing to talk about," he says, crossing the room to his dresser, where he drops his towel and slides into a pair of boxers.

She undresses and crawls into bed in her underwear, slipping under the sheets. "It obviously had to do with that picture." The slam of the drawer makes Rosario recoil.

"You know," he starts, scowling at her, "the day you and I met, I spent the morning at my mom's nursing home. I was talking to her about Calliope. But when I went to find the picture I'd brought for her, left in her room, it was gone. I thought maybe she'd misplaced it and it was lost somewhere in the center. But then there it was, just sitting on the counter of her house."

"I feel like someone is trying to fuck with me. They're saying, 'Haha, I have access to you, your mother and this fucking shameful shithole house of yours and what are you going to do about it?'"

"It's probably Sofie," Rosario blurts. "She's the only person in your life who had deep access to this stuff. Who knows, she's probably the one who sent us the home movie."

"Sofie is not the brightest bulb—she barely knows how to turn a computer on, much less digitize a VHS for uploading."

"And yet she managed to steal thousands of dollars from you. You ever think you underestimated her and she played you? She tricked us into believing Calliope was alive out there with the Order."

Ulysses rakes his fingers through his hair, grumbling to himself. "I need to tell Dr. Okafor I'm not coming in tomorrow." He sits on the bed, taking his phone from the end table. His thumbs go to work on a text, his haggard expression illuminated by the glow of the screen. "I think instead of going to work, I should go see my mom. It's been a while. I was so angry with her but, it feels misplaced now. If there's a conspiracy, she's not behind it. I don't even know if it involves Calliope or what happened to her. I'm even more confused than I was when we started this thing."

The words drive a stake of remorse into her heart. If it wasn't for her insistence on his involvement in this story, Ulysses wouldn't feel so overwhelmed. She feels a surge of guilt. "I'm sorry. I never should have pushed you to do this."

Slipping into bed beside her, his hand comes to rest gently on her cheek. "I'm sorry I implied anything. This isn't your fault." He takes her chin and turns her face to look at him. "Finding you makes this all worth it."

"We almost broke up today."

"No we didn't. We had a fight. Couples fight."

"I don't want to fight."

"I don't either. I just want to be with you. But it's the podcast, babe. I want to move on with my life."

Chapter Thirty

THE FACILITY IS SET up like a small village. Offices are dressed up like shops. There's a beauty parlor, a post office. In the lobby, photos of group outings line the walls. Scribbling her name beneath Ulysses's on the sign-in sheet, Rosario wonders what it must be like to go through life in a fog—not knowing who you are, not remembering anything about your life or your loved ones.

It's memories that comfort us. Memories that give us joy. Without them, Rosario isn't sure whether she'd find life worth living. She can't imagine anything worse than spending her life with someone, only to one day forget they existed, forget a lifetime of happiness. The thought makes her emotional before they even make it beyond the locked door.

"Going to warn you, it does not smell great back here," he says as an aide leads them in with a beep of her key card. It doesn't take more than a moment for her to understand why.

An old man shuffles over, looking confused. A wet spot stains the front of his khakis. "You had an accident?" a nurse asks. He blinks at her, mouth open as if he planned to say something but isn't sure what. They continue past him down a hall.

A small white-haired woman giggles and smiles like a child, her fuzzy slippers with rubber soles squealing against the shining linoleum floor. Making eye contact with Rosario, she pretends to hide behind a corner and presses a finger to her lips. "Shhh," she says. "No one can find me." Behind her, an aide looks at Rosario with a bored expression and counts out fruit cups. Rosario holds up a finger to her lips, letting the woman know her secret's safe with her.

A bedroom door is open, and a woman inside sits in a chair, looking out the window. Ulysses stops at the threshold and knocks, getting the woman's attention. "Mom?"

Eleni turns and smiles at him, a hint of recognition flickering in her eyes. "Ulysses?" she says tentatively. Her smile is cautious, yet warm.

His eyes soften, crinkling in the corners. "Yes, Mom, it's me, Ulysses." His voice is gentle, carrying a hopeful note that she'll hold on to this moment of clarity.

"And this is Rosario," he continues, gesturing toward her.

"Lovely to meet you," Rosario says. Taking in Eleni's features, it's remarkable how youthful she still looks. Her skin still holds hints of youth, few wrinkles and not a gray hair to be found.

Eleni nods. "Likewise." Her tone is gracious but tinged with uncertainty, as if her connection to the present moment is dangling by a fragile thread. When their eyes meet, Rosario feels a strange chill. *Nerves*.

Ulysses waves toward the bed made up in white linens. "Can we sit?"

"Of course," she says, and they each sit at the edge. She studies him. "You look well."

He laughs with surprise. "Thank you," he says. His weary eyes reveal he's anything but, yet he keeps a smile on his face. "Do you remember Calliope?"

She frowns.

"Your daughter," he says. "You remember her?"

"My angel."

Something about the word and the way she says it makes the hair on the back of Rosario's neck stand up. In that moment, her mind is at odds with her senses. Everything about this place and what she knows about Eleni tells her one story, and yet her body feels like it's on high alert. Rosario touches Ulysses's thigh, and he turns to her. "Can I ask her a question?" she whispers.

He searches her face for a motive, then gives her a reluctant nod.

"What about John Russell Thorne?" she asks. "Do you remember him?"

Eleni's eyes, momentarily sharp, lock onto Rosario's with an intensity that belies her frail appearance. "John," she says, her voice dropping to a hush. "No, I'm sorry."

"Calliope's father?"

Ulysses quickly turns his head and snaps at her. "What are you doing?"

Despite Ulysses's defense, Eleni answers through a chortle that suggests Rosario's question was absurd. "Celestial beings have no fathers."

"You're confusing her," Ulysses hisses.

His sharp reaction gives her a flush of embarrassment, and her face heats up. It wasn't her intention to complicate things, but as soon as she walked into that room, her mind went back to her lunch with Detective Harris back when she was covering the Carla Whitman murder. He described that ominous sensation, an instinctive warning that he was in the presence of pure evil. It's what reminds her she'd completely forgotten to reach out to the detective upon returning home safely.

Ulysses drives them back to his apartment after their visit. Sitting in the passenger seat, she sends Harris a text.

> Sorry I didn't text sooner, but I'm back in Tampa.

That night, she pays Shawnee a visit at her first-floor condo in a two-story, thirty-unit suburban apartment building in South Tampa.

The wrought iron gate creaks, and gnats congregate around a bird-bath poised at the center of a display of dwarf palms and colorful shrubs. It's hot and the air is thick with humidity. She knocks on the door, noting a Chinese takeout menu crammed into the door handle. Shawnee opens the door wearing a white tank top and a pair of cotton shorts, an ensemble Rosario recognizes as sleepwear.

"You been derping around all day?" Rosario asks.

Shawnee shoots her a cold look, running a hand through her unwashed hair. "Yeah, well, when your business partner would rather play house with her new boy toy than work, it's kind of discouraging." The blinds are all drawn and it's gloomy inside. Rosario hadn't considered how all the time she's been spending with Ulysses might have affected Shawnee.

"I have new information, that's why I'm here."

Shawnee perks up. Clearing off the couch of the stacks of books and notepads, she sets them on the coffee table next to a large bowl of popcorn, giving Rosario a place to sit.

"Uly and I went to see his mom earlier."

"How'd that go?"

A knot of anxiety tightens in her stomach, and she rubs her palms on her knees. "I don't know. It was weird."

"Weird how?"

"You know how Deputy Harris said when he met Eric Mitchell Vernon he got a cold chill and all the hair on the back on his neck stood up? He just knew there was something off with him?"

"No way." Shawnee smiles, seemingly pleased that Rosario was apparently creeped out by Ulysses's mother. "What happened?"

"She recognized Ulysses, which made him *so* happy. She remembered Calliope and…she called her a celestial being with no father."

Shawnee rolls her eyes though her amused grin never leaves her face. She's loving this. "These people are nuts. What do you think she means by celestial being?"

"Angels," Rosario explains, adopting a mocking mysterious tone to her voice. "They're not of this world."

"So you think she had something to do with Calliope?"

A sour taste builds on the back of Rosario's tongue. Of all the bullshit relationships she's avoided in her life, opportunities she shut down, she fell for Ulysses—a substance abusing former cult member with mental health issues and a mother who made Rosario feel physically ill while in her presence. "Yeah. Something's not right there. It's horrible to think, but I kind of wondered for half a second…what if she's faking?"

"Dude. No way. You think she's faking?"

"Who would fake this? I mean, she lives in a truly awful environment. And I know these dementia issues can happen to people her age, but she's not elderly. She's like fifty-two. Definitely the youngest person in that place."

"Why would she fake it?"

Rosario had thought about it all afternoon. "Maybe she'd done something so horrible, and the evidence against her was so damning, the consequences so unthinkable, the safest option was to pretend to lose her mind."

"Wow. That's a stretch. Even for me."

"I know, but you should have met her. I wouldn't rule anything out."

Shawnee stands up, pacing the room with the restless energy that always comes over her when a story starts to unfold. "Alright," she says excitedly, as if they're back in the game. "We need to dig into Eleni, Thorne and the church's background. Find out where they broke off from the Order, any properties they own, events they've held. Anything that'll give us a clue."

As Shawnee lights up, Rosario sinks into her seat, an ache spreading in her gut. Ulysses was so vulnerable today. He invited her into this private part of his life. But he would be interested in the truth even if it was terrible. Wouldn't he? Rosario's phone vibrates. It's Detective Harris.

It's about time. Thank you for confirming, but I checked up on you a couple of weeks ago.

The surprise sends her head jerking back, and a laugh involuntarily escapes her lips. Her reaction catches Shawnee's attention. She leans over and looks at Rosario's phone as she types her response.

What do you mean?

"Is that the deputy?" Shawnee asks.

Rosario's smile lingers over her screen a moment longer before answering Shawnee's question. "Yeah. Deputy Harris. Well," she corrects herself, "Detective Harris now."

"Oh my," Shawnee pokes. "Detective, huh?" She pauses pensively. "Damn. I hope he still wears that uniform though. That was something special."

"Hush," Rosario says, playfully shoving against Shawnee's shoulder. Shawnee doesn't budge, dampening any satisfaction Rosario might have gotten from it. Her phone vibrates again.

That's official police business.

Then a moment later.

I talked to your doorman.

She gasps. "He went to my apartment. That creeper. How does he even know where I live?"

Shawnee reaches into the bowl on the coffee table and grabs a handful of popcorn. Shoveling a fistful into her mouth, she talks as she chews. "I'm going to go out on a limb here and say he found out easily because he's a detective."

The thought of him finding her, checking up on her without her knowing is a little unsettling. But then it dawns on her, that's exactly what she did to Ulysses. *Hmm.* His points on boundaries are starting to make sense. Though there's something oddly endearing about it. Maybe it's because she knows his intentions were good; he silently confirmed her safety for his own peace of mind, but was respectful enough to leave her alone until she was ready to reach out herself. Thinking about it sends a flood of warmth into her chest, and she tamps it down. She sets her phone into her purse, leaving his text unanswered.

Chapter Thirty-One

Chapter Thirty-One

PODCAST: **Mysteries of the Southern Gothic; Episode 53: Calliope and the Church of the Ninth Order Part III**

[Intro music fades out]

SHAWNEE LEWIS (NARRATOR): Welcome back to Mysteries of the Southern Gothic. I'm your host, Shawnee Lewis.

[Sound effect: Heavy equipment motors, construction sounds]

Shawnee: The American Dream. Homeownership. While out of reach for many today, in 2004 a single mother of two could buy a three-bedroom home in a nice suburb of Saint Petersburg, Florida, on her clerical worker wages. Granted, it was the Wild West of lending practices back then, but Eleni Katsaros was finally able to move her family out of the Water Oak Mobile Home park. A dream come true. But sadly, her daughter Calliope never got a chance to live in that house.

[Eerie music starts softly and continues under Shawnee's narration]

In our last episode, we told you about my harrowing encounter with the Church of the Ninth Order and the young woman I met there, who we believed to be Calliope Katsaros. We've since been able to identify this woman as Mary Roy, daughter of Erma Roy, and stepdaughter of Orson Roy. Her biological father? John Russell Thorne, the Order's former leader—currently wanted on murder charges—making Mary the half-sister of Calliope Katsaros. Having met her, I'll tell you the resemblance is uncanny.

Mary's story is woven into the Order's violent history. Let's go back to April 11, 2004, where a congregation, including the Katsaros family, gathered in church for Easter mass. At the pulpit was the so-called Prophet John Russell Thorne.

[Sound effect: Whispers]

Easter fell in the midst of a scandal. The Roy family had been rocked by a revelation. Mary's fair features—blonde hair and blue eyes—were a genetic impossibility if Orson Roy was her biological father. Upon learning his wife Erma had succumbed to Thorne's charisma, Roy was outraged. He lobbied members of the congregation to his cause. It was time to overthrow Thorne and elect a new leader. Rumor has it, on that fateful Sunday morning, Thorne called Roy up to the sanctuary and…

[Sound effect: Gunshot and frightened screams]

Thorne tried to calm the congregation, calling the murder an atonement for Roy's sin of dissent, a means of upholding the Order's moral and spiritual integrity.

[Sound effect: Rumbles falling silent]

Our sources tell us the church divided. Thorne went his way, and the Order relocated, realigning itself to its so-called peaceful purpose. What does this have to do with Eleni and her proud moment of home ownership?

Shortly after Part II of the Calliope series was released, Mysteries of the Southern Gothic received an anonymous email with a link to a home movie of the Katsaros family. That video shows Eleni, Ulysses and Calliope proudly claiming their piece of the dream. But why were we sent the video? We're determined to find out.

[Mysterious outro music fades in]

We are going to take a quick break to hear from our sponsors. Stay with us after the break, when we will recap the facts as we know them so far.

[Outro music fades out]

* * *

Mysteries of the Southern Gothic Forum

Subject: Episode 53: Calliope and the Church of the Ninth Order Part III

———

ExplodingDevon *2 hours ago*

i've been out to the order. they don't do technology so they sure as shit didn't send the video. any guesses who did?

⬆ 2 ⬇

———

Albright_Alright *2 hours ago*

None of Uly's friends sound smart enough to send an email.

⬆ 1 ⬇

———

ShaneCatSweaters *1 hours ago*

Maybe someone who left the church? Had to be close to the family to know the video even existed. But if it's a clue, what does it mean?

⬆ 1 ⬇

———

A_hole_for_uly *25 mins ago*

I think someone close to the family took Calliope and is fucking with them. Like some kind of a sick game. Also, did you see the new pics of Uly? My ovaries exploded.

⬆ 1 ⬇

—

RedChucks *10 mins ago*

Same. Is it possible for a photo to get you pregnant?

⬆ -1 ⬇

—

ForensicGuy92 *8 mins ago*

thirsting over a guy who probably murdered his sister is ick.

⬆ -3 ⬇

—

A_hole_for_uly *5 mins ago*

Dude he was a kid. No way he would have gotten away with it if he did.

⬆ 1 ⬇

—

ForensicGuy92 *2 mins ago*

His demented mother helped him cover it up. duh.

 3

—

Goodwitch *now*

in part one when he told Sofie he would have given her the money
if she asked I almost died. he's so sweet. you must not be paying
attention.

Chapter Thirty-Two

One Month Later

DR. OKAFOR WARNED him to avoid his triggers. Listening to that godforsaken podcast was one of them, and yet he can't help it. He worries the world might learn a sordid detail of his dysfunctional life before he does. He'd known of the scandal surrounding John Russell Thorne. He'd heard Thorne and his mother argue about it, heard his mother weeping. He didn't fully understand it then, but now, Ulysses wonders how his mother could have invited him back in. One day, Ulysses helped the elders scrub the blood from the church carpet, and the next, the man who'd caused it to spill poured himself a bowl of cereal at the breakfast table. Any wrong move, any sinful act could be Ulysses's undoing.

"Don't tell anyone he's here," his mother had warned, taping tin foil to the trailer windows. "We answer to a higher power than the police."

The memory of that summer feels as if it might suffocate him. A scream simmers and boils up, caught in his throat. Pressing his face into his hands, he lets it out, the heat of this mouth and tears steaming up his face. It echoes in the dark. Fades into the wind.

There's not a damn person on the planet that understands what he's lived through. His mother's mind is clean, his sister a ghost, and when he dies, there won't be a soul left to light a candle for him. Rosario and Shawnee air his pain for the entertainment of their scummy listeners, relishing in others' shameful secrets.

Dr. Okafor warned him, but Ulysses gave into temptation. Now, he's sitting on the yellow porch swing, nursing a bottle and wondering if being back here will help him remember where it all went to shit.

This place was supposed to be pure. Sacred, his mother would say. The stench of rot replaces the memory of home-cooked meals. Spiders have staked their claim to every dark corner, and wasps nests sprout from the siding like papier-mâché. The chains holding the swing creak and groan under his weight. John Russell Thorne, that bastard. Never did show his face here. Ulysses tries to picture it. It's a blur but for his eyes. He'll never forget them. They were Calliope's eyes. Mary's too, he remembers. Piercing blue. They shone bright under a pair of bushy black brows. He'd felt suspended in them.

"What have you got there, boy?" Thorne asked from the doorway. The door having been taken off the hinges, it was easy for him to be watched at any hour of the day. It was summertime, and the damp air was heavy, not a hint of a breeze stayed his suffering. Ulysses sat at the edge of his twin bed listening to music through his headphones. He had bought one of those water spritzer fans from the Dollar Tree and was using it to cool his neck. Sliding his headphones down, he held the fan up cautiously, wondering what crime he might have inadvertently committed.

Thorne scoffed, his linen guayabera shirt stuck to his damp skin. "Enjoy it while you can," he taunted, approaching Ulysses slowly. "It's a lot hotter where you're going if you don't get right with God. What are you listening to?"

Remembering it now, Ulysses feels a chill just as distinctly as he had that day.

Secular music wasn't allowed, and Slipknot's Corey Taylor screamed in his ears. "Nothing," Ulysses said, just as the headphones were yanked from around his neck. He watched, powerless, as Thorne examined his CD player with a look of disgust. Bringing the headphone to an inch from his ears, he sneered. "This is the devil's music." Without another word, he hurled the Discman against the floor. The hard plastic shattered on impact, sending fragments into the air. The homemade CD spilled out, a mix labeled with Sharpie markings. Thorne picked it up and snapped it in half. "I'm doing you a favor," he said.

Could have been worse, Ulysses tells himself. Thorne could have blown him away like Orson Roy. Thorne left midsummer, and his mother bought Ulysses a new Discman once he was gone. Thinking of it now, it was a way to placate him. Like a guilty gift a parent gives their child in exchange for forgiveness. A bald attempt at bribery. Staring down at his hands, he pictures them soaked in blood. He rubs the soft scars where his fingers meet his palm and struggles to remember where they came from. He was so angry that summer.

Had he done something? Had he hurt Calliope? Maybe Eleni blamed herself for exposing him to violence, excused his heinous act out of shame for having raised a sick child capable of atrocity. His hands were wrapped in gauze for weeks, he recalls. Thinking of the woven fabric sends a flash of Calliope, her delicate features peeking through wrappings, and the acid in his stomach rises, forcing its way out of his mouth.

No. No. No. It can't be. Wiping the vomit from his lips, he unlocks the front door. His mind is a tricky thing, a deep and darkened well of memories that had been poisoned by fear and pain. Entering the house, he decides he'd sooner drown in them than live another day not knowing the truth.

Chapter Thirty-Three

SHE'D HEARD STORIES. The kind where a man says he's going to the store to pick up some milk and he leaves town, never to be heard from again. Rosario never saw Ulysses as capable of such things. She especially never envisioned him as someone who would abandon his dog, but almost twenty-four hours ago he said he was going for a walk to clear his head, and he still hasn't come back. Even Domino showed his unease, letting out high-pitched whines and walking in circles until he tired and lay by the door. Calls go straight to voicemail. Texts are unread. Has something happened to him?

Worried sick, her stomach bubbles with acid. She hasn't rested, and her eyes burn from lack of sleep. Watching the clock, she waits and prays for his safe return.

Her prayers evaporate once he walks through the door with slight limp in his gait. He's disheveled—wrinkled clothes, hair unkempt, a haunted look in his eyes. She's given him grace for all that he's been through, but seeing him return with all the telltale signs he's gone on another bender guts her. Her first thought is to strangle him. If this is the kind of shit Sofie had to put up with, it's no wonder she left.

Domino is the first to react, leaping up with excitement, his tail wagging furiously as he bounds toward Ulysses. But Rosario is frozen, her relief at seeing him alive warring with the anger simmering just below the surface. "Where have you been?"

He slows his stride, seemingly taken aback by her sharp greeting. Letting out a long exhale, his body visibly vibrates with what looks like anxiety, but she can't be sure. One of his hands is bloodied. He doesn't look like the Ulysses she thought she knew.

His eyes avoid hers. "I can't do this right now."

"Do what? Tell me why you had me worried sick?"

"I feel bad enough as it is. I don't need a lecture." Tears form in his eyes, and he blows out a puff of air. He seems to try and ground himself, but his hands tremble. He'd been doing so well. Not a drop of alcohol. He'd thrown himself into his workouts, focused on his art. But he'd listened to Shawnee's retelling of Orson Roy's murder, and it shattered a fragile part of him.

"I'm not trying to lecture you, I'm trying to understand. I want to know that you're okay."

Ulysses looks up, his shame-filled eyes meeting hers. "I don't know if I'm okay," he admits softly. "I don't want to lose this—us." He gestures feebly between them

Rosario reaches out, her hand finding his, lifting it to get a better look at his raw knuckles. "What happened?"

"Don't remember. Probably punched something."

Rosario's heart clenches at his admission, a mix of fear and concern washing over her. She leads him to the kitchen, and under the brighter light, she carefully examines his fingers, the water from the faucet running cool to soothe his wounds. "You don't remember?" she probes gently.

Ulysses shakes his head, the pained look in his eyes deepening. "I went to my mom's. Woke up there." His voice is a low whisper, imbued with confusion and despair.

"Why would you go there?"

"I don't know." He sighs. "I was trying to remember…" His eyes flutter and he chokes on his breath, the sentence ending with unspoken anguish. Shutting off the water, she dries his hand with a towel, then wraps him in a hug. He smells like mildew, like mold spores.

"Remember what?" Her mind races with possibilities, and it unsettles her stomach.

He's crying, sniffling softly. Pulling up a kitchen stool, he falls onto it. Pressing the heels of his hands into his eyes, he draws in a deep breath, seeming to find the strength. His voice is tight. "What if it's not the truth?"

It sets her nerves on edge. She expects the next words from his mouth to be that he killed Calliope. Then what will she do? That would mean she doesn't know him at all. It would mean he's dangerous.

"I just want this to be over." His voice wavers, and he stops to gather himself.

Her unease grows, spreading like wildfire through her core. Looking at him, she wonders if she'd been blind. He looks detached from reality, and as she's gotten closer when he speaks, she can smell the hint of liquor on his breath. Her heart pounds in her chest.

"Are you still drunk?"

His face falls into his hands, and he breaks down into tears. "You didn't let up. You stalked me. You showed up at my place uninvited. On more than one occasion. This is the one time I'm fucking losing my mind, and I need you to be on my side."

"I am on your side."

He wipes his face with his forearm. "Lang Randall should have killed me. I think I wanted him to. I think that's why I went there." Raking his fingers through his hair, he rocks subtly.

Despite her earlier bitterness, looking into his eyes, seeing him crumble like this, she pities him. Sitting beside him, she wraps her arms around him, and he collapses against her breast, weeping. After, she helps him into the shower, washing the smell of mildew from his hair.

It's late afternoon when they lie in bed together, letting the sunlight pour in over them. He closes his eyes, and being with him like this feels like the emotional reprieve they need.

"I'm sorry I scared you, baby," he whispers in her ear. "Sorry I made you worry."

In these silent moments, it becomes clear to Rosario that unearthing Calliope's story is slowing killing him. She's the one who dragged him into this. She could stop this at any time, tell Shawnee to move on, but she can't. Not until she finds the truth. Beneath the anxiety, the guilt, she can't shake the feeling there's something he's not telling her. The unspoken words lingering between them steals the oxygen from the room, and she can't breathe. She's got to get out of here.

"I know, babe. Get some rest."

* * *

LEAVING Ulysses to sleep off his intoxication, she distracts herself with errands. She mindlessly wanders the aisles of a Publix in her sweatpants and a cropped tank top and pushes an empty shopping cart around, the smell of fresh baked cookies a small comfort. She catches her reflection in the bakery display fridge filled with cakes. Dark circles have formed under her eyes from lack of sleep. Her focus shifts to a boxed slice of carrot cake, and surrounded by strangers and the sound of light pop music over the grocery store speakers, all the feelings come flooding in—being sick with worry all night, watching Ulysses stumble in and fall apart. She tried to be strong for him, but now, a lump rises in her throat. Her purse rests in the shopping cart, and a muffled buzz vibrates from inside it. She pulls her phone out and glances at it.

Detective Harris

I haven't heard from you. Figured I must have freaked you out.

Get in line, buddy, she thinks.

Dropping her phone into her bag, it vibrates again.

She spins around and scans the faces of every nearby person. Why is it that when she gets her hair done, she never runs into anyone she knows, but her luck would have her look like warm garbage the day she runs into this man at the grocery store? She sees him ambling toward her with a green handbasket. He's out of uniform, yet he exudes something heroic. Maybe it's his broad shoulders. Is he taller than she remembered? Smiling at her, he reveals a dimple in his cheek.

"I'm sorry, I couldn't help myself," he says. His smooth southern twang is exactly as she remembered it.

She combs through her hair with her fingers and crosses her arms over her body, feeling suddenly exposed. "Uh, hey. Didn't know you lived in the neighborhood."

"Ah, you thought this Publix was safe, huh?" he chuckles.

Glancing in his basket, she sees he's carrying a loaf of bread, a jar of peanut butter and a bunch of bananas. "Big plans this afternoon?" she jokes, nodding toward his basket.

"Oh yeah. You ever had a peanut butter and banana sandwich?"

"Can't say that I have."

"My goodness, you are missing out. I highly recommend it. Put a little drizzle," he starts, then looks around and leans in as if he's telling her a secret. He lowers his voice. "Just a little drizzle of honey on there. Mm." His penetrating baby blues hold a glint of humor.

She bites her lip to hold back a smile.

"So I hear you and that cake are getting pretty serious," he says, gesturing toward the fridge.

A flash of heat trickles up her neck at the thought of him watching her pale faced and dressed like a hobo, staring at desserts. "I just meant I have a boyfriend."

The amusement begins to wane from his expression, leaving only a friendly hint behind. He clicks his tongue. "Shame." They exchange a glance and she looks away, her teeth not quick enough to catch her lip and prevent this smile from being seen. "We can still be friends, can't we?" he asks.

"Of course."

"Good. Speaking of, how's Shawnee doing?"

"Oh, she's great. I'll let her know you asked."

"Please do. That last episode. Man, y'all are really onto something with this series. You've done a great job. I'm riveted. Got it set to auto download."

For some reason, even though he'd helped the show more than once, she didn't think he ever listened to it. It gives her an unexpected swell of pride. "Glad you're enjoying it. That means a lot."

He hesitates, as if he's not sure he should say what he's thinking. "Y'all cover some dark subjects, don't you? I know you're a tough cookie, but take it from someone who's seen a lot of bad shit. Make sure you're taking care of yourself, okay?"

Of course. She must look like she's having a nervous breakdown. She laughs slightly and shakes her head. "Just having a weird day, that's all. I must look a mess, ogling carrot cake."

"That's not what I meant," he says apologetically. He looks her up and down, his hands drawing a silhouette in the air. "You *always* look beautiful. I just meant you seem a little down is all." He holds up his hands, palms out. "It's none of my business, but I'm here if you ever need a friend. I mean that sincerely, not in a creepy way. It can be hard looking into these kinds of things, seeing the evil people are capable of. Just know you've got someone in your corner who understands. And anytime, day or night, call and I'll listen."

The offer is so earnest, so devoid of any pretense, that Rosario struggles to hold back the emotions that had been bubbling up to the surface. *Don't you dare cry in Publix.*

"Hey," he says, seeming to notice her emotions. He waves toward the fridge. "You like carrot cake?"

"Yeah," she replies, voice tight. "I love carrot cake."

"Me too. Whoever came up with making something that grows in the dirt into a dessert is some kinda wizard. Would you like to have some carrot cake with me? There's a little cafe over here. Two friends. Eating vegetable cake. Exchanging war stories."

She nods, wiping a tear from her eye. "Okay."

They sit around the corner from the bakery in the cafe between the deli and fresh flowers. Her spirit wants to unload the burden of the last few weeks, what happened with the house, and how freaked out she's been about Ulysses's mom and his drinking. But she can't bring herself to talk about it. It's too private. Instead, she asks him for his theories on the case.

"As awful as it sounds, I don't think she's alive. And when a child's harmed that way, it's more often someone the victim knew. Family member. Acquaintance."

Swirling her plastic spork in a dot of cream cheese frosting, she debates whether to disclose any information. It's surreal being there with Harris eating cake and talking about a missing child while the incessant *boops* of groceries being rung in by nearby cashiers plays in the background. It's all too normal. "I've met Eleni, Calliope's mother. She's in a memory care facility. Something about her just didn't sit right."

He nods slowly, pensively. "How so?"

"Well, it felt like she had this aura of darkness. Gave me goosebumps, you know?"

"I do. That's your intuition. You gotta follow it. But intuition will only get you so far. You can't convict someone with a gut feeling." He leans back thoughtfully, the idea drawing him into the depths of his experience. "In a case like this, without the digital footprints we rely on today, we have to go back to basics. Old case files, photographs, personal diaries or letters. Anything that could give you a snapshot of the relationships and dynamics at play at the time."

Rosario isn't sure what might have survived. From talking to Ulysses, she assumed there were a few things stored away, sentimental items. She just needs a chance to dig through them. But Ulysses is so sensitive about giving her access to things like that. She'll have to broach the request gently. She clears her throat. Every word that escapes feels like a perilous confession. "Ulysses, you know, the brother?"

"Yeah," he acknowledges, the prongs of a plastic fork disappearing into his mouth.

"Well, he's the one I've been seeing."

Harris stops chewing and looks her over before letting out a pensive hum. He swallows and wipes his mouth with a napkin. His expression is unreadable, but she winces slightly, worried he'll think less of her. It wasn't a good idea to get romantically involved with Ulysses, she's known it from the beginning. "He's been really sensitive lately," she continues, careful about what she reveals. "All the episodes and prying into his personal life, I think it's wearing on him."

Harris sets the napkin aside, his demeanor softening. "I get that. But this is about Calliope, isn't it? Finding out what happened to her?" He leans forward, elbows on the table, fixing her with an insistent gaze. "You're not poking around just for the heck of it."

Of course she isn't. Hearing someone else say it feels like a weight lifted. Talking to Shawnee, it's like she relishes in the chase. She can't investigate without getting blood on her teeth. But Rosario can't shake the pictures of that little girl. If Calliope's life was cut short, if she was taken somewhere, she deserves to have her story told. She deserves justice.

As they finish their cake and say goodbye, Harris stands, his chair scraping gently against the floor. "I'm really glad I ran into you."

Rosario stands too, feeling a reluctance to end the encounter. "Me too. This was just what I needed. Thank you, Detective."

"Please, call me Beau."

"Thank you, Beau," she says, the informality of the name feeling awkward leaving her mouth. He smiles, that dimple making another appearance.

"Anytime. And remember, I meant what I said. If you need a friend, I'm here."

As he walks away, Rosario watches him go, a mix of emotions swirling within her. Detective Harris's—*Beau's*—insights, his offer of support, have given her a renewed energy in her search for the truth about Calliope's disappearance.

Chapter Thirty-Four

"I JUST CAME OUTSIDE to walk Domino, and there's a bunch of people standing around staring at me and taking pictures," Ulysses mutters. Rosario's still in bed. He's called her, as he often does during his morning routine before work.

"Hold on," Rosario says, jumping into another app on her phone. "I'm recording."

Ulysses lets out an annoyed sigh. "They're looking at me right now. A group of teenagers across the little retention pond at my complex. Just staring at me and taking pictures like a bunch of weirdos." The wind whips against the phone, and Ulysses shouts off angrily into the distance. "What are you looking at?"

"Don't engage them, babe. They're just kids."

"I'm so tired of this. Hold on, I'm taking a picture of these fuckers," he says, the sound of his voice becoming distant. "How do you like it, assholes?"

Rosario sits up in bed, throwing her legs over the edge to touch the floor. Rising, she makes her way to her closet to get dressed, phone in hand with Ulysses's on speakerphone. "I think you should stay with me for a little while," she says.

Ever since the Calliope series started, the Mysteries of the

Southern Gothic podcast has grown its listener base. The TikTok kids that had been flocking to the Order started following their story, and consequently, Ulysses would get the occasional batch of uninvited visitors at the art center or to his neighborhood. Although Rosario prefers Uly's cozy love nest, security at her place is much better.

"Really?"

"Yeah. We spend every night together anyway. Just pack a bag."

The sound of his breathing fills the silence for a pregnant moment, and she second guesses her invitation until he finally says, "Okay."

THAT WEEKEND, Ulysses arrives to Rosario's with a black case. He unzips it on the bed. "Have you ever fired a gun before?"

"You brought a gun?"

"Guns, plural," he says, opening the case. "Left the other one in the Jeep."

"This isn't over the kids, is it?"

"No," he says dismissively. "I'm not worried about a bunch of kids. Here." He sets the gun in her palms. "It's not loaded, but you always treat a gun like it's loaded."

The cold metal carries a weight that feels heavier than it looks. If he'd shown her this a few months ago, she'd have asked him what he needed guns for. But knowing what the Order, or at least their former leader, John Russell Thorne, could do to a person, she understands.

He points to the components with his index finger. "This is the safety. Once that's disengaged, it'll let you pull this trigger back. Don't pull it unless you intend to fire, okay?"

"Okay."

"This is the magazine," he says, pressing a button. "It's empty now. This is where you'd load it, if you ever needed to. I'll show you." Reaching for a box, he opens it, revealing rows of stacked bullets. He plugs them into the magazine, loads it, then reengages the safety. "See? Safety's on."

He sets it back in her hands, and an uneasy feeling settles in her gut. Kind of like standing at the edge of a tall building. A wrong move could spell disaster. The fear she can't trust herself not to jump. She passes it back to him. "I don't like it."

"Well, you don't have to like it. But I'm going to put it up here," he says, motioning toward her end table. "And if someone comes in here, you get it. Try to get out of here, but if you can't, hide with this and fire if you need to. Understand?"

She nods, and he does as promised, tucking the gun away in the drawer, bullets beside it. Eager to move on from the thought of a deadly weapon living in her apartment, she helps him unpack.

If someone would have told her six months ago that she'd meet a man who makes her knees weak and after one month of dating they'd be practically living together, she'd have died laughing. But the next morning, Ulysses sets a hot cup of coffee on her bedside table so she can drink it in bed. That night before they go to sleep, they take their melatonin gummies together and watch *The Great British Baking Show*.

"Bit stodgy," he mimics against her hair.

"Unda-proved," she replies.

She doesn't know exactly when she fell asleep, but wakes up from the sensation of movement beside her. Ulysses is on his back, mumbling something. His arms seem to jump as if being shocked with an electrical current.

"Please, Momma," he mumbles. "I'm tired." His body twitches with slight jerky movements. "I wanna go home."

She inches carefully toward him, trying not to make a sound. His breath is short, rapid. "I can't dig anymore." It must be a traumatic memory from Eleni's medieval method of discipline, making kids dig holes until their arms gave out.

She passes comforting strokes over his arm. "You okay?"

He settles in deeper, nuzzling the pillow. "Mm," he hums and rolls over.

The morning after, Rosario watches him over the rim of her coffee mug. He's quieter than usual after taking Domino for his walk. She notices him tracing the rim of his cup, lost in thought, before snapping back to reality with a start when Domino nudges his hand for attention.

"Were you dreaming about digging last night?" Rosario asks, trying to keep a playful note in her voice.

He forces a smile that doesn't quite reach his eyes. "Was I having a puppy dream? Chasing bunnies and digging holes?"

"Maybe. You were twitching and whimpering a bit," she pokes. She takes a sip from her coffee and lets the humor wane. "You were saying something like, 'Mom, I'm tired. I can't dig anymore.'"

"Ah," he says, and offers a knowing nod. "Yeah. One of those dreams." He chuckles to himself. "I didn't get in trouble a lot back then, but when I did, my mom didn't fuck around."

"She made you dig holes."

"Yup."

"Until your hands bled, Brody said."

Letting out a humorless laugh, he says, "Sometimes, yeah," and looks down at his hands. He rubs along the ridge where his fingers meet his palm as if he can still feel the callouses, the scars. His eyes cloud over with a distant look. After a beat, he shakes himself out of it. "She was a single mom raising a boy all on her own. I can't fault her for that kind of stuff."

Clearing her throat gently, she raises a question she hopes he'll answer honestly. "If one of your clients told you they had a recurring dream about their punishments as a child, what would you think that means?"

Ulysses pauses, the question hanging between them like a thread about to snap. He sets his cup down, the clink of ceramic against wood punctuating the shift in the room's atmosphere. For a moment, he looks like the counselor he is, analyzing, calculating. Then he sighs, a deep, resigned sound that seems to carry the weight of years.

"It could mean a lot of things," he starts, his voice taking on a softer, reflective tone. "Dreams are the mind's way of processing—working through memories. Recurring dreams, especially about something like childhood discipline, could suggest unresolved feelings, maybe even trauma."

Rosario watches him carefully, noting the clinical detachment in his voice as he talks about potential trauma, as if he's discussing a hypothetical client, not his own experiences. "Those punishments seem to have had an effect on you," she says. "They seemed a little harsh. Don't you think?"

His nostrils flare as he draws in breath, then exhales with a derisive huff. "What's your problem with my mom?"

It shocks her. He'd never mentioned anything about it before, never seemed to pick up on the uncomfortable feeling she'd get anytime he spoke fondly of her, or how being in the same room with her made her nauseated. "What do you mean?"

"You're always picking. I mean, she's not perfect but she did her best, you know. I don't know why you want to vilify her all the time."

"I'm not trying to vilify anyone," she says, her voice steadier than the irritation she's holding back. "But I can't help but think that maybe some of her methods, getting mixed up in the Order…"

Ulysses leans back in his chair, scrubbing a hand over his face. "Your mom's a professor, your dad's some kind of successful businessman. Cool. Good for you. Maybe my mom didn't follow a conventional path, but she wasn't some brainwashed idiot. She read all the time, studied poetry and Greek mythology. Everything I learned, I learned from her."

The room temperature drops, the space between them wider than the table that separates them. She watches him, trying to find the right words to bridge the gap, to pull him back from whatever ledge he's inching toward in his mind. "I'm not the enemy, Uly," Rosario finally says, her voice firmer than she intends. "I'm just worried about you. I can see you struggling, and I want to help you."

"Help," he repeats with a subtle sneer. Ulysses looks at her, and there's a flicker of something—frustration, maybe, or resentment. "I'm fine. I don't need you to fix me."

The accusation stings, more than Rosario wants to admit. She's taken aback by the bitterness in his tone, by the implication. "Is that what you think I'm doing?" she asks, hurt creeping into her voice. "Trying to fix you?"

Ulysses doesn't answer. He stands up, his chair scraping against the floor with a sound that feels like a period at the end of a sentence—a full stop. He collects his things, his movements brisk, efficient, as if he can't wait to escape. "I should go. I'm going to be late."

And just like that, he's gone, leaving Rosario sitting alone at the kitchen table surrounded by the remnants of their breakfast. She's left staring at the empty space he's left behind, the silence echoing loudly in her ears. The doubts that had been whispering at the back of her mind grow louder, more insistent. Is their relationship strong enough to withstand this?

As she cleans up the kitchen, Rosario's movements are mechanical, her mind elsewhere. Why can't he see she just wants to understand him? She needs something that will uncover the truth about Ulysses's past, and the role his mother played in it. The day stretches out, long and empty, filled with Rosario's restless thoughts. She tries to distract herself, to focus on the everyday tasks that demand her attention—feeding Domino, ordering groceries, doing laundry—but her mind keeps circling back to Ulysses. The more she thinks about it, the more convinced she becomes there's something deeply wrong, something Ulysses is either unaware of or unwilling to confront.

She needs evidence, something concrete to show Ulysses her fears aren't unfounded, that there's a reason for her concern. It's not just about proving a point; it's about protecting the man she loves from a past she suspects is even more troubled than he's willing to acknowledge.

But how? All their research efforts have turned up nothing. Eleni has few possessions at her nursing home, her memory now supposedly wiped clean. Her home festers with decay, no possessions inside. There must be something. Photographs. More home movies. Something to prove Rosario's instincts aren't misguided.

* * *

There's no harm in a visit. She'll just sit with her for a little while. Security here leaves something to be desired. No one asks for identification. She signs in as Lisa Simpson, and no one flutters an eyelash. As she navigates through the artificially cheerful corridors, her mind's a whirlwind of doubts. She's not even sure exactly what she'll ask. The scent of antiseptics mixed with faint, unsettling odors meets her as she enters the more private quarters of the facility. She passes residents lost in their own worlds.

Approaching Eleni's room, Rosario pauses, gathering her courage. She doesn't knock; instead, she stands at the doorway, watching Eleni stare out the window. "Ms. Katsaros?" she says.

Eleni turns slowly, her expression one of mild curiosity but no recognition. "Yes?" she says.

"Hi, I'm Rosario. I came to visit with Ulysses once, do you remember me?"

Eleni narrows her eyes. There's not a hint of anything behind them. She can't be sure if it's confusion or emotional detachment, but it chills Rosario to her core.

"Who?"

Maybe Rosario has lost her sense of compassion, maybe she's lost her own mind, but there's something about Eleni she doesn't buy. "Your son, Ulysses," she says firmly. Stepping into the room, she sits on the edge of Eleni's twin bed, made up nicely with clean linens. "Of course you remember Uly. He's the man who visits you, pays for you to live here."

Eleni's eyes widen and her lashes flutter. "Who are you?"

"I'm Rosario. Uly's girlfriend."

She scrunches her nose and small burst of derisive laughter escapes her lips, but she says nothing. Rosario pulls up the home video on her phone and shows it to Eleni, waiting to hit play until she's sure her eyes are on it. "Do you remember this day?"

Eleni leans forward slightly, her gaze flickering toward the screen as the images begin to move. For a moment, she's silent, watching the scenes of a younger version of herself doting on Ulysses and Calliope in a sun-drenched plot of land. Her face softens, a hint of nostalgia, or perhaps confusion in her expression. "Where did you get this?"

The question surprises Rosario. Is this a moment of clarity? Of sincerity? "Someone sent it to me. Someone out there seems to think this video will tell us something about what happened to Calliope."

"What is there to know?" Eleni asks.

A knot tightens in Rosario's gut. "She hasn't been seen alive since July 16th, 2004. Do you want to know what I think? I think you know what happened. I think it's so awful that you'd rather forget."

Eleni's eyes widen. "I don't know what you're talking about. Who are you?"

She raises her voice, and Rosario peers out into the hallway. There's no one around. "I'm someone who's interested in the truth about Calliope. About what happened that summer."

Looking away, Eleni focuses on something outside the window that Rosario can't see. The silence stretches between them, heavy and uncomfortable. Rosario knows she's pushing boundaries, but the stakes are too high to back down now. "I understand it's difficult," she continues, "but any piece of information can help. Even the smallest detail."

"You understand nothing," Eleni says, still looking out the window.

"Was it John Russell Thorne? Did he harm Calliope?"

Eleni turns slowly, almost theatrically, to face Rosario. The transformation is startling; the frail, confused woman is gone. In her place, a figure of unsettling composure, her gaze sharp and calculating. "Dead men can do no harm," she declares with a precision that belies her supposed condition. Then a smile, sinister and knowing, curls the corners of Eleni's lips. "My son doesn't love you," she says, the malice in her voice unmistakable. "If he did, you wouldn't be here asking foolish questions."

Rosario, grappling with the gravity of her discovery, presses on. "Whatever happened to Calliope is going to come out."

Eleni's facade of frailty shatters completely now, her eyes wild. "Leave," she hisses, a venomous command. But emboldened by the weight of her mission, Rosario stands her ground, unwilling to back down. The standoff between them crackles with silent tension, a battle of wills in the sterile quiet of the room.

It's in this moment, with the truth hanging precariously in the balance, that Eleni's control snaps. "Leave!" Eleni's scream tears through the silence, a shocking explosion of sound that ricochets off the walls. The scream is not just a command; it's a weapon.

Rosario reels back, the force of the outburst sending a jolt of fear through her. The elderly residents and staff, alerted by the commotion, begin to converge toward the source of the disturbance, their expressions a mix of concern and curiosity. Realizing the situation could escalate, Rosario makes a quick exit.

* * *

It's not breaking and entering if she has a key. Right? She carefully turns the cold metal key in the lock of Ulysses's apartment door, telling herself that her actions are justified. This isn't about the show, this isn't about Shawnee. This is for Uly. For love. For the truth he deserves and for the peace Calliope's memory demands. The haunting encounter with Eleni—the way her cold, calculating stare cut right through her, the unnerving scream that echoed in her ears as she was forced to leave—lingers in Rosario's thoughts, fueling her resolve.

She can't afford to wait for Ulysses to come around to seeing the truth. His blind loyalty, a result of a lifetime of deception by his own mother, is too deeply ingrained. If there are answers to be found, Rosario knows she must unearth them herself. She steps into the apartment with a heavy heart, driven by a mix of love, fear, and an unwavering commitment to uncover whatever truths have been buried for far too long.

Outside, rain gently patters against the windows. The sky is shrouded in gray and little light filters in through the closed blinds. The lack of sun and low temperatures make the inside cold, and she stretches her fingers to let the blood flow. Turning in a slow circle, she scans the room for ideas. If he's stowed away keepsakes, where would they be? It's a small space, every inch used purposefully and economically, and he seems to keep only the essentials.

She treads quietly to his bedroom and opens the closet. As she hoped, there are bins neatly stacked one on top of the other. She lugs them out, moving shoes and canvas out of the way to form a path. They're too heavy to lift, so she drags them across the beige, low-pile carpet with a few hard tugs.

Opening the first bin, she receives instant karmic punishment. Sitting prominently atop a stack of books is photo album of Ulysses and Sofie. The glossy cover is designed to look like an old map, stained yellow with age. A square in the center holds a photo of them gazing lovingly at each other. *You are my greatest adventure*, it says. The plastic-lined pages are filled with four by six photos. They're smiling, kissing. Everywhere—at the beach, in the mountains. Years of memories. A shared history of decades.

A sting rises to her eyes. Why would he hold on to these if he didn't still love her? The thought of Sofie lying in wait, patiently anticipating Rosario's inevitable blunder, steals the oxygen from her lungs. Just one fight that breaks them apart, and Sofie will be his first call. Slamming the album shut, she tosses it aside onto the bed and continues her search.

Old drawings. Report cards. Art competition ribbons. Track medals and trophies. All things that are insights into the man she loves, but nothing that would solve this mystery. Putting things back as they were, she lifts the top bin with great effort, setting it down on the floor beside the rest of the stack.

The top of the next bin is labeled *Mom's things*. She unlocks the plastic tabs and pries off the lid, setting it aside. The scent of old perfume wafts up and makes her cough. It's strong and unpleasant. An old etched-glass jewelry box is wrapped in a thin, hand-stitched quilt. Some kind of a family heirloom perhaps. Inside are cheap-looking, tarnished trinkets, many featuring angels—cherub faces, angel winged pins, and charms. She closes it and wraps it up again so that it appears undisturbed.

Then books. Many variations of the Bible, poetry, Greek mythology. A thick journal bound in red leather. It must have at least five hundred pages. A clasp holds the book shut like a belt buckle, a brass prong through a tiny punched hole in a strip of hide. She holds it with both hands feeling its heft. The deep dents embossed in the leather, the resistance she's met with when unbuckling it, all suggest it's been a long while since it's been opened. Would Ulysses ever have read this? *Boundaries*, he always says. One of his favorite therapy words. He's big on setting them, respecting them. This is a red line he probably would never cross. It's one of the things that sets them apart. And now, with Eleni's evil glare still looming in her mind, she feels an urgent need to cross it.

With a quick glance over her shoulder, she opens the journal. Flipping through the pages, she finds it nearly full. The dates are written at the top of each entry in a fanciful cursive handwriting with blue ink. They span years.

As she flips through the journal, Rosario's heart races—not just with the fear of being caught, but with a growing dread of what she might find. Sitting at the edge of the bed, she turns on a side table lamp and sets the book in her lap, flips to a random entry to start, and begins to read.

March 3, 2004

Today John and I picked out paint colors for the exterior and shingle color for our roof. Mediterranean blue for the siding and Sundance yellow for the front door. They're bright and optimistic. The neighborhood is vibrant too. Our neighbors have the cutest lawn ornaments—fluttering butterflies and peacocks. While we pray for the collapse of the immoral world, there are still glimmers of beauty here. This could be a chance to shepherd a new flock into the congregation of the Order.

Returning home becomes more difficult each time. I know it's a sin to covet, to long for material things, but I want my yellow front door, to listen to butterfly wind chimes twang in the wind. Instead, I return to find the fat little girl from across the road bouncing a tennis ball off our trailer. Ding up your own tin can, I told her. We can't move soon enough. I truly hate it here.

The lender calls every other day with questions. A letter for this and a statement for that. I've sent them a dozen paystubs. It's the only income John and I can verify, tithes being a cash arrangement and all.

I haven't told the boy. Even to suggest we'd be moving away from the Randall family nearly brought the fragile thing to tears. I do wish John would spend more time with him. Even if he didn't get his weakness from me, a male influence might toughen him up a bit. I worry about that boy. He'll be going into high school in a new neighborhood, with a higher caliber of student. I can't have him falling to pieces every time anyone looks at him cross-eyed. I wonder if I've made his life too easy.

The children are asleep, and I'm off to bed. Tomorrow is a new day, a day closer to freedom and the victory of purity over the temptations of the devil. A day closer to my cheerful front door. Maybe I'll paint a porch swing to match.

It makes Rosario sick the way Eleni talks about Ulysses, how she calls him 'the boy.' She feels a pang of sympathy for him. This is the person who raised him, the person he defends even today despite how she's mistreated him. Flipping a few pages ahead, she continues.

April 8, 2004

He's made a fool of me. For years I've bent for him. Bent until shape-less, then further and further still until finally he's broken me. Erma Roy. A married woman. She didn't need the security of a man. Orson isn't the most handsome man in the world, but he's a provider. He's a faithful man and a natural leader. I admire his determination to weed out wrongdoing and seek justice, but I am humiliated by the gossip.

When I was expecting Calliope, I protected John. I lied. A sin of the tongue. A sacrilege to suggest there was some divine force that blessed our family. That God himself touched my belly and there Calliope grew. Like

Zeus and Danaë, a mystical rain penetrated my womb and impregnated me. The absolute fool I've been. I want to scream but the children are sleeping.

It sickens me to imagine the spawn he's created, who they've named Mary no less. A disgrace. Through no fault of her own that child is damned. To think, when we lay together on those nights he'd visit, he was tainted by—

ROSARIO HEARS a noise coming from the other room and slams the journal shut. Standing, she slides her phone into her back pocket and looks around at the mess she's made. She never expected him to come here in the middle of the workday. In a hurry, she puts things back where she got them, pausing for a moment as she contemplates returning the book to the storage bin. This is the clearest insight she's had into this case since they started, and she doesn't want to risk losing access to it on a fluke. She shoves the journal in her bag and closes the lid to the storage container in which she found it. She returns the stack of bins to the closet, then drags her foot across the carpet to erase the trail it left.

Footsteps. *Shit.* What is she going to say? She opens the door quietly and creeps out, hoping not to frighten him. Her pulse races and her brain runs through a list of plausible excuses at record speed. A clamor in the kitchen. Did he come home for lunch? Late lunch maybe, it's almost three in the afternoon. Peeking around the corner, her heart sinks. Sofie.

"What the fuck are you doing here?"

The sound of Rosario's voice makes Sofie jump up and scream. Recognizing Rosario, she clutches her chest and takes a breath, her eyes closed in a moment of relief. "Uly said I could."

"Oh really?" Rosario says skeptically.

"I'm not lying. I have the texts to prove it." Without Rosario having to ask, Sofie pulls out her phone, taps and swipes for a moment, then extends it out to her. "See."

I don't know what to do. I can't go back there. You know how momma is. She's making my life hell.

I'm not using my place right now. You can crash there for a little while, but you need to find a permanent solution.

Thank you so much Uly you're the best. Are you at work?

Yeah, busy now but if you swing by after 4 I'll give you a key

Okay, I'll see you then.

ROSARIO HAD no idea they still texted each other, that they saw each other just a few days earlier. When she started seeing Ulysses, she never imagined Sofie would be a constant presence in their relationship. But she's like a stubborn stain; no matter how hard Rosario scrubs, this little bitch won't disappear. To house his ex-girlfriend like this, provide for her. It nauseates her.

"I don't have anywhere else to go right now. Please. I'm working on finding a place, but if you yell at Uly about this, he's going to make me leave and I'm—"

"Forget it," Rosario says. "You didn't see me and I didn't see you."

Sofie's chest seems to sink with relief. "Thank you."

Pulling her bag over her shoulder, Rosario silently retreats. A dull ache swells within her. He's being helpful. That's what he'll say, she's sure of it. '*It doesn't mean anything. You saw the way Nadine slapped her, that's the way it is at that house. I felt bad for her.*' She plays the argument in her head before they have it. But it was a lie of omission. Rosario is his girlfriend, and she deserves to know if he's still doing favors for his ex. Not a small favor, like forwarding her mail, but giving her a place to live. Letting her sleep in his bed.

When she finally ambles in, Domino greets her with excited jumps and turns. Ulysses is barefoot in his painting shorts and ratty T-shirt, art supplies strewn across the foyer. An easel holds an extra-large canvas the size of a forty-inch television. The entry was the widest open space in the house that didn't pose a risk of destroying a piece of her furniture with oil based paints. *Their* furniture.

When he catches sight of her, he brightens. "Hey, there's my plantain princess." He sets down his brush. The glasses he wears when he's working come off, and he hooks them into the collar of his shirt. He kisses her. "How was your day?"

The weight of his mother's stolen diary weighs heavy on her shoulder. "Good. You?"

"Busy. Missed you."

"Missed you too," she says, sweeping through the foyer toward her bedroom. She shuts the door.

Chapter Thirty-Five

THAT WAS A LITTLE ABRUPT, he thinks. She must be angry at him. *Shit,* what'd he do now? He can never tell if it's real anger or the pouty thing she does when she wants him to chase after her, to shower her with apologies and affection until the brilliant sex that ensues makes them forget what they were upset about.

It's his first night off all week, and he'd just gotten a second wind to paint. As he sorts through aluminum tubes of pigment, he wonders if he should say *fuck it* and let her get over her hurt feelings herself or go after her. After setting up and staring at the blank white canvas for a while, he's too distracted. He sighs and marches to the bedroom.

Slipping inside, he closes the door behind him just loud enough to announce his presence. Rosario's sprawled across the bed, her face buried in her arms. She's changed into her pajama shorts and plain cotton T-shirt. When she lifts her head to look at him, her eyes are swollen and pink. She sits up, seeming to make an effort to steady her hitched breaths.

"Honey," he begins sweetly, then sits beside her at the edge of the bed. "Hey," he says, taking her cheek with his palm. He wipes a tear away with his thumb. She won't look him in the eye. "I'm sorry about this morning."

She sniffs, and her voice is tight as she says, "She's your mother. Of course you want to defend her. But Uly—"

"Thank you for understanding," he interrupts. He slides a hand down her back, finds her waist and pulls her close while shifting himself closer. "And I know you just want to help. I know it's coming from a good place, and I'm sorry I got so defensive."

Rosario's arms, tentative at first, wrap around him in return, her body leaning into his with a sigh that feels like surrender. He continues. "I shouldn't have snapped at you or left that way."

"It's not just this morning," she finally says.

"Then what is it?"

She glares at him, searching his face.

What has he done this time? The longer she holds him in that sharp gaze, the deeper his heart sinks with unease. His mind draws a blank, and he attempts to retrace his steps. He was rude this morning, but that wasn't it. Last night they were fine, they cuddled in bed. "Babe, seriously, I don't know what I did wrong. Help me out here."

"Sofie," she says.

A one-word answer that speaks volumes and makes his eyes close with realization. *Shit.* His mouth falls open in an attempt to explain, but nothing comes out but a choked sound. Sofie needed a place to stay. He had a place. It just seemed like a quick fix to a problem. "I didn't think it was that big of a deal. She's just staying there temporarily."

"Why is it your responsibility to solve her problems?"

"It's not. But I was able to, so I did." He pauses, wondering how this managed to ruin her day. "How do you even know she's staying there?"

"You're asking me how I found out that you were keeping this from me? I went by."

"It wasn't a conspiracy," he nips back. "I just didn't think it would come up."

"Well it did."

Ulysses nods. "You're right. I should have told you. I'm sorry for making you feel like I had something to hide."

Caressing his chest with her hands, she says, "Thank you."

"Does that mean you forgive me?" He presses a kiss to her jaw. Drawing a trail down her neck to her collarbone, she responds to his touch with a shiver, the tension between them shifting, becoming something else.

"It means I appreciate your apology, but——"

"But nothing," Uly interrupts. If she wasn't always just a little difficult, a little unruly, she wouldn't be Rosario. He smiles against her neck, letting his warm breath fall there. When she first showed up at his door unannounced all those months ago, he thought it was about her podcast, about getting him on board with this investigation. But now that they're together, feeling the way she holds her breath when he touches her, he knows that it was for him.

"Let me make it up to you," he whispers, then drags his lips along the spot where her neck meets her shoulder, that sensitive spot she likes the most. "You know you always feel better once you're properly fucked."

He pulls her into his lap so she's straddling him, and he can feel the heat coming off her from between her legs. She wants him. It channels something instinctive. Sliding his hand into her shorts, he finds the hem of her panties and forces past it, reaching his hand inside.

"Stop," she cries.

Pulling his hand back, he pauses a beat before he forces her off him. She starts to cry. He cannot win today. "Are you serious? What's the matter now? *Fuck*, I barely talk to Sofie. Okay? She mostly texts me about bullshit, and I don't respond. She's having a hard time. Her family is dysfunctional. We both grew up in a screwed up place, and she doesn't have a lot of people who understand her. That's all."

The sheets rustle, and when he turns his head toward the sound, she's gotten up and is walking toward the bathroom. What does she want from him? He's not a cruel person. He doesn't have to be in love with Sofie to feel pity for her. Of course he understands why she'd feel a bit of jealousy. Ulysses has the luxury of not having any exes to contend with. But she has nothing to worry about. After the way Sofie violated his trust, nothing would ever bring them together again. Nothing.

Chapter Thirty-Six

ONCE HE'S FALLEN ASLEEP, Rosario creeps out of bed and retrieves the journal from her bag, carrying it into her office. At her desk, she begins to read, picking up where she left off.

> *It sickens me to imagine the spawn he's created, who they've named Mary no less. A disgrace. Through no fault of her own that child is damned. To think, when we lay together on those night's he'd visit, he was tainted by Erma Roy's sin. God help me. Relieve me of this agony. What's more, deliver me swift justice. I pray for an answer, for a solution. I cannot go on this way. He must pay.*

A woman scorned. This entry would have been just before that Easter service where Thorne killed Orson Roy. This supports the idea it was the rumors of the affair that culminated with his murder. Eager to see what happens next, she skims the pages, looking for references to Calliope. Since Eleni's April entry, she writes cryptically about the Easter troubles, the fallout at the church, and Ulysses's nightmares. Finally, Rosario finds the next entry with Calliope's name.

May 29, 2004

How can Calliope have the heart of an angel but the eyes of a demon? I've been processing the shame of the last several weeks. While writing usually gives me peace, the quiet now only delivers more turmoil. I've kept busy, always at work, constantly moving. There's no rest because once I have a moment to think, the voices flood in. They tell me to do terrible things.

I can't help the boy with his moods right now. Since the Easter troubles, he cries all the time. At night, usually, just before bed. Like me, it's when his mind has a moment to wander that the dark thoughts creep in. He asks more about death, what happens when we die. It's as if he hasn't been paying attention all these years. I reminded him it's a hierarchy. Mortal men and women who enter this life and live it purely will ascend to the Order of Angels. The Ninth Order. The closest of the heavenly beings to engage in human affairs. We'll come back, and when we do, we will be the celestial force that saves humanity from itself.

When we talk about it, it seems to give him comfort—the idea that death is not the end, that we will return somehow and for a greater purpose. Calliope in particular. I worry about her presence here among us. Her heart is pure, but human eyes never grow, they don't ever change. They'll be a constant reminder of the fool he made of me. She deserves a mother who can nurture her, not resent her. It's not her that I despise. It's her eyes. Her DNA. The parts of her that are him.

For now, I try to focus on the work that needs to be done. The extra shifts. Checking in with the builder. We're nearly next in line to break ground. With or without John, we'll have our home, our porch swing, our yellow door. There is hope yet.

The words weigh heavy on her chest. Eleni hated Thorne so much after he betrayed her that she began to resent Calliope. She looked too much like her father. Mary too, apparently. It's why Shawnee was able to mistake them for each other. Knowing what she knows now, Rosario is reluctant to continue, afraid of what she might read next. Ulysses is sound asleep in the next room. Is it possible he's never read these entries? Remembering the condition of the book when she first opened it, it did seem like it had been shut for a long time. But these entries are twenty years old. There were so many years of opportunity for Ulysses to have stumbled upon these pages. Had he truly blocked this out, or is he being willfully blind to his mother's evil? Swallowing hard, she skims the pages that follow, short nonsensical entries about angels and the impending collapse of the world. A longer entry catches her eye.

June 20, 2004

John never expected consequences to arrive, but here they are. Since his Easter tantrum, members of the congregation could conceal his sins no longer and the authorities are circling. He's been hiding, moving from home to home and relying on the faith of his loyal congregants. With nowhere left to turn, he has returned to me for protection. Though, publicly, I have denounced him and his evil acts, I've offered him a private refuge in my home. God has presented me with an opportunity which I cannot squander. The children have been warned their lips must remain sealed. Any indication that John is hiding here will most certainly be disastrous and deny me my chance to fulfill God's will. I will be his sanctuary, for now. Just as a Venus flytrap's mouth is a sanctuary for a fly. Prayers are answered in mysterious ways, and divine intervention is not the hand of God reaching down and moving the chess pieces into the ideal position. He has touched my mind, my will and blessed my hand with the cunning to deliver the only fitting form of justice. An eye for an eye, a foot for a foot. I will bide my time, and the false prophet will be condemned to hell for eternity.

But a question remains unresolved, a prayer unanswered as of now. He has always doted on Calliope, and she adores him. Their resemblance seems to grow stronger each day. Writing this, I fear I've received my answer, but I am not equipped to accept it.

A plan has laid itself out in my mind, a map and a series of steps. An aligning of stars. I can see hundreds of miles ahead and suddenly it's clear what I must do.

The hints have revealed themselves each day, glinting with a special light, demanding to be acknowledged. The stunning display of red, white, and blue streamers, banners and party favors lining the aisles at the pharmacy today. A poster pictured a sky lit up with colorful fireworks. Beside it

*were necklaces and sunglasses in patriotic colors, and a T-shirt that read
'Sorry, can't hear you over the sound of freedom ringing.' On any other day,
they'd be ignored. But today, they spoke to me. I know what I have to do,
now I just need the courage to do it.*

"Holy shit," Rosario says aloud, her whispered voice breaking
the dead silence of her office. Checking the time, it's nearly three in
the morning, but she can't stop now. Her stomach stings with anxiety. Taking a deep breath, she continues to an entry dated July 5.
Scanning the text, a sinking feeling settles in. Bile rises up in her
throat. *No. No. No.*

Her hand flies over her mouth, and a nauseated feeling sends
pulses of sick through her veins. *Oh my God.* A sting rises to her eyes.
The things she did. The things she made Ulysses do. It's no wonder
he's an alcoholic. Not just to forget the things he'd done, but the
things he's lived with every day, how he'd be reminded of it. How
could anyone forget this? It's not possible. *My God, the way he defended
that evil woman.*

Pacing the office, she tries to steady her breathing. *Calm down.* A
bitter taste coats her tongue. She has to call the police. What will she
say? Is she even in any real danger? The gun in her bedside table.
Had he brought it here to protect himself from the things Rosario
might discover? No. That's impossible. It was her who invited him
to stay here, he'd never asked. He'd always complain about those
people watching him, though. Could that have been a lie? Had he
used her kindness against her? She'd ignored every red flag, blinded
by her feelings for him. Even if this isn't his fault, even if he was
forced, how could he conceal it all this time? She doesn't know him
at all.

Her pacing could wear a path on her office floor, but she can't
be still. The knowledge she's holding threatens to burst through her.
The things she still doesn't know, especially whether Ulysses can be
trusted, twists her stomach into knots. The room seems to spin, to
shrink. She can't do this alone. Reaching for her phone on the desk,
she calls Detective Harris. She waits, counting each ring and
praying he'll answer.

"Rosario?" he says, his voice slightly hoarse, likely from being woken from a deep sleep. She's not sure if she's making a mistake, if she's making a bigger mess of things, but she doesn't know what else to do.

"Deputy—Detective Harris. Beau. I'm so sorry to bother you."

"What's wrong?"

"I've just found something horrible, and I'm scared."

"Did he hurt you?" She can hear the change in his voice, the sounds of him rustling out of bed and into action.

"No, no, nothing like that," she says, hardly able to catch her breath. "No, he's asleep. It's a journal. Calliope's case. Ulysses's mother." Her hysterical mind spins out of control. Strangled by the revelation, her choked words spurt off between gasps. "S-she did something terrible. He helped her. Was he lying to me? Oh my God. I don't know what I'm going to do."

"Are there weapons in the house?"

"Yes. A gun. It's in my bedside table. He's in the bedroom."

"Can you get somewhere safe? The lobby? Somewhere secure and wait for me?"

"I'm in my office with the door locked. He's asleep."

"Okay. I'm on my way. I can be there in fifteen minutes. Can we stay on the phone?"

"Yes."

Chapter Thirty-Seven

JOLTED awake by Domino's shrill barks, Ulysses reaches for Rosario, but touching the sheets on her side of the bed, he finds them cold. The sound Domino makes is frenzied, the kind of barking reserved for a warning—when there's someone new and unfamiliar nearby. Ulysses sits up in a panic, and his mind runs through a list of potential threats. *The Order. One of their sympathizers. One of the podcast's crazy fans.*

Still muddled in a cloud of sleep, he tries to force his mind to sharpen and keep pace with his racing heart. Lurching for the end table, he pulls the drawer open. His hand drops inside and searches by feel until his fingers make contact with the cold steel of his pistol. Glancing at his phone on the table, he sees it's after three in the morning. The room is shrouded in blackness. The distant city lights do little to illuminate the bedroom. His feet hit the cold floor and he gets up, cautiously approaching the door, the weight of the gun in his grip.

He creeps out from the bedroom into the hall toward the living room. Domino's barks have calmed, but his anxious breaths pant in short quick bursts. Ahead, the living room is blindingly bright. *Strange*, he thinks. He remembers they'd turned off all the lights before bed. Rosario must have gotten up, but Domino wouldn't have barked at her like that. Is she in danger? Then he hears the bass of a man's voice and points his gun toward it. Figures in the hall. Rosario and a man he doesn't recognize. Why would a strange man be here at this hour? Ulysses starts to lower his gun. "Rosario?" he calls.

Rosario and the man both spin toward the sound of Ulysses's voice.

"Police! Drop your weapon!" the man shouts, quickly drawing a gun of his own.

Ulysses's heart hammers in his chest as the command slices through the fog of his exhausted mind. His grip on the gun loosens, the realization the situation could quickly spiral out of control dawning on him.

"Please don't shoot him," Rosario pleads.

"What's going on?" Ulysses cries. The last time a gun was pointed in his direction, the whiskey in his system hadn't allowed him to feel the depth of the trepidation he does now. His legs tremble beneath him. The man doesn't look like a police officer. He's dressed in jeans and a T-shirt.

The man steps forward, his own weapon trained on Ulysses, his eyes steady, assessing the situation. "Police! I said drop your weapon!" he shouts again.

Domino panics at the sound of their loud exchange. His tail low and stiff, a deep threatening growl rumbles from throat. The rare sound of his aggression drives Ulysses closer to the edge.

Ulysses looks to Rosario. The fear in her eyes is unmistakable.

"Who the fuck are you?" Ulysses shouts, his finger resting on the trigger.

For a moment, time stands still. Then a burst of light flashes from the man's gun as a punch of energy slams into Ulysses's chest, followed by a deafening pop and Rosario's screams. Domino's frantic barks. A fire spreads across Ulysses's chest. Falling to his knees, then on his back, he tries to makes sense of why he's looking at the ceiling, tries not to panic from the sensation of warm blood dripping down his sides, up his neck. *I've been shot.*

"Uly!" Rosario screams.

He can't move, can't lift his head. His vision blurs and becomes tunneled in black as he loses consciousness. *I'm going to die.*

Rosario hovers over him. "Call an ambulance!"

"What did I do?" Ulysses pleads for answers, his mind racing. How had things gone so wrong so quickly? His gaze flickers to Rosario, searching for an explanation in her eyes.

"I told you to drop your weapon goddammit," the man says, crouching over him. "Stay calm. Help's on the way."

"I'm so sorry," Rosario whimpers. Her lips press against his forehead, her tears trickle into his hair. The tunnel narrows and the world fades to black.

Chapter Thirty-Eight

PODCAST: **Mysteries of the Southern Gothic**; **Episode 54: Calliope and the Church of the Ninth Order Part IV**

[Intro music fades out]

Rosario Martinez (Narrator): Welcome back to Mysteries of the Southern Gothic. I'm your host, Rosario Martinez.

[Audio: rustling, Rosario's muffled talking from a recording setting up a mic]

Rosario: We started this podcast not to entertain but to get the truth. We're not journalists or law enforcement. We're just people who took solving puzzles a little too far. But you've ridden along with us on this journey, and somehow we've managed to share these really incredible stories with you over the years. Calliope's story in particular has been one of the most challenging cases we've taken on and, for me, has become the most personal.

We don't really talk about ourselves on this show. In fact, while we pry into the personal lives of the people we cover, you probably know next to nothing about me and Shawnee other than our voices and whatever we share online. It's not what you want to hear, right? You're here for the crime.

Well, sorry for the detour, but I promise it'll make sense soon enough.

[audible sigh]

I've been decidedly single forever. My entire adult life. Not because I'm afraid of commitment or anti-relationship, but I'm one of those women who's overly romanticized meeting "the one." If I wasn't struck by lightning when I met him, I wasn't interested.

And I meet people all the time. Not just personally. When we look into cases, I've met victims' families and friends, talked to law enforcement. It's never been a problem until a few weeks before Christmas last year.

I walked into the Ybor City Fine Arts Center expecting to convince this guy to participate in our investigation. To be on the show and introduce us to people who would have more information about his missing sister.

But then…

[Sound effect: lightning strike and rolling thunder]

I was struck by lightning.

I can't explain it, but something about him wiped every intelligent thought from my head, and I didn't know what to do. Ulysses was teaching a class there at night, and instead of doing what I went there to do, I pretended to be an art student. It was the first of many dumb things I did, but I panicked. What made it worse was that he recognized me. He couldn't figure out from where exactly, and even though I hadn't cared a few minutes earlier, I was suddenly worried he might actually be annoyed I showed up to his job to dig into this old wound.

It wasn't until about a week later when he was trying to get rid of an old bookcase that I met with him in private to tell him the truth.

Once he remembered where he knew me from, it did *not* go well. He was pretty angry, actually. And understandably so. I'd lied to him, and I'd previously offered some commentary on his sister's case that wasn't complimentary. It hurt him and his family. Honestly, I thought that was the end of our investigation into Calliope's disappearance.

But I'm nothing if not persistent. My tactics amounted to stalking. It was not good. But luckily, instead of getting a restraining order against me, like he probably should have, Ulysses let me in to have a conversation.

That's where it started, and if I were a real journalist, I would have told you sooner that Ulysses and I started a romantic relationship after Part I of the series aired. Shortly after Part III, we were effectively living together.

That's where this gets complicated. When your live-in girlfriend is also investigating a case you're involved in, things can get a little blurry.

And they did. He trusted me, and I violated that trust to try to solve this mystery. In my heart, I wanted to solve it for him. I swear that's the truth. But I'm also here with all of you, telling you what came next, and I can't do that without sharing with you the things I learned as a result of this intimate access I had to Ulysses.

The facts we discovered were sinister and must be brought to light out of respect to Calliope, the victim in this case. A smart little girl with a promising future ahead of her, tragically cut short.

[Eerie music starts softly and continues under Rosario's narration]

Eleni Katsaros's home was a metaphor for the woman. A pleasant, charming exterior, but inside was ravaged by rot. Her mental infirmity led to its gradual destruction. Small floods of her own making destroyed the floors and mold consumed the space. Every inhaled breath threatened harm and burned my throat walking through it. It was dangerous. It's why Ulysses ultimately moved his mother into memory care, a facility he provided to her at great personal expense. And indeed, his utility was what she'd been counting on when she spared his life.

Ulysses did his best with the home, donating what was salvageable and packing away personal affects for posterity: her jewelry; a homemade quilt; her favorite books. And her journal.

[unsettling music intensifies]

I'd often heard from the people we've interviewed that they experienced a distinct feeling upon coming into contact with the perpetrator of an egregious crime. The sensation of every hair follicle perking up, skin tingling, a sick feeling in the stomach. I felt all of those things when I met Eleni face-to-face for the first time.

But you don't tell the man you love that his mother gives you the creeps. I chalked it up to nerves at first, but I couldn't shake it. So I returned and visited her alone. Sitting with her, face-to-face, I saw her façade of the confused, fragile woman crumble, and a cold, calculating monster stood in her place.

There was only one place to turn, and even though what I found was horrifying, I'm not proud of how I came to find it. After Ulysses left for work one day, using the key he gave me to his apartment, I went in without him knowing.

[Sound effect: door creaks open]

A good and respectful son, Ulysses never pried. He carefully organized his mother's things in storage containers and tucked them away in his closet. That's where I found it. Her journal.

Was it a violation of her privacy to read it? Absolutely. But I had to remind myself, we were after the truth. Calliope deserves justice.

So, I read it. The entries started off hopeful. Strange, but generally optimistic about the future Eleni was planning with John Russel Thorne, Calliope's father and then leader of the Order. But soon, her words confirmed what investigators had previously suspected—Orson Roy was murdered because he stood up to Thorne about Thorne's affair with his wife, an affair that resulted in the birth of Mary Roy. Listeners of the show will remember Shawnee's encounter with Mary at the Order, who she believed at the time to be Calliope.

Eleni was shattered by the news of Thorne's infidelity, and the resulting child. Her entries show her as feeling betrayed, outraged, disgusted. But they also contained a tone of resentment against Calliope, a little girl who resembled her father and adored him. As I read the entries, my anxiety continued to mount. It seemed like the temperature was rising, and we were reaching an inevitable boiling point I prayed wouldn't arrive. Then I read the entry dated July 5, 2004.

[Audio clip: Voice actress reading the journal entry July 5, 2004]

The false prophet is dead, his offspring ascended to the Ninth Order. My angel, having entered this life and lived purely, has joined the celestial force that will save humanity from itself. My hands were guided by the stars. Taurus .380. With each burst of colorful light sparkling in the night sky, I fired. I can still hear the high-pitched singing in my ears.

Thorne was no God, no prophet. He loved only pleasure, only himself. He was an evil to be purged and now we're free. On Independence Day was made a cosmic alignment to God's will. To think he laid with Erma Roy, a married woman. The disgust nearly choked me. Her bastard daughter, born from sin, will never sing in the choir of angels alongside my Calliope.

Thorne left a mess for us all. The gore, a labor in and of itself to cleanse and prepare. Limbs to be separated. Bound in fabric. My arms and back still ache from the physical labor. But my boy is too young to understand. The laws of mortal man require this difficult work to be performed alone and in secret. I had to sterilize it for him. Make it clean enough to stomach.

God will forgive their shared grave, as what remains are mere vessels, meant to return to the earth. Return they shall, and we will build our holy home upon them, the soil enriched by their bones and anointed in blood. No holier ground would exist in this Newest Testament, the story of the restoration of purity to the world after the inevitable collapse of morality.

I will keep the boy in my prayers. A fragile one. He is pure at heart, and I admit I've kept him here selfishly. I prayed on my doubts. Had God willed me to deliver them both to him? But His message was clear. A mother needs a son.

Ulysses, unaware of the burden that destiny has placed upon my shoulders, sleeps soundly. He is a necessity for my future. In the quiet moments, a truth whispers to me—as the years advance and my strength wanes, who but my son to care for me?

This morning, with the remnants of Independence Day celebrations still littering the streets, I found another useful purpose for the boy. His fascination with fireworks had to be redirected toward something of divine significance. His punishment for firing off dangerous mortars without permission, I decided, would serve a higher purpose. I instructed him to dig a hole, as deep and as wide as he is tall. A task daunting for his tender age, yet necessary for the lesson it would teach and the purpose it would serve. Just as Michelangelo lent his talents to St. Peter's Basilica, the boy, an artist in his own right, built this holy tomb.

As Ulysses toiled under the summer sun, his shovel biting into the earth, I saw in his labor not just a punishment, but a preparation. This grave for the false prophet and his offspring was also a baptism for Ulysses—a rite of passage from the innocence of boyhood into the solemnity of his future role. In each scoop of dirt, he prepared the ground that would hold the remnants of our liberation from sin. Then, in crossing over to manhood, he carried their bundled remains, shrouded in gauze linens. Piece by piece, he rested them into the earth. We did our best to restore their earthly shapes, to place them into their final resting places in proper order, head to toe.

As I end this entry, I pray once more. Not just for guidance or forgiveness, but for understanding. May my son one day see the necessity of my actions, the weight of my choices, and the depth of my devotion to God. Not just as a mother, but as a harbinger of a new dawn for humanity.

[Mysterious outro music fades in]

Rosario: We're going to take a quick break to hear from our sponsors. Stay with us after the break, when we will read you the next entry in Eleni's journal.

[Outro music fades out]

* * *

Mysteries of the Southern Gothic Forum

Subject: Episode 54: Calliope and the Church of the Ninth Order Part IV

—

InTheTreehouse *1 hour ago*

"I have no journalistic integrity but it's okay because I'm not a journalist" what a joke

⬆ ⬇

—

ForensicGuy92 *45 mins ago*

Who gives a shit? I'm not even mad at Rosario. At least she stepped up and got her hands dirty for once. She solved the fucking case dude.

⬆ ⬇

—

Rosario4ever *40 mins ago*

Yeah wouldn't you want to know if your mom was a psychopath

⬆ ⬇

—

FoxyPodcastLvr *35 mins ago*

I knew it. Eleni was always going to be the killer

———

CrackedSpine *20 mins ago*

The way Rosario went about it was dishonest. The ends don't justify the means. It's not like she's bringing Calliope back.

———

ForensicGuy92 *15 mins ago*

This is a true crime podcast, they're not necromancers. They wanted to find the truth and they got it.

———

Ulysgirl03 *15 mins ago*

Poor Ulysses. He deserved better. His ex stole from him, his mother was a murderer and Rosario used him for entertainment value then got him shot.

———

MegLuvsPodcasts *10 mins ago*

He knew what he was getting into seriously like what did he think was going to happen? He agreed to the show. She's doing her job.

Beau_813 *now*

This is Calliope's story. She deserves to have her story told, not covered up to spare feelings. This little girl is getting justice because of the difficult choices Rosario made.

Chapter Thirty-Nine

PODCAST: Mysteries of the Southern Gothic; Episode 54: Calliope and the Church of the Ninth Order Part IV

[Intro music fades out]

ROSARIO MARTINEZ (NARRATOR): Welcome back to Mysteries of the Southern Gothic. I'm your host, Rosario Martinez, with the second half of Part IV. Before the break, you heard the words of Eleni Katsaros, the mother of Calliope and Ulysses. In her journal entry, she describes how she shot, killed and dismembered the Order's former leader, John Russell Thorne, and Calliope, then forced her thirteen-year-old son, Ulysses, to dig a hole and bury their remains under their home, which was under construction at the time. A home she later destroyed, strange acts thought to be a sign of her dementia, but under this new light, seem like she'd been driven mad by the horror of her own crimes.

Those of you who followed this case might remember Calliope was not reported missing until July 16th. This next journal entry explains why.

[Audio clip: Voice actress reading the journal entry July 15, 2004]

That nosy Nadine ought to sort her marriage out and rein in that juvenile delinquent son of hers instead of worrying about my family. Her husband is destined to fill the void left by Thorne's absence. She'd be doing her family a service to stop resisting and accept the path God has chosen. Yet she concerns herself with our business. The incessant questions will not end.

Ulysses is forbidden from discussing our family with them. As far as the public is concerned, Calliope is just outside playing, or inside having a snack. It's none of anyone's business what we do.

As much as they bickered, it surprises me how often Ulysses asks about his sister. It seems at times he forgets. Perhaps he's chosen to push it from his mind. She's spending the summer with her father, I told him. It seemed like an easier truth to accept. Though, it's insulting the way his shoulders slump. His obsession with a male figure is offensive. Have I not done my job? Am I not enough for him? Soon he'll be starting high school, and I worry about his weakness. He's too soft, cries too easily. He didn't learn these things from me.

Now, with the school year approaching, I have prayed for guidance. The school district will wonder about Calliope. Of course, I could tell them she's moved away to be with her father, but considering he's a man wanted for murder, that did not seem like a viable option.

Thankfully, God has led me to a solution. Just yesterday, a child was carried out of the woods a few towns over, abducted by some pedophile and left for dead. An awful thing, of course, though ripe for opportunity. It's nothing if not plausible. Nadine and her prying eyes will be redirected, her suspicions drowned in a sea of communal panic and sympathy.

I've begun to lay the groundwork. The beauty of this plan lies not just in its simplicity but in its utility. The sympathy of neighbors, once a nuisance, will become a shield, protecting us from further scrutiny. And as for the school district's inquiries, what better excuse could there be than a child tragically, mysteriously taken from us? Their prying will be silenced by their own decorum in the face of our "grief." Ulysses, bless his heart, his genuine confusion and despair will lend credibility to the ruse. His tenderness will serve a purpose at last.

[Eerie music starts softly and continues under Rosario's narration]

While their friends and neighbors searched for Calliope alongside Florida authorities that summer, Calliope was already dead and buried. By then, the ground above her was covered with a concrete foundation, concealing Eleni's crime. Ulysses went on to live in that home, built up on his sister's remains, for seven years. Listen to Tampa Police Department Chief Paula Shipherd at a press conference announcing the discovery of the remains.

[Insert Tampa Police Department Press Conference audio clip. Voice of Chief Shipherd.]

Today, the Tampa Police Department is announcing a significant development in a long-standing cold case that has deeply affected our community. Acting on information received from a credible source, our investigative team conducted a search beneath the foundation of a home belonging to the Katsaros family. This search led to the grim discovery of human remains, which have since been forensically identified as belonging to Calliope Katsaros, an eight-year-old girl reported missing in 2004, and Mr. John Russell Thorne, aged fifty."

Subsequent to these findings, Eleni Katsaros, who before being taken into custody was a resident in a specialized memory care facility, has been formally charged with two counts of first-degree murder, as well as charges related to the dismemberment and concealment of the bodies of her daughter and Mr. Thorne. The case, which began as a statewide search for missing Calliope Katsaros nearly two decades ago, has been brought to a close through the diligent efforts of law enforcement and contributions from the community, including significant leads provided by the Mysteries of the Southern Gothic podcast.

Reporter: Can you clarify what role, if any, Ulysses Katsaros played in this case? Was he aware of his mother's actions, and is he facing any charges related to this crime?

Chief Shipherd: Regarding Ulysses Katsaros, our investigation has determined that in addition to being a minor at the time of these crimes, Mr. Katsaros was also a victim of the horrendous actions perpetrated by Eleni Katsaros. It's important to clarify that Mr. Katsaros had no knowledge of, nor involvement in, the murders or dismemberments. Our findings show he was manipulated into assisting with the burial under duress and without understanding the true nature of his actions. The Tampa Police Department recognizes the profound impact this case has had on him and offers our deepest sympathies.

Reporter: Chief Shipherd, can you comment on the incident where Ulysses Katsaros was shot by a detective responding to a call at his home? How did this situation arise, and what steps are being taken regarding the officer involved?

[Audio cuts off with a click]

Rosario: Ulysses was asleep when I slipped out of bed to my office to read the journal. When I read Eleni's confessions that night, I was horrified. Terrified. All this time, he'd told me he didn't know the truth about what happened, yet I had just read that he participated in it. Now, I understand that he was just thirteen years old, and I can't imagine the trauma he must have endured. But at the time, the thoughts that were running through my head were darker. I didn't know what to believe, who to trust, or whether I might be in danger.

That's why I called my friend Detective Beau Harris. You might remember him from the Unaccompanied Minors series involving the murder of Carla Whitman. He was Deputy Harris back then, but his good work bringing Eric Mitchell Vernon to justice in that case led to his well-deserved promotion to detective. Detective Harris didn't hesitate to respond to my call.

[Insert Tampa Police Department Press Conference audio clip. Voice of Chief Shipherd.]

Chief Shipherd: Detective Beau Harris, although off duty at the time, responded to a phone call from Ms. Rosario Martinez. Upon arrival at the residence, Detective Harris, who was not in uniform, encountered Mr. Katsaros, who was armed. The situation escalated rapidly, resulting in Detective Harris discharging his weapon and wounding Mr. Katsaros.

[Sound effect: gunshot]

Chief Shipherd: I want to be clear—this incident is deeply regrettable, and we are committed to a full and transparent investigation into the circumstances leading up to it. Detective Harris has been placed on administrative leave, as per protocol, while the investigation is underway.

It's important to understand that law enforcement officers are trained to make split-second decisions for the safety of themselves and others. In this instance, the officer was faced with an armed individual in a highly tense situation. We will ensure that a thorough review is conducted.

[Audio cuts off with a click]

[Mysterious outro music fades in]

Rosario: We're going to take a quick break to hear from our sponsors. Stay with us after the break, when we will fill you in on Ulysses's condition.

[Outro music fades out]

Chapter Forty

THE FORCE of his consciousness crashes into him like an asteroid, ripping Ulysses from the peaceful place of his warm bed and psychological oblivion. His lungs burn, feeling too full, too forced. Panic flares as he becomes acutely aware of an intrusive pressure against his throat, a foreign presence thrusting air into his lungs. The rhythmic clicks and gasps of a machine.

His eyes snap open to a blinding assault of fluorescent light, causing them to fiercely water. Through the blur, he sees unfamiliar shapes and shadows. He feels restraints on his wrists holding him down. Instinctively, he struggles with a raw, animalistic desperation to be freed.

A shrill alarm pierces the room, mingling with the frantic beep of the monitor by his bedside.

Firm hands press down on his shoulders. "Easy, easy," a voice urges, the tone low and soothing, though there's an underlying note of urgency. "You're on a ventilator; it's helping you breathe. Try not to fight it."

Ulysses tries to speak, to scream, but the tube in his throat stifles any sound. Tears stream down the sides of his face, pooling in his ears. Every instinct tells him to pull, to remove the invading tube, but the restraints make it impossible.

The nurse, whose face hovers above him in a halo of light, is speaking again, voice edged with both command and compassion. "I need you to calm down. You're safe. I'm just going to give you a little sedative, okay? This will help you relax."

Gradually, as the minutes stretch on, his wild thrashing lessens. The terror doesn't disappear, but it recedes enough for him to take in his surroundings. The sterile room, the machinery, the distant murmur of voices. All seem to dull and become unimportant.

What happened?

His body is etched into the sheets with sweat. It feels like death. Like not being allowed to die. In the depths of his drug-induced haze, Ulysses occasionally hears voices—muffled and far away, as if underwater. Memories drift in and out.

Over the course of the next few days, as the fog of drugs and the weight of reality churns through his mind, he begins to piece together his situation.

Vision still slightly blurred, Ulysses can't see the doctor's face behind his mask, just that he stands over him, a foreign figure dressed in white. Ulysses gasps between choked coughs, realizing the tube has been removed from his throat. Once he catches his breath, he mutters a rasped, "Where's my dog?"

"I don't know anything about that," the doctor says, not looking up from his notes. "There were some complications during surgery. You suffered significant blood loss from the gunshot wound and required mechanical ventilation to ensure adequate oxygenation of the tissues. But you've been off the vent all day. You've been stabilized. Vitals look good. We're moving you out of ICU."

"Okay," he says, still confused and mostly in the dark about the events that brought him there.

As the doctor exits, Rosario enters. "Oh my God," she says, rushing toward him. "I'm so glad you're okay." She reaches toward him gently, navigating a maze of tubes and wires to embrace him.

Ulysses blinks at her, a mix of confusion and relief washing over him as he processes her presence. The sight of her brings a sliver of normalcy to the chaos of his current situation. "What happened?" The last clear memory he has is of the confrontation, the blinding flash of a gunshot and then darkness.

Rosario hesitates, her gaze dropping to their intertwined hands. "You were shot, but you're going to be okay now," she reassures him, squeezing his hand a little tighter. "You've been through surgery, and the doctors have been monitoring you closely."

"Who shot me? The police?"

She looks away, eyes falling to the floor. "Detective Harris. He came over because…Uly, we need to talk, but I don't think now is the best time. You're still healing, and I don't want—"

"I want to know."

She sits on the edge of the bed and draws in a deep breath, staring at her hands. "I just wanted to help you get answers. All I wanted was to tell Calliope's story and to get justice for her. I didn't mean for this to happen, but I freaked out. I got scared, and I called him because…" She trails off, hesitating.

"Because why?"

She shakes her head, as if she's auditing what she should say. "Your mom kept a journal. It was in one of the storage bins in your closet."

"You went through my stuff?" His muscles tense and he flushes. She winces and draws back. He's repeatedly asked her to respect his privacy. She never fucking listens. Drawing in a deep breath, he tries to steady his rising temper.

"Uly, the journal says things. About what happened to your sister."

Ulysses's heart rate spikes, each beat a loud echo in his ears. "What things?" His voice is a gruff whisper, fury and fear warring within him.

Rosario's eyes meet his. "It... It implicates your mother in Calliope's disappearance. And not just hers." She pauses, struggling with the weight of her next words. "Thorne's too."

The room seems to spin around Ulysses, the beeping of the machines by his bedside now a distant sound. His mother. His sister.

The fragments of his family story suddenly threaten to suffocate him.

"She was losing her mind. She says things sometimes, crazy things. I mean, how do you know it's even true?" His question is a lifeline for some semblance of doubt, some chance of misunderstanding.

Rosario reaches for his hand again, her grip steadying. "The police found evidence." Her voice breaks on the last word, and she takes a moment to compose herself. "They found human remains under your old house. They've arrested your mother."

The words hit Ulysses like a physical blow, leaving him breathless. Human remains. Arrested. His mind reels, trying to reconcile the accusations laid before him. "I...I need to see her. I need to talk to her."

Rosario's expression softens, her thumb brushing against his hand in a comforting gesture. "I know this is upsetting. But right now, you need to focus on getting better. There will be time for everything else later."

Ulysses struggles against the tubes for a moment, but his exhaustion quickly drains the fight from him. Frustration brings heat to his eyes. He's helpless. And even with this explanation, he wonders why he's here. "I still don't understand why that guy shot me. Why was he in your apartment at all?"

Rosario reaches out, her touch gentle. "I'm so sorry, I was just so scared. We'd been having problems and...we had a bad night. I was worried you'd been lying to me."

Ulysses closes his eyes, a desperate attempt to block out the reality crashing down on him. The sedatives, the pain, and the overwhelming revelations merge into a maelstrom of confusion and despair. "So you called a detective to arrest me?"

"Not to arrest you, to protect me."

"Protect you from me?"

She nods. Suddenly he remembers the fearful look in her eye. The look that made him doubt whether he should drop his weapon. She was afraid, and that man didn't look like a police officer. His instinct had been to protect her. But she wasn't afraid of that man, she was afraid of him. The man was there to protect her from him. Somehow this revelation hurts most of all.

"How could you think I'd hurt you?" His voice is barely audible, choked with emotion.

"The things I'd read. You'd lied about Sofie and—"

"You were sneaking around and looking into my stuff. What the hell's the matter with you?"

"But, Uly, the drinking. You'd get violent sometimes. It was scary. Okay? I didn't expect you to come out with a gun. He told you to drop your weapon."

Hearing her repeat those words sends a chill through him. "I thought you were in danger, Rosario. Domino was freaking out. I thought the guy was the threat. As far as I'm concerned, I got shot trying to protect you. I would never hurt you. Ever."

"I'm so sorry. I really am."

"I need some time to think. Alone."

As Ulysses's gaze bores into her, Rosario crumbles. She stands slowly, the room heavy with regret. Without a word, she moves toward the door, her steps quiet, deliberate. Pausing at the threshold, she casts a lingering look back at him, then steps out, the door closing with a soft, final click. Ulysses is left alone, her presence fading into the sterile air of the hospital room.

Hours pass, marked with brief rounds by nurses. He receives a short visit from Dr. Okafor, who seems to intentionally avoid any troubling topics. Trays of food that come and go. There's a *Family Feud* marathon on whatever channel the television in his room is set to but there's no sound. He's starting to doze off when he hears the door click open again. A flash of hope blooms that a nurse will come in and tell him he can go home. But instead, a man enters. The man who shot him. He's holding a striped box that looks like it might have some kind of treats inside. His eyes are remorseful, tentative.

"Ulysses?"

"Yeah."

"I'm Detective Beau Harris. Can I sit with you for a few minutes?"

"If I say no, will you shoot me again?"

He sighs. "The last thing I wanted to do was shoot you. But you were pointing a gun at me."

"Yeah, I remember how it went. What are you doing here?"

"I came to tell you how awful I feel about this. And I brought you some cookies."

Ulysses, in his exhausted state, chuckles softly at the absurdity of it all, then waves him over. Harris lumbers toward him and hands him the box. Opening it, he finds it's filled with an assortment. Thumbprint cookies with strawberry jam, sugar cookies with colorful sprinkles, and chocolate.

"I know cookies don't make up for taking a bullet." The detective's awkward sincerity seems genuine.

"No. They don't. But thank you anyway," he says, picking out a thumbprint cookie and taking a bite. It's good. The texture dissolves like sugary sand against his tongue. As he chews, he gets a better look at Harris. Tall, broad, clean cut. This was the guy Rosario had on speed dial to come to her rescue, huh? "How do you know Rosario?"

He shoves his hands into his jeans. "Worked on a couple cases with her in the past. Nice girl. She's told me how much she cares about you. I hope you won't hold my split-second decision making against her. She never wanted you to get hurt."

Ulysses pauses, the cookie halfway to his next bite. "It's more than that. Don't know why she needed to call you in the first place."

Harris nods solemnly. "Well, I can't answer that. But I do know she was afraid, and fear doesn't always make sense."

"No. It doesn't." He leans back against his pillows, tired. The effort to stay angry, to hold onto the resentment, is draining.

Harris gives a slight tilt of his head, acknowledging the concession for what it is. "I'll leave you to rest then. Again, I'm truly sorry." He moves toward the door, pausing briefly as if he wants to say more, but decides against it. He exits, leaving Ulysses alone with his thoughts and the box of cookies. A small, inadequate token of an apology, but a gesture nonetheless.

Chapter Forty-One

One Week Later

REENTRY into the world was like taking a time machine to 2004. Reporters were waiting for Ulysses outside the hospital, outside of her apartment building. Except now, the questions they shouted at him were much different. *Why didn't you tell the police your mother murdered Calliope? Why did you help bury the bodies?* He never thought he'd prefer lying in a hospital bed to freedom, but hearing their questions, seeing the way people looked at him, eyes filled with curiosity and disgust, he wanted to be anywhere but there.

Logically, he knew the person he should be most furious with was his mother. Yet he couldn't shake the feeling that none of this physical and emotional agony would have happened if not for Rosario's intrusion. He prayed this bitter feeling would wane, especially as he regained his strength and she helped him navigate life— getting in and out of cars, into their building, where she and Shawnee used their bodies as shields to protect him from the biting questions. Yet, he wasn't sure he could go back to the way things were. He'd planned to gather his things and return to his old apartment, at least until he could get his head on straight.

Taking a moment of rest on the living room couch, Domino lays in Ulysses's lap, at peace and basking in affectionate pets. Ulysses finally asks the question that had been plaguing him while in his hospital bed for weeks. What sordid details have been broadcast to their listeners? Considering the news coverage, surely Rosario and Shawnee were eager to ride the momentum and drop an episode covering the utter disaster his life had become.

"Was there another episode?" he asks.

Shawnee shoots Rosario a look before answering for her. "Yeah, but the series is over."

In a way, the information is a relief. That podcast had been chipping away at him, sanity and spirit, for months. Now that it's over, he might finally get a moment to grieve, to heal.

"Can I listen to it?"

"Babe, are you sure you want to do that?" Rosario asks. The term of endearment grates at him, a sign he's far from forgiven her for all that's transpired. He rotates his stiff shoulders and feels the sting of his still-healing muscles where the bullet ripped through him. "I'm sure. Let me hear it."

She disappears for a minute, returning with her laptop, which she sets on the coffee table. Pulling up the episode, she hits play and backs away. Her backlit figure paces as her voice streams through the speakers. It's overcast outside, shading the interior in gray.

Listening to her romanticize their story, as if it was love at first sight, all while she was deceiving him, he goes numb. The way she describes his mother, comparing her to the rotting condition of her home, a home he never wanted to show her to begin with. The visceral reaction she had to his mother that made her physically ill. She glosses over the many ways in which she violated his trust and then reads his mother's journal entry for the world to hear. Hearing it for the first time himself, it's even worse than he'd imagined.

He remembers shooting fireworks with the Randall family that year. How he felt normal being surrounded by people for an outdoor barbecue. They lounged in lawn chairs in the dirt and watched the colors explode across the night sky. Calliope wasn't allowed to go, but he didn't know why. He'd been glad then, actually. For once, she was the one on punishment and he was free to go. To think it was because his mother planned to kill her turns his stomach. Even hearing it retold in a voice eerily familiar to his mother's, it's like it happened to someone else.

Then, a commercial. The horror of his life juxtaposed with a thirty-second ad for web hosting services. His temper rises but he holds it back, listening to another entry. His jaw tightens, muscles growing rigid at more revelations broadcast to the world. He was a pawn. A useful idiot. All these years, he'd loved a woman capable of horrors and now the world knows. It's too much to bear. Rising to his feet, he picks up the laptop and throws it at the wall. It crashes and sends keys and fragments flying into the air. Rosario yelps, and Shawnee quickly jumps to her feet, her eyes zeroed in on him.

"We're done," he says coolly to the both of them, then retreats to Rosario's bedroom to gather the few things he'd moved in. He should have known better than to help her, than to trust her. He packs his things, lifting and sorting with a burning pain in his arm and chest. He probably reinjured something with that throw; he gave it every ounce of force he could muster.

When he finally wheels his bag out, he whistles for Domino and ignores the sounds of Rosario's sobs. She clings to Shawnee, curled up with her on the sofa, her face buried on her shoulder. Shawnee shoots him a pained look. Another liar not to be trusted. He'd have been better off never knowing them. Hooking Domino up to his leash, he taps his pockets and finds his phone. Without looking back, he rolls his bag out the front door.

Returning to his apartment, he finds it in a disarray. A bag of chips sits open on the coffee table next to used cups and mugs. A cat walks across his kitchen counter to sniff at a stack of dirty plates. The bedroom door creaks open, and Sofie slips out wearing one of his T-shirts and a pair of panties. "Hey."

"Hey."

"I wasn't sure if you'd want me to visit you in the hospital. Thought I might make things worse."

"Don't worry about it." He shakes his head. "Place looks like shit."

"I know. I was just fixin' to clean," she says, but he knows better. It's a line she's used often. "I'll change the linens."

"Thank you," he says, and for a split second, he wonders if she's been sleeping with someone else on those sheets. He sits on the couch and watches Domino and the cat inspect each other. Fortunately, it seems to be going peacefully. "You got a cat?" he shouts to the other room. She left the door open, and he can half see her making up the bed.

"She's not mine. I just feed her sometimes and we hang out."

Ulysses scrubs his face and laughs to himself. She emerges from the bedroom with an armful of sheets and walks them over to the washer, shoving them inside and starting a cycle. She approaches him cautiously and stops in front of him, just staring. Her hair is in disarray and he can tell she's not wearing a bra.

"Why are you looking at me like that?"

"Can't I look at you?"

"I'd prefer you didn't."

"I'm just glad you're here, that's all." She sits beside him. "I'm glad you're okay. I was worried."

"Couldn't have been that worried if you didn't visit."

"You wanted me to visit?"

"No."

"You finally break up with that Puerto Rican girl?"

"I'm not going to talk to you about that."

"So you did, huh?" She scoots closer, and he eyes her suspiciously. "Is it because she got you shot?"

"It didn't help."

"Can I see it?"

"No."

"Come on. Pretty please. I've never seen a bullet wound before."

He sighs wearily and pulls off his shirt. The wound is covered in gauze and tape. "I don't want to open this with all the bacteria and shit you got flying around here."

She drags a finger over the edge of the tape, picking at it with her fingernail. "Just let me peek at it."

"You're so weird."

She giggles and pulls it back, wiggling closer to get a better look. "Ew," she says, quickly covering it. "Ruined your tattoo. Or made it more badass. I dunno, guess it depends on who's looking." They laugh together, faces inches apart.

"I'm glad you're home," she whispers, her big doe eyes inviting him.

He's been so despairing the last couple of weeks, so lonely. Something about being with her feels normal, comfortable. He reaches around her neck and pulls her face to his, kissing her. She hums against him and slips onto his lap.

He pulls up her shirt, confirming his earlier suspicion, and buries his face in her breasts. Reaching for the button of his jeans, she undoes it, and he raises his hips to force them down his thighs with his boxers. Hooking a finger into her panties, he shifts them to the side, and she impales herself on him. He lets out a groan. "Fuck, I missed you," he says, gripping her hips.

She rides him slowly, and he watches her. They lock eyes, and he can barely hold on. It's been weeks without any intimate contact with anyone, including himself, and when she picks up her pace, he loses control. He withdraws quickly, pressing himself against her thigh, spilling onto her skin. She laughs softly and climbs off him to clean up.

"I'm sorry."

"It's okay," she says. "That was fun."

"Did you get to…"

"No, but we can try again."

He tucks himself away, expecting to feel a modicum of guilt for walking out on one woman and entering another within an hour. But he doesn't. Maybe Rosario wasn't forever after all. He remembers caring for her so deeply, but now there's nothing. It seems his feelings couldn't weather the force of the storm the last few weeks had brought them. Watching Sofie walk around his apartment undressed, he reflects on their breakup and the things she did.

Distant wounds with pain that's all been spent. It makes him wonder if one day he'll forgive Rosario, if there's any chance they'll be together again.

"Come on," Sofie says, waving him into the bedroom. He follows.

That night, Sofie is in his arms tracing shapes on his chest when his phone vibrates on the pillow beside him.

Rosario

I'm so sorry I hurt you. That was never my intention. I can't imagine the pain you must be in after everything you've been through. I'd do anything to make it right. You're the only man I've ever loved. Please come home.

For the first time since he left, he feels a wave of shame.

Sofie lifts her head. "Is that her?"

"Yeah."

She rests her head down again and kisses his chest. "You're mine, Uly. Always have been, always will be."

He scoffs, letting out a long bitter exhale. "You left me. Left me homeless. You forget that?"

"Don't start that up again. We both know that never would have happened if you'd just stop paying your mother's way like I asked you to. And I left because you were falling to pieces all the time. Going off on benders and stuff. That's not okay."

"I know that. I'm sober."

She props herself up on her elbow, the light from outside outlining her silhouette. "It's easy to be sober when you're bedridden in the hospital. But all this, it's come out for a reason. It needed to happen. And now that it's been brought to light, I hope you can finally forgive yourself."

"Forgive myself for what?"

"Protecting your mom. You felt like you were betraying your sister."

"What are you talking about?" he asks, his heart beating faster.

"Baby, this is me you're talking to. You can drop the act."

"What act?" he asks, sitting up. "Did you know about this?"

Frozen in a cautious expression, she searches his face. "You really didn't remember, huh?"

A deep feeling of unease rushes through him. He holds his breath, waiting for her to say something that makes sense.

"You know Calliope was never really there that day, don't you? She was never really missing."

He knows what he heard. What Rosario announced to the world, what the news said. Until now, it was some remote idea, detached from any connection to reality. Sofie's worried face returns him to that day. Bloody linen bundles—an arm, a leg, a head. Remembering the strange sensation of their weight in his hands sends a chill down his spine. He must have made himself forget.

The clients at Palms, the younger ones especially, just want to feel like they belong. His mother was the only person Ulysses belonged to then. Of course he'd be too frightened to face losing her. Even if she was a monster, she was his. Without a father, where would he have ended up? She'd have been in jail, and he would have been raised in foster care. But it was too much to bear, the feeling he'd selfishly denied his sister justice. Now, it all comes flooding back.

Ripped from bed by her shouting. His mother had never told him he wasn't allowed to shoot fireworks. It never came up. But suddenly his heart was pounding out of his chest, his cloudy mind, still half asleep, trying to make sense of what he'd done wrong. Before he knew anything, they were on the road with a shovel and two large coolers in the backseat. He didn't understand why she'd taken them to the site of their soon-to-be-built home. The holiday kept the construction crews away, and all the lived-in homes filled with neighbors prying eyes were situated away from their small plot. No one even noticed as he dug in the sweltering heat so long he nearly fainted from exhaustion and dehydration, his hands bloody.

But how could it be true? Four children knew this dark secret and kept it for years? He's almost too afraid to ask, to acknowledge how much he'd forced from his memory. "Did Brody know? Warren too? All this time."

"No, not at the time. That day, when you told everyone Calliope was just outside, they believed you. We all did. It wasn't until your momma started losing her mind that she told me the truth. I confronted you then, asked you to stop paying for her tithes, her care. You really don't remember?"

Warren said he saw Calliope that day. Brody too. They'd run through the story so many times, heard Ulysses retell it again and again. The power of suggestion likely painted an image so vivid they remembered it as if they'd seen her with their own eyes. Swallowing hard, his mind races. "It was you, wasn't it?"

"What was me?"

"The home movie. The photograph. You did that."

She rolls onto her side and faces him. "What difference does it make? It's been solved, hasn't it?"

He settles onto his back. "You made me think I was losing my mind."

"They were spinning their wheels. I thought they'd have enough sense to ask a damn question out there with Daddy instead of causing a scene."

The exhaustion of the last few weeks reduce the lies she told and the havoc it caused to a minor offense. "I'd never met Mary before."

Had he? Now he's not so sure.

"I'm sorry." She rests down again and throws an arm across his stomach. "She really looks like Calliope though, don't she?"

"Yeah."

"All I'm saying is, I'm glad it's finally out there in the open. Justice will be done, and you are on your own now. Things can finally get better."

He kisses the top of her head, then sets his phone on the end table, Rosario's text unanswered. "I hope so, Sof."

"Glad you're home."

"Me too."

Chapter Forty-Two

AFTER A FEW DREADFUL days weighed down by an insurmountable sadness, Shawnee forces Rosario into the shower and takes her to the Apple store to buy a new laptop. She wanders, the ache of her broken heart ever present in her chest. Shawnee lights up over a new MacBook. "Look. This one has fourteen-core CPU and thirty-core GPU."

Rosario shrugs weakly against the heaviness of her despair. "I don't even know what that means," she mumbles.

"It means it's fast. You could do a lot of things at the same time. Imagine how easy it'll be to edit audio and video on this thing."

She lumbers down the aisle, scanning laptops that all look exactly the same. "Just tell me which one to buy and I'll buy it." What difference does it make? She already told Shawnee she's done. She's never making another episode again. The show ruined her life. Ruined her. She doesn't like the person she becomes when she's chasing down a case.

Shawnee perks up again, but this time, it's not over the system specs of a new computer. "Oh my goodness. What a small world. Look who it is." Tall and broad-shouldered, Detective Harris cautiously approaches them in plain clothes.

"Imagine running into you here," he says, waving awkwardly with one hand, the other shoved into his faded jeans.

A heat rises to Rosario's face. She's zero for three on presentability with their encounters, but at least this time, Shawnee could have warned her. It's so obvious she set this up on purpose. She would have dabbed on some under-eye concealer at least. Done something with her hair. Now, she feels out of place. The last time she was set up by a friend to meet a boy at the mall, she was twelve years old. She's rusty at this.

"Was thinking about finally getting an iPhone," he says, an obvious lie.

He's so bad at it, it makes her crack a smile for the first time in weeks. "Oh?"

"Mm," he says in confirmation. "Every time I go to get one, they say they're about to come out with another one. Thought I'd finally buck up and pull the trigger," he says. Biting his lip, he nods at her, acknowledging what he's just done. Takes a beat. "My goodness, I could not have picked a worse choice of words, now could I?"

"No, you couldn't have."

Shawnee glances at the both of them. "Oh no," she says, looking at her phone. "I just remembered. I have this other thing."

Rosario's eye pop, and she sucks in a surprised breath. She knows what's going on but is far too embarrassed to say anything to stop it. Her internal screams for help are futile, her telepathic efforts to stop Shawnee in her tracks ineffective as she says her goodbyes, backing out of the Apple Store like the traitor that she is and leaving Rosario and the detective alone. They look at each other, but she can't face him for long.

"Look, I'm sorry about the dubious tactics. I wanted to see you, and Shawnee thought it would be good to get you out of the house."

A tingle creeps up her neck, and she takes in the yellow stitching on her combat boots. She's such a mess, her friends had to forge a plan to get her sunlight and social contact. Crossing her arms in front of herself, she finds the courage to look at his face. "I'm sorry I haven't responded to your messages. I just feel like I ruined everything. With your job, with Uly."

"It's okay. I know you're feeling pretty bad about what happened. And I am too. But I'll be fine with work. It's just a formality."

"I should have thought it through before freaking out and calling you in the first place."

"I'm glad you called me," he says. "You didn't feel safe. Now, I'm not a therapist or Dr. Phil, but maybe if he didn't make you feel safe that was part of the problem."

Rosario shifts uncomfortably, the weight of her emotions and the past few weeks making it hard to stand still. She hadn't considered her actions in that light before. The idea she might have been reacting to a deeper, more instinctual sense of danger in her relationship with Ulysses hadn't fully dawned on her until now.

She buys the laptop Shawnee fawned over, and to her surprise, Harris buys an iPhone. Making small talk, she learns this is the first time either of them has been to a mall in a long time. "I have a hankering for some really bad mall food," he says.

"Want to go to the food court? Was actually kind of daydreaming about a hot pretzel."

"Heck yeah," he says with an enthusiasm that's contagious.

They wander through the mall together, his shop bag dangling from one finger. They get pretzels and beer cheese and sit at a small table in the noisy food court.

"I know things didn't go according to plan, but wow, that was a fantastic series."

She wishes she could agree. The show's been getting loads of attention. BuzzFeed reported on it. It made national news.

"I mean that. Set aside Uly's feelings for a minute. An innocent little girl's getting justice because of the work you did. People are going to know her story because of you. Be proud of that."

Rosario picks at her pretzel, the salt and the warmth of the dough a small comfort. She nods, making her shoulders a little sturdier. "I know, and I am. I guess it's just been hard. Setting aside

Uly's feelings. I love him. But I ruined everything and now he's gone."

"You know," Harris begins, a thoughtful expression on his face as he twists the plastic lid on his drink. "I heard that part in your podcast about meeting him. Being 'struck by lightning' and all." He glances at Rosario, seeming to gauge her reaction.

She gets strangled inside thinking of how intensely enamored she felt with Ulysses, how she still feels. It brings a heat to her face, a blur to her eyes.

"You've been camping, haven't you?" he asks, his voice tinged with lightness that seems designed to overcome her moment of gloom.

"Me? No, never," she replies, a bit surprised by the question.

"Really? Never?" He seems genuinely taken aback.

She shakes her head, confirming.

He nods, then launches into his explanation, his voice carrying a hint of enthusiasm. "Well, I just mean to say that lightning is intense, sure. It's a brilliant flash of light—*boom*—but then it's gone. I like to think of relationships kind of like a campfire. First, you need that initial spark. It might be small, but with a little care, it catches, right? And if you nurture it, give it time, that little flame grows. You have to be patient, keep tending to it. If you do, you'll get a strong fire going. And as long as you keep feeding it, it can burn for as long as you let it. Hell." His tone shifts, a playful edge creeping in. "If you're not careful, it might just get out of control, might even burn down half the town." His story, earnest at the heart but capped with his unique brand of humor, trails off. He offers a small smile, lightening the mood.

But then his expression falls and the mood shifts. His usual playfulness gives way to a more serious demeanor. "I know when we first met it wasn't like being struck by lightning for you," he admits, his voice dropping a notch, tinged with vulnerability. His eyes, usually so full of mirth, now shimmer with a blend of hope and nervousness. "That's fine. Of course. But for me, I felt something. A spark. And honestly, I feel it now. Just being here with you, spending time together, it's like a sparkler goin' off right here," he says, his hand moving to his chest, over his heart.

"Detective——" she starts.

"Beau," he corrects.

"Beau, you're sweet."

Before she can finish her sentence, he sinks back slightly into his chair. His expression steels as if bracing for her inevitable rejection, then he holds up his hands in defense. "Look, I'm not asking for anything. I'm sorry." Beau looks up, his eyes meeting hers. "I know you can't snap your fingers and be over this. Trust me, I get it. I just want you to know that I'm patient. And I'm okay being friends. I'd just really like to get to know you better, learn about you. And you could learn about me, that's all."

"I'd like that."

After their pretzel, they head out to the parking lot, where he leads her to a gleaming white Chevy Silverado pickup truck. He rushes ahead to pull open the passenger door. "Here, let me take that," he says and extends a hand to help her set her shopping bag in the back. It's lifted and she struggles to get in.

"I never understood why people jack up trucks so high," she says, slightly annoyed by the challenge of climbing in. She hasn't gotten much physical activity lately, lying around feeling sorry for herself.

He shuts her door and lets himself inside the driver's side. Starting it, he says, "For clearance. You know, when there's flooding. Especially after a hurricane or a rough storm, a lot of the roads here can get pretty bad. I'm usually out here helping to clear paths."

"Oh," she says, feeling a little foolish. She always thought people just wanted their trucks to look like they were in a monster truck rally. "That makes a lot of sense."

"I bet you drive a zippy little sports car."

"Guilty as charged."

"Well, I use this to help pull those zippy little sports cars out of the road when Tampa floods to high hell."

She smiles sheepishly. "Alright, I get it now." His cheek dimples, and he shoots her a friendly wink letting her know he's just having fun with her.

"So," she starts. "Are you from around here?" His accent was almost a little too southern for Tampa, a city full of northerners tired of the cold and military families hailing from other parts of the country.

"Alabama, actually. Parents moved out here while I was in the service. When my time was up, I wanted to be near them."

"You were in the military?"

He nods. "American by birth, Marine by the grace of God."

The sun shines bright and high in a cloudless sky. Drawing in a deep breath, she takes in the smell of a new car air freshener. Glancing at his infotainment system, she wonders what would start to play if she resumed whatever he was last listening to. She leans forward slowly, trying to give him a chance to smack her hand away. But he doesn't, and when she presses play, a talk station comes on. Dave Ramsey. It plays just long enough for her to hear him say something about mutual funds.

He quickly stops it. "Something you want to listen to?"

"Is that what you listen to?"

He shrugs. "Smart guy."

Beau is beautiful, but at times, he's got the sex appeal of an AARP commercial. He narrows his eyes at her with a playful cautiousness. "What about you, plantain princess, what do you listen to?"

"Who told you about that?"

He laughs. "That's for me to know and you to find out, sugar."

It was Shawnee, of course, but the term of endearment in his drawl makes her swoon a little. Even if he's sweet on her, his affectionate words seem to simply be a southern thing. It's just the way he talks. "Music, usually."

"Go ahead and put something on then, whatever you want."

She taps the screen, scanning through channels until she finds an alt rock station. Nirvana's "In Bloom" plays and her gaze flits to him for judgment. He nods with approval, and she feels a bit of relief.

When they pull up to her apartment, he parks. "Don't you dare touch that door," he says before hopping out. She has a moment of confusion, then looks at the door wondering if it's boobytrapped or something. He opens it and extends a hand to help her out. As he does, her boot slips off the rail and she slides against him to the ground. His arm hooks around her back to steady her. She feels a flash of heat.

They say the best way to get over someone is to get under someone else. The thought of going up to an empty apartment fills her heart with dread. His hand at the small of her back, he draws her closer, pressing a gentle kiss to her cheek. She's a moment of desperation away from asking him upstairs when he whispers in her ear.

"I meant what I said." Then he pulls back and presses a hand to his chest. "Campfire." There's a twinkle in his eye, so unabashedly earnest.

Her immediate cringe response probably says more about her than him. She smirks, searching for a glint of irony in his expression. Finding none, she shakes her head, more out of bewilderment that a man so handsome could simultaneously give her the ick. It makes her hate herself a little. *He's just being sweet, what is wrong with me?*

"Campfire," she says, shooting him a pair of finger guns.

She takes her bag and heads upstairs, facing her empty apartment alone for the first time since Ulysses left. No Shawnee. No excited click of Domino's paws pattering her way. No Uly. It chokes her all over again, and she fights back tears.

Chapter Forty-Three

One Month Later

COCOA, the newest member of the Martinez family, isn't house trained, so Rosario enrolled him in the Tampa Canine Academy to teach him the basics. Every Monday, Rosario takes the auburn-coated lab mix to his obedience class. At three years old, Cocoa wasn't eligible for the puppy class, but he's doing just as well as the dogs his age that graduated from the puppy academy. He's a quick learner.

She returns home after class and finds Shawnee waiting outside. "Sorry I'm late," Rosario says. "I was signing Cocoa up for the doggy graduation ceremony."

Shawnee scratches behind Cocoa's ears. "Please tell me you're getting him a cap and gown."

"Oh, I'm way ahead of you. It'll be here tomorrow."

They settle into her office and get to business. Shawnee starts. "Alright, so it's been a while since we've released an episode, and the people in the forums are going to start an uprising if we don't come out with some more content soon. I think we have enough to get started on an episode of this Belladonna case."

Rosario falls into her chair and crosses her arms over her chest. "Fine. Let's hear it."

"As you know, the case starts in Miami." Standing up, she waves her hands theatrically to set the scene. Grabbing a grease pencil from her bag, she starts to draw on the window glass. The new move makes Rosario chuckle.

"Wow, very CSI of you."

"Thank you," she says. "The Ramos family was calling for police to reopen the investigation into the death of their son, George Ramos, because they believed it was a homicide." She draws an X on the glass followed by a *G.R.* "Official records say he died from acute anaphylaxis. But the family believes he was poisoned. They said the cops were quick to close the case because the guy had been accused of raping a girl in the neighborhood."

"Jesus," Rosario says. "You didn't tell me that. Not a very sympathetic victim, babe."

"Listen, hear me out. This is just where it starts. The mother, Eileen Ramos, who was the one making a big stink about all this, dies in her home years later." She draws another X on the glass, followed by an *E.R.* "According to the reports, her cause of death was listed as chemical asphyxiation. But no signs of foul play."

A smile slowly spreads across Shawnee's face. "It itched my brain. The reports kept referencing a girl who was the last person to see George Ramos alive. I called the family attorney. He'd heard of us and was excited we'd taken an interest in the case. He doesn't represent the family anymore, but he sent me the records they gathered to try and get the case reopened."

"That's amazing."

"Belladonna left Miami when the family starting pushing to reopen the case. Moved to California seven years ago." Shawnee excitedly raises her eyebrows and spins to mark on the glass. *X*, followed by *A.K.* "Ana King. The socialite. The focus was all on the husband, some kind of a talent agent who was having an affair with Belladonna."

"We already knew all of this."

"Yes, but I'm trying to paint a picture here. Imagine the episode.

All of these circumstantial details will make the case." Shawnee pulls up a PDF file on her laptop and scrolls. Finding a paragraph, she highlights it and reads aloud. *"Ten Strange Facts Surrounding Ana King's Disappearance.* Get this. *Just one week before her disappearance, Ana King was rushed from the Beverly Oaks Country Club to Cedar Sinai Medical Center, where she was treated for acute anaphylaxis."*

"Holy fuck."

"Yeah, dude. And I haven't even shown you the best part."

Rosario rises to her feet and starts to pace. Damn Shawnee for tempting her this way. She told herself she was done with the podcast. "What's the best part?"

Shawnee's fingers dance over the keyboard. She spins it around and there's a YouTube video loaded on the screen. It's from 2017. There's a beautiful young woman in her garden, kneeling next to a potted plant. A young Belladonna. Shawnee hits play.

"See this beauty? It may seem innocent, but this invasive species is a killer." The woman drags a finger over the plant's fruit. Her big amber eyes are filled with a contrived innocence. Rosario swallows hard. There's something strange about this one.

The woman continues. "Not only is it highly poisonous, the *ricinus communis* is merciless at suffocating and stealing resources from its native counterparts." Her voice carries a sweet, ethereal quality. "Nature is brutal, isn't it? It's impolite. It takes what it wants, and it doesn't ask permission. Given the option to shrink or thrive, it will choose to thrive no matter the cost."

Shawnee slams the laptop shut for dramatic effect. "She poisoned the fuck out of these people."

"Oh my God." Rosario feels like they're holding on to explosive information. "Why hasn't anyone done anything about this?"

"George and Eileen were never ruled homicides. They never found Ana, and the husband"—she consults her notes—"Ben Deluca, became very rich as a result. And I'm not talking plantain chip money. We're talking like a quarter of a billion dollars. That kind of money buys a lot of silence."

It sounds dangerous. "So what's your plan?"

"Well, that's why I wanted to meet."

"You don't have a plan?"

"Not yet. Do I have to do everything around here?"

Rosario wraps her arms around herself, her mind rushing with possibilities. Los Angeles feels like a world away. "So what's up with them now? It's been more than half a decade."

"That's what I'm still trying to work out."

Rosario's fully charged, they both are. Her battery has been depleted for so long, it's nice to be excited about something again. They eagerly get to work, pouring over case files and diving into internet searches. The light outside begins to fade. Rosario peeks at her phone to check the time. It's after eight. Her eyes drift to an unanswered text.

Beau

What you got going on tonight princess?

Her eye rolling muscles get a workout every time she looks at it. She's been playing it cool with deputy dimples. They text every now and again. Sometimes he'll call her when he's driving home from work, or just before bed. It definitely wasn't lightning. In fact, she was still waiting for a moment where the tinder would catch, when she would exhale with the confidence the flame was strong enough to burn on its own.

For every sweet term of endearment made in his drawl that made her melt, there was a dad joke that made her want to hang up the phone. They haven't even kissed. She let him down as gently as she could. She's not ready. She isn't sure she'll ever be ready.

And then four days ago, Ulysses broke no-contact.

can we talk?

Her heart sank. She'd stared at the message for hours, debating whether to text back. He's probably hurting. But if she responds, it would open up lines of communication. Even though she ultimately decided not to reply, she can't bring herself to delete the message.

God, she just wants to heal. When will it finally stop hurting?

It doesn't help that Shawnee is always picking on her. Taking a break from their research, Shawnee asks Rosario about how things were going with Beau. When Rosario tells her, her response is less than supportive.

"Girls like you make me sick. It'd be one thing if you didn't like him, but I know you do. What are you afraid of?"

Rosario goes limp in her computer chair, her arms hanging over each arm, legs sprawled across the floor. "Being bored to death. Being strangled with virtue. He's too good. It makes me feel…I don't know. Bad."

"That's really poignant stuff. Did you just come up with that? You should use that in our next episode."

"Fuck you," she mumbles without any venom.

Shawnee pushes her glasses up the bridge of her nose with a chortle. "God's gift to the earth over here thinks a man's going to wait around like patience on a monument." With a slow, persnickety shake of her head, she taps away on her laptop. "Imagine running into him and a new girl. Won't that burn your ass?"

"A little."

"Then go out with him. It's just a stupid date."

hey. shawnee and I are bouncing around case ideas if you want to come by

"There. I invited him over."

When he arrives, he's got a board game tucked under his left arm and a brown paper bag gripped in his left hand. In his right hand, he perilously balances three fast food soft drinks in a cardboard drink carrier.

"What's all this?" she asks.

"Stopped by Arby's on the way. Thought y'all might be hungry."

She sighs and forces out the words as sincerely and warmly as possible. "Thank you." It's considerate, she reminds herself. Silencing the part of her brain that wants to make fun of him, she tells herself it's sweet he showed up with a bag full of roast beef sandwiches. She leads him to the office, and he sets the food and the board game on the coffee table before getting comfortable in an armchair. "So, what are y'all digging into now?"

Shawnee repeats her performance, and Rosario watches Beau learn each of Belladonna's theoretical victims. He makes the occasional nod, and Rosario can see his gears turning.

"Have you reached out to anyone handling Ana King's case? LAPD? Family attorney?"

"Not yet."

"I'd be interested in what they gathered. From what you've said, it seems like they looked at the husband pretty hard. With that kind of money involved, it's no surprise. What did these folks do again?"

"Show business. The husband is a talent agent or something. Ana was a socialite. It was her father's money."

"What do you mean her father's money?"

"He owned a bunch of businesses: a production company, management firm. She inherited a portion when he died."

"When did that happen?"

Rosario pulls up the timeline she'd been putting together in a document. "Um, it looks like Charles King died a month earlier. Beverly Hotel. Heart attack it said. But there was a bunch of speculation because apparently he'd invite women to his hotel room to audition, and well, it wasn't really an audition."

"I see." He gets up to stare at the glass with the shapes and letters, then leans against the edge of the desk, his eyes distant, lost in a quiet thought. "This woman. She an actress?"

"Social media personality."

"And the husband was her agent?"

"Yeah."

"And he worked for the father?"

"Yup."

He looks at them expectantly, and they wait blank-faced for him to fill them in on the punchline. "Come on, ladies," he drawls with a playful yet knowing smirk, as if he's about to help them see something painfully obvious. He ambles toward the window where Shawnee drew out the victims in white grease pencil. He takes an Arby's napkin, crumples it and hovers over the glass as if to wipe it clean. "May I?"

"Knock yourself out," Shawnee says.

As he moves to wipe the glass clean, his muscles subtly flex beneath the fitted fabric of his T-shirt, accentuating the lean, defined physique underneath that moves with a graceful, assured ease. He draws a circle and writes *B.D.* inside. Above it, he draws two circles side by side, *A.K.* and *C.K.* marked respectively. He taps the circle with the husband's initials. "I'm this guy. I've got a hot side piece, a wife I can't stand, and a father-in-law that owns my ass. He ain't going nowhere without losing money, a career, or both. That's your motive." His vowels rise and fall in pitch, spoken like a slow song that makes her toes curl up in her socks.

He draws an *X* over the *C.K.* "His femme fatale has a specialized skill set. She's gotten away with it before, she can get away with it again. There's your means." He takes a step back, surveying the letters and shapes on the glass. "Hubby sets up an audition, and sweet thing makes it look like a heart attack. Now daddy's out of the picture, the husband can leave his wife without worrying about his career. That's your motive, means, and opportunity right there." He licks his lips and a broad smile slowly spreads across his face, dimples winking at them. "I think we found us a serial killer."

A flash of heat engulfs her, spreading like wildfire. She swallows hard. Glancing over at Shawnee, she's gnawing away at her lip, apparently deep in thought, before she posits, "If the point of killing Charles was to get him out of the way, then why make the wife disappear?"

He taps the grease pencil against his knuckles. "To get the money."

"No," Rosario says, causing Beau to raise his eyebrows. "That's not her style. Let's say she did kill Charles King. She made it look like a heart attack. George Ramos, allergic reaction. Eileen Ramos, chemical asphyxiation. Her crimes hide in plain sight and she gets away with them. That's the thrill of it."

Beau nods pensively. "She tried, though, didn't she? We're assuming the incident that put Ana in the hospital a week before her disappearance was this woman's doing too. Maybe she failed and had to change it up."

"Or she didn't fail. She was just laying the groundwork."

His eyes widen. "Yeah. Yeah, maybe." He turns again toward the glass. "Dang, Rosario, I think you might be on to somethin' here." He points a finger to the glass. "We got G.R., don't nobody give a damn about him. He's the town rapist. That one was easy. Then an old woman dies in her house with some chemicals. No sign of foul play, no problem. But Ana King. A socialite. Someone in the public eye. Someone young. This one wasn't going to be easy."

Rosario gets up, standing beside him to get a look at the glass, to see it how he's seeing it. "Exactly. A coroner only looks under certain circumstances."

He turns to her, an intensity in his eyes that almost makes her lose muscle strength in her legs. "She wanted 'em to think it was a repeat of what happened before. Another allergic reaction."

Her gaze fixed on him, she can't look away. It's thrilling to watch him work. His expression softens, glancing at her lips. He lowers his voice a touch. "Goodness gracious, Ms. Martinez. I'm impressed."

"Have you seen the pictures of the husband?" Shawnee chimes in from behind them. It slices right through the tension.

Rosario turns to her. "Yeah, he's a beefcake. So what?"

"No, I mean from around the time it happened. Look." She walks her laptop over and presents it to them. On the screen is a photo of Ben Deluca leaving the police station with his lawyer, hand raised to shield himself from the reporter's cameras and questions. "This was just after she was reported missing. His face is bruised."

"She put up a fight, huh?" Beau says. "Good for her."

"It was him," Rosario blurts.

"Think he killed her in a fight?" Beau asks.

"Yeah. Belladonna wouldn't kill that way. But if she was in love with him, she'd help him clean it up. What I can't wrap my head around is why Eileen Ramos's death and Ana's disappearance happened so close together. Why go back home to kill a woman after all those years? If she wanted her dead, she could have done it before."

"That's a damn good question," Beau replies with a frustrated sigh. "I'll make some calls. See if I can't get some more information, get them to cooperate and share info."

"Really? That would be incredible," Rosario says.

"Belladonna's not her real name, is it?" he asks.

"No, it's," Shawnee starts, consulting her notes. "Elyse Santiago."

"Reaching out to the LAPD about a seven-year-old case is a long shot," he admits, a hand scratching the back of his neck. "I don't exactly have any pull over there." He pauses, looking at Rosario with a determined glint in his eyes. "But it's worth a try."

It's the early morning hours before they run out of gas. Beau peeks at his watch. "I've got to start gettin' ready for work. Early shift and a court appearance today." Rosario looks at the time—three a.m. "I'm so sorry. You're not getting any sleep?"

"Ah, don't you worry about me, darlin'. I've done a lot more on a lot less." The sweet melodic quality of his voice gives her butterflies. She walks him out and Shawnee follows. He kisses Rosario's cheek and hooks his arm around her waist, gazing down at her. "I'll call you tonight, let you know how it went."

"Thanks, Beau."

"Anything for you."

She closes the door and falls back against it.

"Anything for you," Shawnee mocks in an exaggerated Alabama accent.

"Shut up."

Chapter Forty-Four

RETURNING FROM THE COURTHOUSE, Beau reaches his desk, a small island in the sea of organized chaos he shares in a quad with three other detectives. He sets his coffee down and drops into his chair. The desk, cluttered with files and a single, framed photo of his niece, is usually a pit stop between interviews, picking up suspects and going out on warrants. Today, after a long exhausting morning in court, it's where he plans to sit and review a few of the many reports in his queue of cases.

His eyes sting from being open, lids heavy from being up all night. He'd do it all over again for Rosario. *Dang* he's sweet on that girl. His eyes lose focus daydreaming about that plump little peach, how he'd love to take a bite. A warm flush washes over him and he catches himself. *Time to get back to work,* he thinks and shakes it off.

He'd sent an email to a detective at the LAPD not expecting to hear back anytime soon. Yet, as he sits and scrolls through a long-winded report of a non-crime, his phone rings.

"Harris."

"Detective Harris, this is Detective Miguel Santos calling from the Los Angeles Police Department. I received your email. Is now a good time?"

"Yes, Detective, thanks for giving me a call. I didn't expect to hear from you so soon."

"Well, I couldn't help but wonder why a detective in Tampa would be interested in a seven-year-old cold case."

It's a fair question, one Beau needs to navigate carefully. He leans back in his chair, considering how best to approach the topic without raising any unnecessary barriers. "Well, we're looking into a suspect's pattern concerning some crimes out here that might link back to the Ana King case, and any insight you could provide would be invaluable." He pauses, gauging the response on the other end of the line, hoping his sincerity and the genuine interest in solving the case shine through.

Santos, for his part, seems to mull over Beau's words, the silence on the line stretching for a moment longer than comfortable. "Well, you could submit a formal request. If it's approved, then—"

Beau closes his eyes, picturing the letters and shapes drawn in white grease pencil all over Rosario's office windows. "Look, I'm gonna stop you there. Between you, me and the wall, we've been working with a civilian consultant on a few cold cases out here. It's less than official. But they have some theories involving this case that sound mighty promising. Of course, we'd keep you in the loop on any findings."

"I can't just send you information if there's not a legitimate purpose."

"Sure you can." He offers a half-smile even though Santos can't see it, hoping to bridge the miles between Tampa and Los Angeles with a bit of warmth. "We don't need nothing tangible now, just information. Detective to detective."

"You said you're working with a civilian consultant?"

Beau peeks over at the quad, his colleagues at their desks too entrenched in their own work to give a damn what kind of deal he's trying to finagle for himself. Clearing his throat, he shifts in his chair as if bracing to reveal a well-guarded secret. "Well, Detective Santos, if I'm being completely honest with you, and because I reckon honesty's the best policy, we're collaborating with the

Mysteries of the Southern Gothic podcast. Now, I know what you're think—"

"A podcast?" Santos interrupts, skepticism thinly veiled in his voice.

"Yes, sir, a podcast. But not the kind you might be thinking about. This one's special. You see, they recently helped us crack a case wide open that's been colder than a well digger's shovel for over two decades." Beau's voice warms with enthusiasm, his Southern charm dialing up a notch. "And I'll be honest with you, Detective, I think they might be onto something with this Ana King case. And not just her, we think this suspect could be tied to the father's death as well."

There's a pause long enough for Beau to wonder if he's oversold his pitch, but then Santos speaks up. "I've suspected that myself. Alright, let me see what I can do on my end. Can't promise anything, but I'll take a look."

Beau's relief is palpable, and he can't help but let a genuine smile spread across his face. "Thank you, Detective. I really appreciate it. And I promise, whatever we find, we'll make sure it's worth your while."

As he hangs up, Beau leans back in his chair, a mix of relief and anticipation settling over him. Rosario will be pleased. Maybe pleased enough to finally agree to a date. It's not like he couldn't find a pretty girl to settle down with if he wanted to. But there's something special about Rosario, and last night it came into full view. Talking through that case with her, seeing her in her element was a rush. And as careful as she's been to keep him at arm's length, he thinks her defenses might be beginning to crumble.

At the end of the workday, he goes out on a limb. It's not usually in his gentlemanly nature to visit someone at home unannounced, but he thinks this special surprise warrants an exception. He waves to the doorman as he strides through the lobby and into the elevator. Knocking at the door, Cocoa's bark announces his arrival, and he waits for Rosario to answer. When she does, the look on her face suggests he's made the wrong call.

"Oh, Beau. I didn't know you were coming by."

"I'm sorry, darlin'. I think we might get some information on the King case. Wanted to give you the good news in person."

"That is good news," she says, gripping the door.

His excitement wanes the longer he stands in the hallway. Why won't she invite him inside? Maybe she's alone and uncomfortable with inviting in a prospective suitor. "I'm sorry, is now a bad time?"

"No, of course not," she says. "I'm sorry."

She's rigid. Nervously opening the door wider, she lets him in. It feels awkward. Maybe he should leave. "Is everything alright?"

She gestures toward the living room. He turns and looks across the room. A chill runs through him. Ulysses is sitting just a few feet from where he stood when Beau shot him.

"Oh." The weight of his dejection is crushing, but he struggles with all his might not to let it show. "I'll get out of your hair," he says.

"Don't go," she says softly. "I didn't know he was coming by." She lowers her voice to a whisper. "Please stay."

He nods. After the shooting incident, Beau felt terrible about hurting an innocent man. Hearing more about his mother's crime, how Ulysses suffered, was heartbreaking. Yet, watching Rosario grieve him, knowing he scared her, made her cry, and broke her stuff made Beau more than a little pissed off. Sure, there were things she could have done differently, done better. Lord knows the poor guy didn't deserve to get shot, but clearly Rosario felt unsafe.

But she was just trying to do what was right for that little girl, trying to make sense of a horrible thing. She might act like a hard-ass with her sassy little attitude, all the skulls and combat boots, but she never fooled Beau. The poor thing was frightened. Of course she was. Ulysses was a drunk who, caught at the wrong moment, was liable to fire a gun or take a swing. Now the bastard thinks he can try to weasel his way back into her life after breaking her heart.

He follows Rosario into the living room. When Ulysses finally notices him, his eyes widen. "Fuck me, it's pistol Pete."

"Ulysses," Beau offers in polite acknowledgment. He sits a few feet from Rosario on her couch, across from Ulysses, who barely nods, his gaze flitting between Rosario and Beau, a clear undercurrent of tension threading through the room.

"I didn't come here to cause trouble. I was kind of hoping Rosario and I could speak in private."

"Sorry," Beau says, his tone jovial. "That's not how things are gonna go."

Ulysses sits up, his posture growing rigid. "Rosario, I'm sorry. I just came here to make amends. This isn't a romantic visit."

"You're damn straight it's not," Beau says, trying to keep his anger out of his voice. "Forgive me, but what do you think you're doing coming back here? Is this for one of your little recovery steps? 'Cause you can write a letter to your sponsor and check Rosario off your list." Turning slightly to Rosario, Beau's voice softens. "You don't have to sit through this if you don't want to." His offer is a lifeline, a chance for her to step away from a conversation that threatens to rip the scab off her still healing wound.

Facing Rosario, Ulysses pleads. "Is this really necessary?"

"Beau," Rosario chides. "Please. It's okay."

Conceding, Beau sits back with a sigh and waves him on. "Fine, let's hear it."

"Look, I've been doing a lot of thinking, and Sofie actually helped me come to realize that I made this all about me. From the beginning. But it wasn't about me. It was about Calliope. And even though it was painful, and I didn't appreciate the way you went about it, what you did was ultimately good."

Beau scoffs so hard he nearly chokes. "Was that supposed to be an apology?"

"Beau," Rosario scolds.

"I was living with this guilt. All you ever wanted to do was help, and you did. Getting Calliope's story out there, holding my mother accountable—it's given me a sense of peace I haven't felt in a really long time. I'm fifty two days sober. I wanted to thank you. And apologize for breaking your laptop. And for not appreciating you and the incredible person you are."

Rosario nods and Beau can see the hurt in her eyes when she says, "Sofie helped you see that, huh?" she asks.

Ulysses nods stoically. "We both come from the same fucked-up place. We understand each other."

Rosario's face hardens, as if she's holding back a surge of pain.

"I'm sorry," Ulysses says softly. "I never meant to hurt you."

She nods, shaking tears loose from her eyes that roll down her cheeks. "Thank you for your apology. I'm sorry too. For violating your trust. I just wanted to get to the truth, but this never should have happened. Us. It was a mistake. I crossed the line."

"It wasn't a mistake. I loved you, Rosario."

The words seem to twist the knife, and she bites her lip, her eyes holding back tears.

Beau's not sure how much more of her suffering he can witness. "You done?" Beau says.

With a resigned sigh, Ulysses scratches the short, scruffy beard on his cheek. His jaw tenses and he slowly rises. "I should go."

Beau follows him down the hall. At the door, Ulysses looks back, and Beau takes the opportunity to leave him with some parting words. "You said your piece, now I'd appreciate it if you stayed gone this time."

"That's not really up to you. If Rosario wants me to be here, I'll be here."

Beau chuckles as the elevator dings and the doors open. Before Ulysses walks into the elevator car, Beau offers a friendly pat on his arm. "Listen here," he says with a good-humored tone. "I asked you nicely to let that girl heal. Next time, I won't be so nice. See, I've killed men a lot tougher than you. You might have dug your sister's grave, but you ever show your face around here again, you'll be diggin' your own. You understand me?"

Ulysses glowers at him, a knit forming in his brow as the elevator doors close.

Returning inside, Beau ensures the door closes firmly behind him before turning back to Rosario. "You alright?" he asks, sitting beside her on the couch.

His question seems to unlock something within Rosario, the composure she's struggled to hold to together so tightly now crumbling. She looks up at him, her eyes brimming with tears that spill over, tracing lines of mascara down her cheeks. For a moment, she attempts to speak, her lips parting in a silent effort to find words that won't come. Then, with a small, almost imperceptible nod, she collapses into Beau's arms, her body racked with sobs that have been held at bay for too long.

Beau wraps his arms around her, pulling her close, offering the solidity of his presence against her heartache. His hand finds its way to the back of her head, fingers threading gently through her hair, a silent vow of protection and understanding. The room is filled with the sound of her crying, echoing the depth of her pain. Beau feels a protective fierceness rising within him, a resolve to stand guard over her in her moment of need.

As Rosario's sobs begin to subside, her breathing grows more even, steadied against the rhythm of Beau's own calm inhales and exhales. Finally, Rosario pulls back slightly, her eyes meeting his. He offers her a small, reassuring smile. "You get it all out?"

She breathes in and then exhales hard, her shoulders relaxing as if she's just set down a heavy weight. "I think so," she says softly. He wipes at the streaks of black under her eyes with his thumb. "Thank you for staying," she says.

"I'm not goin' anywhere until you make me," he says, a touch of humor in his voice.

He's close enough to kiss her. Every muscle in his body is willing him closer, willing his mouth to press against hers, but he can't. She's vulnerable. The tears he'd taste on her lips were cried for Ulysses. She smiles at him, a lovely sight after watching helplessly over her grieving the loss of a man she loved. A kind of love she might never have for Beau.

But he'll be damned if he's not going to try.

Chapter Forty-Five

ROSARIO'S red lips hover an inch from the black fabric of the mic's pop-filter. "Welcome to Mysteries of the Southern Gothic, a podcast that examines real-life crimes and unsolved mysteries. I'm Rosario Martinez. This episode is called 'The Candy Bandit.'" Clearing her throat, she tries it again, changing her inflection a little.

"I liked it better the first way," Beau says, stubbled cheek propped up on his fist. His lower half twists back and forth under the table on the rotating seat of the desk chair.

"Yeah?"

"Sounded more natural."

It's late afternoon on a Sunday. The sun, low in the sky, shimmers across the water. The weather is mild, and Rosario has left the balcony door open to take in the breeze. She plays the audio back through her headphones. Beau's right.

Shawnee groans at her laptop before slamming it shut. "This is dumb."

"I think it's kinda cute," Beau says.

Shawnee perks her head up to face Rosario and motions toward him. "See," she says. "Cute isn't what we're going for. I'm tired of waiting around. Let's pound the pavement."

"What pavement?" Rosario shoots back. "You want to go door-to-door looking for mysteries?"

Shawnee sulks back in her chair, the life seemingly draining from her.

Beau, looking bored, scrolls through his cell phone. "Oh no," he says, a bit of shocked disappointment in his voice. "Y'all seen the guy from all the *Bloodbath* movies died?" He holds out his phone, and Rosario leans forward, squinting at the screen. The news straightens out Shawnee's posture with interest.

"I'm pretty sure the movie was *Bloodoath*," Rosario says. "And that was a couple months ago I think."

"Hmm," he says skeptically. "You sure about that?" His fingers go to work on his phone.

"Positive."

"How'd he die?" Shawnee asks.

"Yeah, it was *Bloodoath*. How am I just now finding out?" He swipes, expression slacked. "They didn't say how. Dang. That stinks. I wonder how old he was."

"He was kind of old. Didn't he play Zeus in that one movie?" Shawnee asks.

"*Prometheus and the Theft of Fire*," Rosario responds flatly, dragging an audio file into place.

"Dang. We gotta take you to trivia night, girl. Win us some free beers or something with all that movie knowledge you got in that pretty little head of yours."

She glowers at him, and it inspires his dimples to emerge. She hits record again. "That's Deputy Beau Harris referring to David Folsom, better known as the Candy Bandit, a home intruder known by his unusual calling card: leaving a trail of spent candy wrappers in his wake."

She plays Beau's audio through the speakers, and he mouths along to it as he scrolls through his phone. It's not the sexiest case they've ever covered, but they weren't going to top Calliope's story immediately, and their listeners needed a palette cleanser.

"Whoa," Beau exclaims, his mindless rocking coming to an abrupt stop.

"What?"

"*Joseph Sierra's estate is a class in wealth planning,*" he reads aloud, eyes fixed on the small screen in his palm. "*Most of his considerable assets were placed into a trust designed to bypass the probate process, ensuring a seamless transition of his wealth to his beneficiaries.*"

"That's smart," Shawnee chimes in.

"No, listen to this," Beau says with emphasis. "*Not all assets were included in this trust. Sierra left a house in Malibu, California, to his ex-wife, and a cattle ranch in Grand Junction, Colorado, to his longtime business manager and close friend, Ben Deluca.*"

Shawnee's mouth falls open, eyes wide and primed on Rosario. They stare at each other a moment before Shawnee finally says, "He left him a ranch?"

"Why would he leave him a ranch?" Rosario asks, but the pieces are working themselves into place in her mind.

"Who knows? Could be a lot of reasons," Beau says. "Or there's *a specific* damn good reason why he left him that ranch." He rises to his feet, walking over to the window where they'd added a timeline pieced together from public records and news coverage. "Husband is checked into East LA medical center. Three days later, husband reports Ana missing. Somebody figure out how many miles it is from Los Angeles to Grand Junction."

Rosario is way ahead of him. She's already searched for the driving directions. On her screen is a map, a jagged blue line connecting California to Colorado vibrant against the black dark mode background. "Just under seven hundred eighty miles. Thirteen-hour drive."

He tugs at his chin. "I'll be damned." Beau shakes his head, exasperated. Turning to Rosario, his stare is intense. She gets up. His magnetic pull draws her close to him when he's putting pieces together.

Shawnee tilts her head back and stares at the ceiling, playing devil's advocate. "Wasn't Ana's car last seen picking the husband up from the hospital?"

"Oh, Ana was in that car alright," Beau says. "But I bet she was in the trunk."

Rosario's heart races. She can't stay still, doesn't know what to do with her hands. Squeezing them into fists, she can barely contain the stream of thoughts and conclusions rushing through her mind. It paints a picture, a film, and the projector is on full speed running through that tape. Rosario and Beau lock eyes, and she can almost see the desert laid out before them. "They drove all night."

Beau nods at her, they're in sync. "Ranch like that, they had to have some kinda heavy equipment."

"Makes it easy to dig a big hole," she volleys back.

"That would explain why they never found Ana's car," Shawnee adds.

"Oh, it's out there," Beau says confidently. He's vibrating. "Look, y'all, this could be a long shot, but—"

"No," Rosario says. "I can feel it."

Thank You

Thank you for picking up this book. If you enjoyed it, please consider leaving a review. Your feedback is invaluable and helps other readers discover my work.

Also by Jessica Carrasquillo

The Manchineel

Some fruits are forbidden for a reason.

Elyse shares nature's beauty and danger with her followers, but behind her smile hides a chilling capacity to kill. When she's introduced to Ben, a married older man and charming Hollywood attorney, an undeniable attraction blooms. As their connection deepens, so do the roots of a deadly plan.

Available on Kindle, Paperback, and Audiobook.

www.jessicacarrasquillo.com

* * *

Chosen Daughters

The cult shattered their faith. Love will pick up the pieces.

Ulysses never planned to return to the cult. The Church of the Ninth Order shaped his darkest memories, and while love drew him back into their oppressive community, heartbreak left him stranded. Clinging to his fragile sobriety, he plans to keep his head down and distract himself with his art. But when he's asked to counsel the enchanting Esme, staying detached is no longer an option.

Available on Kobo, Kindle, Paperback

About the Author

Jessica Carrasquillo is an attorney living in South Florida with her husband and two pugs. Drawing upon her observations of human nature, she crafts stories that explore the intricacies of love, justice, and morality.

Sign-up for updates:
www.jessicacarrasquillo.com

Trigger Warnings

Please be advised this work contains themes and scenes that depict, mention, or discuss: abduction, alcoholism, assault, child abuse, child death, cults, death, gun violence, hospitalization, murder, PTSD, unhealthy relationships, violence. It is important to approach this work with caution if you find these topics particularly distressing. Remember to practice self-care and seek support if needed.

While every effort is made to capture all potential triggers, the above list may be updated after publication. For the most up to date trigger warnings, please visit: www.jessicacarrasquillo.com/triggers